BLOOD SACRIFICE

BLOOD SACRIFICE

A Mystery of the Yucatán

GARY ALEXANDER

A Perfect Crime
Book

DOUBLEDAY
New York   London   Toronto   Sydney   Auckland

A PERFECT CRIME BOOK
PUBLISHED BY DOUBLEDAY
a division of Bantam Doubleday Dell Publishing Group, Inc.
1540 Broadway, New York, New York 10036

DOUBLEDAY is a trademark of Doubleday,
a division of Bantam Doubleday Dell
Publishing Group, Inc.

*All of the characters in this book are fictitious,
and any resemblance to actual persons, living or dead,
is purely coincidental.*

Book Design by Dorothy Kline

Library of Congress Cataloging-in-Publication Data

Alexander, Gary, 1941–
Blood sacrifice : a mystery of the Yucatán / Gary Alexander. —
1st ed.
p.   cm.
"A Perfect crime book."
I. Title.
PS3551.L3554B58   1993
813'.54—dc20   92-37070
CIP

ISBN 0-385-46895-4

PRINTED IN THE UNITED STATES OF AMERICA
July 1993

First Edition

1   3   5   7   9   10   8   6   4   2

For the real Esther and Rosa, and Tracy too.

For Cathleen Jordan, who first published
Luis Balam and *Bamsan Kiet.*

Whosoever therefore resisteth the power, resisteth the ordinance of God; and they that resist shall receive to themselves damnation.
—Romans 13:2

If his heart was to be taken out, they conducted him with great display and concourse of people, painted blue and wearing his miter, and placed him on the round sacrificial stone, after the priest and his officers had anointed the stone with blue and purified the temple to drive away the evil spirit. They then seized the poor victim and swiftly laid him on his back across the stone, and the four took hold of his arms and legs, spreading them out. Then the executioner came, with a flint knife in his hand, and with great skill made an incision between the ribs on the left side, below the nipple; then he plunged in his hand and like a ravenous tiger tore out the living heart, which he laid on a plate and gave to the priest; he then quickly went and anointed the faces of the idols with that fresh blood.
—Friar Diego de Landa,
*Account of the Things
of Yucatán* (1566)

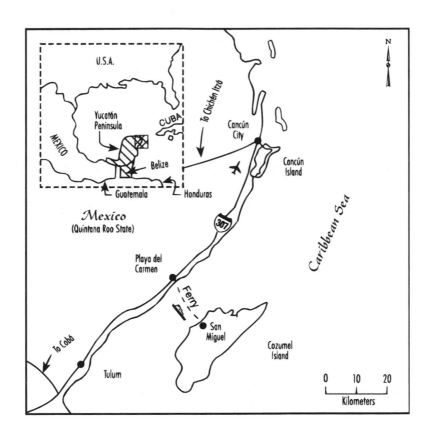

BLOOD SACRIFICE

CHAPTER ONE

ou," said a plump sixtyish woman with two cameras. "You're that upside-down guy!"

Luis Balam smiled and said, "He was Maya, I am Maya."

"Doesn't the blood rush to your head?" someone else asked.

After the laughter, Luis explained the "upside-down guy," a wall stucco of an ornately attired figure who seemed to be either standing on his head or falling. "He is guarding the doorway of his namesake, the Temple of the Descending God. Some historians say he's the Bee God. Others say the Diving God. Nobody will be certain until the glyphs are completely translated."

A gangly, bespectacled young man at the rear of the group shook his head in emphatic disagreement. He had been a dissenter throughout the tour, thankfully a silent dissenter.

The woman with two cameras aimed a clunky Nikon with a fish-eye lens and snapped Luis's picture. Through her viewfinder she saw a thirty-seven-year-old Yucatec Maya of average height: five feet three. She saw the round face, prominent cheekbones, aquiline nose, and almond eyes that had been brought across the Bering land bridge millennia ago. She saw a deceptive musculature, she saw stockiness without fat.

Luis Balam was short but not small. Belligerent drunks and defiant prowlers had learned that distinction to their dismay while Luis was a police officer. Before the trouble, before he was forced out.

"The hieroglyphics are still being deciphered, aren't they?"

"Continuing every day," Luis said, leading his group to the largest structure at Tulum—El Castillo (The Castle). "A sizable fraction is now known."

"Can you read them?"

"I *speak* Maya," Luis answered. "When the Spaniards came to Yucatán, they destroyed our writings. Many times I've asked these walls to talk to me."

"How come on some of these temples the doorways are so low, like three feet high?"

"To force those entering to bow or crawl in homage, it is believed."

The silent dissenter rolled his eyes.

Luis took his eight tourists slowly up the steps of El Castillo. With the exception of the silent dissenter, who wandered off, they were middle-aged, red of face, and short of breath. They were dressed in vivid shorts and printed pullovers. It always amazed Luis how much varicosity and cellulite North Americans were willing to display.

At the top they rested and gazed out at the Caribbean. The midday sun was lost above puffy clouds but not forgotten. Its vertical rays turned the sea to blue topaz. Temperature and humidity nudged triple digits.

Luis said, "Tulum is the largest fortified site on Mexico's Quintana Roo coast. Tulum means 'wall' in Maya. The walls around us are as much as seventeen feet high and twenty feet thick. The cliff we overlook is forty feet above the water."

"A helluva fort. What else was it used for?"

"Tulum was a trading center. The reef that parallels the coastline is hazardous," Luis said. "There are slots in the wall on the seaward side of El Castillo. Fires were built at night behind two high windows. A mariner who could see both was steering through an opening in the reef. He saw one or none—he had a problem."

The group murmured approvingly. North Americans, Luis thought; they worship technology in any form, from any era.

"The Spaniards came to Tulum too, didn't they?"

This was Luis's favorite part. "Yes. In 1511 a Spanish warship struck the reef and sank. Most survivors died of disease or were sacrificed. One who lived married a Maya, fathered three children, and commanded warriors who drove off the next Spanish raid, in 1517."

"Human sacrifice," a man said, winking. "Mind-boggling. That's not a modern custom, is it?"

"We have stopped doing it," Luis deadpanned, then added after a pause, "Regularly."

Silence. They usually laughed, albeit nervously. Nothing now, though, nothing but blank stares. Almost at once he realized his blunder. The woman with two cameras said, "That poor little stewardess gal. Remember? In the autopsy they dug out a flint particle. They figure that Gilbert plunged that Mayan flint knife in her chest so hard he chipped it on a rib. No offense, but people are speculating that this Gilbert killer, he's Mayan."

"Then it follows that a murder committed with a German Lugar is committed by a Nazi war criminal," Luis countered.

"I'm just saying what people are saying. Are the police close to catching him?"

"I have no idea," Luis said.

"She was last month, early May, name of Alison something, I think," said the woman with two cameras. "Flew for American out of Dallas. She was number three. One in March, one in April. Each in a different Cancún hotel."

"This is June. Aren't you worried?" a man asked.

Nervous laughter.

"I'd damn near be flattered," said the woman with two cameras, cackling. "But I'm safe. Gilbert kills young skinny lookers. Dark-eyed, dark-haired knockouts."

"Maybe I'm naive and uninformed, but who is this Gilbert?" asked another woman. "I hear the name. I hear there's been trouble. I never did learn the full story."

"You must not watch the news," a man said. "After the third, the flight attendant, it made the nationals."

"How do you think you got such a good deal on this trip?" the woman with two cameras asked. "It's the off-season, but Gilbert's made it the off-off-season. I don't know where you're staying in Cancún, but where we are the rates are rock bottom and you just rattle around."

"Well, the news is so bad these days I don't bother to keep up. It's too depressing," the naive woman said defensively.

"I got wind of Gilbert at the check-out line," said the woman with two cameras. "I buy those tabloids and I'm not ashamed to admit it. They've covered Gilbert since April, when he killed the time-share condo saleslady. Say what you want, those scandal sheets keep on top of things."

"Who nicknamed him Gilbert?"

"It just kind of caught on. Sick humor if you ask me," the woman with two cameras said to Luis. "The hurricane was when? I forget."

Luis knew he had lost control. He knew it was pointless to continue the tour. History and scenery had been obscured by the bloody shadow of a madman. "September of 1988. Hurricane Gilbert was the strongest storm measured in the Caribbean in this century. It did billions of dollars of damage to Jamaica before it hit our coast."

"Damn near wiped out the Cancún tourism industry. Some of the hotels, the sand was washed off their beaches," the woman with two cameras said. "This killer, he's doing the exact same thing."

"Flint was the material used for sacrificial knives in the old days, wasn't it?" Luis was asked. "How come not iron or bronze? You people, if you could build these temples and pyramids and invent a calendar and stuff, it seems to me you could do some pretty slick metalwork."

"Flint, yes. Obsidian too. The lowland Yucatán is a

limestone shelf flat as a tortilla. We have no metal ore. We barely have topsoil. My forebears traded for what metals they had. Thank you, ladies and gentlemen, for allowing me to be your guide at the Tulum ruins."

"Thank you," the woman with two cameras said. "And may I say, you speak marvelous English."

"Thank you," Luis said. "And may I say, so do you."

Laughter.

Outside the wall, in a seedy bazaar offering everything from clothing to postcards, from jewelry to ice cream, Luis Balam recounted his money. Eight people, seven U.S. one-dollar bills. There was always a deadbeat.

But he was not complaining. It was the beginning of summer. North Americans could lie on their own beaches, burn under their own sun. Subtract potential vacationers frightened elsewhere by Gilbert and multiply by the rabid competition among guides in these lean times, and he knew he had been fortunate to snag these eight at the wall and organize them into a group.

He conceded an edge, though—his resemblance to the "upside-down guy." Most of the other guides were mestizo, of mixed European and native ancestry. Luis could think of no other advantage a full-blooded Maya would have over a mainstream Mexican. He was a living curio, and because of it, seven dollars richer.

"Excuse me." The silent dissenter extended a hand. "Dave Shingles. Can you spare a minute?"

Luis accepted the handshake and said, "My lecture amused you."

"I meant no disrespect. It's just that, you know, you

were inaccurate in a couple of areas that kind of jumped out at me."

Up close, he appeared even younger, twenty-five at the oldest. Downy chin stubble heroically imitated a goatee. His breath was rancid and his waxen complexion bespoke a life spent indoors staring at pages and computer screens. Luis knew the type. This boy could argue all day about nothing.

"I have appointments," Luis lied. "I can't stay and debate with you, much as I would love to."

"I came to apologize for my rudeness and to do you a favor."

"How much will the favor cost me?"

Dave Shingles grinned. "Nothing. Honest. Could we move from here for a minute?"

They were in the infield. Tulum was the most visited archaeological site in Mexico. Despite Gilbert and summer, a line of tour buses howled at fast idle, to run air conditioners for shopping and sightseeing passengers. The noise was deafening, the air dense with fumes. Luis nodded and walked with the strange young man toward a row of shops.

Shingles unfolded a piece of paper, a drawing, saying, "I took a course at college in Mesoamerican history. I was hooked. The Aztecs and the Incas, they were okay, but you Mayas, man, you're something else."

Luis had seen the drawing before. It was of a king surrounded by Maya iconography.

"Okay, what do you see?" Shingles asked eagerly.

"Lord Pacal, ruler of Palenque. He died in A.D. 683. This is the carving on his sarcophagus lid," Luis said. "Very famous."

"Yeah, but don't you *see?*"

A shopkeeper rolled and unrolled a woven hat to demonstrate its pliancy. "Pan-e-ma," he told a browser. "Genuine Pan-e-ma."

Luis returned the drawing. The nature of Shingles's strangeness had been revealed. He was not the first of his inclination to accost Luis. Tulum and Palenque were their holy cities.

"Well, it's obvious," Shingles said. "The propulsion unit he's sitting on, the thrusters beneath, the control panel he's operating."

"You see rocket innards in the glyphs," Luis said. "I see language. Erotic gossip maybe."

Dave Shingles was undeterred. "Historians and archaeologists, I don't understand why they can't get their facts straight. You know the real reason for the low doorways like on the Temple of the Descending God? I know you do."

"Genuine Pan-e-ma," the shopkeeper persevered. "For you, only sixty thousand pesos. Cheap. Almost free."

"A god is tumbling from the heavens. Our ancestors were extraterrestrial dwarfs. They could pass under without brushing their heads," Luis said, turning away. "Go to Palenque. Its flying saucer men are taller."

The hat browser was also leaving. "For you, amigo," the shopkeeper called out, "Fifty-nine thousand. Below cost."

Shingles walked alongside Luis. "Palenque is three hundred miles from Tulum as the vulture flies. I'm a lone wolf and Palenque believers come in packs and hang around. They're a bunch of fruitcakes. Besides, Palenque isn't the place. They're as screwed up on their facts as anybody."

"No, Mr. Shingles, Palenque is not for you. You should not associate with such crazy persons."

"The Maya calendar predicted the end of the universe, you know. When the great cycle of the long count ends on December 24, 2011, it's all over. Or on December 21, 2012. That's an alternative calculation."

"Give or take a year," Luis said, fluttering a palm. "Nobody's perfect."

"Uh-uh," Shingles said. "Not Palenque, not twenty years in the future, not the end of the universe. I have my own calculations."

"I imagine you do."

"Tulum is the place. The universe isn't ending. The date's when they're coming for us."

Luis stopped. "Who is coming for whom?"

"The alien spacecraft, for the believers. I'm camping at Xcacel beach until then. The favor is that I'm tipping you off. It's a selfish favor. You look so much like them, you might, you know, be my ticket aboard. Keep it quiet, okay? They won't have room for everybody."

"When?"

"A week from Tuesday, at dawn."

Luis Balam rubbed thumb and fingertips together. "You owe me a dollar."

Shingles fumbled in a pants pocket. "How did you know I was the one?"

CHAPTER TWO

rchaeologists sought Luis's past. Anthropologists sought his present. Evangelicals sought his pagan soul. Tourists sought his advice on safe drinking water.

Impersonal as their probings were, they were at least directed to the Maya, individually or as a society, today or yesterday. But to the ancient astronaut cultists, Luis thought, we were and are dumb Indians. Our ancestors could not possibly have erected twelve-story-high pyramidal temples. We could not have developed sophisticated writings, mathematics, and calendars.

Enter the short, dexterous Venusians.

Why do they deny the ingenuity of humans?

Luis was so preoccupied by injustices he nearly drove past Black Coral. His brakes caught with a gritty squeal. He turned in front of a truck into the parking lot, thudding through potholes. The jolting impacts muffled the truck's bleating horn.

Black Coral was eight kilometers north of Tulum on Highway 307, the coastal highway. Divers harvested antler-shaped black coral from a reef skirting nearby Cozumel Island. Jewelers on the island crafted the material into irresistible merchandise, affordably priced bracelets and necklaces, mementos of an unforgettable vacation.

Trouble was, Black Coral shared its generic name with numerous competitors. This shop consisted of a large tent, a hand-lettered BLACK CORAL sign, and, inside on folding tables, plastic trays of jewelry made from hematite, silver, lapis lazuli, turquoise, amber—and yes, black coral. Luis Balam was Black Coral's proprietor.

Business was slower than slow. Tour buses drove the economy along the highway. Luis and fellow merchants bribed drivers to stop en route to Tulum and the vast inland ruins of Cobá, to afford passengers a sampling of indigenous handicrafts. There were too many shopkeepers, too few buses. Supply choked demand.

Between his shop, Tulum, and occasional freelance detective assignments, Luis Balam was clinging by his fingernails. Things would get better, he told himself.

For a change, he thought happy thoughts. Gilbert would eventually be arrested and winter would return to North America. The maniac would be subjected to a prompt trial and a firing squad, then forgotten. Snow blizzards would blast Chicago and New York, and ice-encrusted citizens would stagger to the closest travel agent.

Luis's teenaged daughters, Esther and Rosa, were minding the shop. They and Luis's parents operated it while he was elsewhere.

"Father. Your driving," Esther said, shaking her head. "You are determined to orphan us."

Esther, aged eighteen, was the daughter of Luis's first wife, who had run off to a neighboring village with an evangelical convert when Luis first went to Cancún, in 1975, to work construction at the then-new resort community. His wife's man did not want a baby around, so Esther was returned to Luis. Because of his long absences, his mother and father had essentially raised Esther in her infant years.

"I had room. That truck did not even scrape my paint. How have we done?"

"One bus, two private cars. A hitchhiking American hippie who wanted to use the telephone and bathroom we do not have," Esther said. "The hippie was older than you, Father. He had a gray ponytail and a headband."

"One sale," said Rosa, his sixteen-year-old.

Rosa was the product of his second wife, who had died of a fever during his second stretch of Cancún employment. Despite the money, Luis had intended to return to his village forever, as the gods had evidently mandated. But Highway 307 had been paved and was open the length of Quintana Roo State, from Cancún to the capital of Chetumal on the Belize border.

Via friendships struck at Cancún, Luis was accepted by the traffic police. He could live with his parents and his babies in Ho-Keh, his village, and still proudly wear the navy slacks and sky-blue shirt of the Tránsito. Heaven had smiled upon him. So he had thought.

"You are grinning," Luis said. "It must have been a big purchase."

"A hematite necklace, Father," Rosa explained. "We priced it at sixty dollars and he paid fifty. Usually we let them go for forty or thirty-five."

"Rosa, our actress," Esther said good-naturedly. "She groaned and covered her eyes at his offer of forty. She said her father would kill her for selling below wholesale. He was a nice, gullible man."

"A North American yuppie man buying it for his mother," Rosa added. "He was cute and had blond hair and a Rolex watch and white goo smeared on his sunburn."

Luis marveled again at their differences. Esther was quiet and serious. She wore the traditional Maya *huipil*, the gaily embroidered white dress. Rosa favored blue jeans and neon blouses. She was addicted to cola beverages and rock music.

He worried endlessly about both his girls. Was haggling with tourists over the price of beads their ultimate? Perhaps. They could clean toilets in the Cancún hotels. They could stay in Ho-Keh, marry corn farmers, and become baby machines. There was much, much more a Maya could not do than do. A Maya female could do even less.

"Who is hungry?" Luis asked, patting his stomach.

"Who is never *not* hungry?" Esther and Rosa said in unison, pointing at him.

Black Coral's tent was segmented. In the rear the Balams sat on packing crates and cooked at a camp stove. Luis enjoyed a lunch of hot tortillas and warm León Negra beer. Rosa's hearing was acute. She scrambled out in response to a noise that escaped Luis and Esther.

"The transit bus stopped," Rosa reported. "Mr. Martínez got off."

They went forward and outside. A handsome man with a mustache trudged toward them. A year ago in a Cancún

City café, Luis had seen an early North American television show entitled "I Love Lucy." Shave the waxed, pencil mustache and Ricardo Martínez Rodríguez could be the twin of Ricky Ricardo, the Cuban bandleader. Ricardo had been Ricky to Luis ever since, whether he liked it or not. Ricky seemed tired and unusually solemn.

"Luis, hello to you and your beautiful daughters," Martínez said, wiping his brow. "If you will buy a telephone, I will buy a telephone. Contacting you for an important job is a major undertaking."

Esther and Rosa giggled. Luis said, "We cannot afford telephones, you and I. We have no lines and poles, and I do not trust microwaves. I would go broke listening to static."

"Yes," Martínez said with a hand flourish. "There must be an easier way for us to communicate. In less than eight years we will be in the next century. The century of Buck Rogers, is it not?"

Ricardo Martínez Rodríguez was a Cancún City attorney with a marginal practice. He could not afford a car. His erratic fees were squandered on glandular women and doomed schemes. Ricky's assignments were often like rainbows, dazzling but ethereal. Luis experienced a certain euphoria whenever a bill he submitted to Ricky was paid.

"Buck Rogers," Luis said. "I met a personal friend of his at Tulum this morning."

"Unless the friend has an urgent legal problem and his planet prints hard currency, I do not care. Luis, is there a drink in your establishment? Cold does not matter. Wet does. Thankfully the bus had no live chickens or vomiting drunks today, but it was an oven nonetheless."

"Save your money, Ricky, and you would not have to ride third class."

"Cannot be helped," Ricky said seriously. "My social life is expensive. My image as a cosmopolitan professional must be maintained."

Esther brought the men bottles of León. Ricky bowed, kissed her hand, sending her inside blushing.

Ricky took a drink and said, "It is good we are alone to talk. I will get right to the subject. You know of Tropical Language Scholars, do you not?"

Luis tensed. "Evangelical missionaries. Fundamentalist Protestants. They supposedly translate the Bible into our languages. Their real goal is our souls."

"True," Ricky agreed. "It is a shoestring operation. They do not make many converts."

"Any is too many," Luis said, reminded of his first marriage.

"I represent Tropical Language Scholars in Quintana Roo State. I am on retainer."

Luis looked at him.

"Unpaid retainer. They are skinflints."

"Unpaid," Luis said. "Of course."

"In the event of legal difficulties, the alleged language translators are instructed to contact me. No one ever did. Not until last night and this morning. Luis, take a long swig of beer before I continue. You will need it."

Luis obeyed.

"Luis, last night, in the Cancún Hotel Zone, at the Club Estrada Hotel, Gilbert killed again. He was captured soon after."

Ricky paused for dramatic effect, which to Luis seemed ridiculously unnecessary.

"Gilbert killed a prostitute," Ricky said. "Gilbert is a member of Tropical Language Scholars. Gilbert is an evangelical missionary."

CHAPTER THREE

*T*hey headed northward in the Volkswagen Beetle that Luis had bought surplus from a Cancún International Airport rental-car agency. Its running gear had been shell-shocked by bad roads, its engine malnourished on 81 octane gasoline. A hundred-fifteen-kilometer trip to Cancún City, to Ricardo Martínez Rodríguez's law office, was problematic. Luis had managed to keep the car running with bicycle tools and intuition. He knew he would soon need magic.

Ricky allowed Luis to drive in dazed silence, to digest what he had revealed. Highway 307 was two lanes and shoulderless. Thick scrub jungle crowded the inland side. Now and again, the Caribbean peeked through on the other. Traffic was light and Luis drove hard.

After thirty kilometers and the Playa del Carmen junction, Luis finally asked, "Who knows?"

"Eyewitnesses, the police, Tropical Language Scholars, us," Ricky replied. "The lid will not stay on long. Rumors are seeping out already."

"Gilbert, the prisoner, contacted you?"

"Through the police. They pounded on my door at dawn. They would have kicked it in and dragged me out of bed if I had not answered. They have no respect for an educated, professional gentleman. The police are handling this case with extreme care, however.

"I went to the telephone company. A lady friend of mine works there. She was able to send a fax to Tropical Language Scholars' home office in Dallas, Texas. On the initial attempt! I waited. They replied in one hour. They instructed me to visit the suspect, which I did, and tell him to say nothing, which I also did. They then said to initiate a private investigation. That is you, Luis. They are sending their own North American lawyer to Cancún, a man named Ringner. You and I are to coordinate with him."

"What happened?"

"The police supplied me bare fragments. Gilbert's name is Proctor Smith. His fourth and final victim is—was—a prostitute by the name of María López. I understand she was very, very beautiful."

"At the Club Estrada Hotel?"

"Not Cancún's finest hotel, but no dump either. I apologize for having to utter the Estrada name, Luis. Your pain is my pain."

"Not your fault, do not apologize," Luis said, squeezing his friend's shoulder. "It was five years ago. My life out of the police force is much happier."

"Raúl Estrada Estrada alive and free and fabulously rich is a slap in your face, Luis. Each minute he is at liberty, it is like he is laughing at you, spitting at you. Life is, as they say, a heartless bitch."

Luis smiled. Ricky, well-meaning, remained a lawyer with a lawyer's penchant for babble. Although the constant resentment was gone, Ricky's chatter dug at the scab. Luis brooded about it periodically. For whatever reason, his mind would not let it rest.

"I *will* repeat the Estrada name. And the story," Luis said.

Ricky sighed. "I talk too much."

"It helps me, it is therapy." Luis tapped his forehead. "Pressure up here is relieved. How many Cancún Hotel Zone hotels do Estrada and his family control?"

"They grow wealthier by the second. Six, seven, eight. Plus four-star restaurants. A travel agency or two, just to steer moneyed North Americans to the proper places. And that is just Cancún. Tally additional holdings in Mexico City and on the West Coast. Acapulco, Mazatlán, Ixtapa. They live in Mexico City on an estate larger than your village. They jet the world. They swim in champagne. They own the fastest, most gorgeous automobiles and women.

"Raúl, is a 'junior,' the spoiled son of a rich, rich man. He is in charge of the family's Cancún holdings. He 'manages' by testing their cafés, bars, and beds. He gets so much pussy I am an envious virgin by comparison. His pet project this year is the new Puerto Estrada resort on the coast. His father's pet project is what it is. A destination resort of magnitude. But the people they have hired accomplish the management and the work. Raúl playacts at being a boss, The Boss. Are you feeling better, Luis? Yes? You are a very strange man."

"Much better," Luis said.

One night, Raúl, drunk and speeding on the highway,

struck a bicycle. The Estrada mode of travel was the Mercedes-Benz. The Maya mode of travel was the bicycle. Mayans could fit more people on a bicycle than anybody.

Luis was on duty. The man and his wife on the bicycle were killed instantly. The bicycle itself was a pretzel. The little boy and little girl were not found until the following day. They were riding on the handlebars. The girl was wedged in the fork of a sour-orange tree, catapulted twenty meters from the road. There were no skid marks. The driver had not touched his brakes.

Luis had investigated. He had reliable witnesses and signed statements. He traced Estrada's Mercedes to a garage. They had fixed it, but he recovered the fender, spent his own money on film, and photographed everything.

Much bigger money changed hands. Luis's report was altered. A phantom driver, it was officially concluded. Luis persisted. He was considered too noisy. Infractions were manufactured against him and he was fired for inefficiency.

"Where were we, Ricky?"

"At the Club Estrada. The López woman had rented a room on the second floor to conduct her business. Our Mr. Proctor Smith came charging out of her room, blood dripping from his hands. He had committed the crucial error of leaving the door ajar. Guests walking by heard groans and moans. They opened the door completely and flicked on the light. Smith virtually trampled them. He is a massive, oafish man who was wrestled with considerable effort onto the plush hallway carpeting. The guests then summoned employees, who held him for the police."

Luis slowed. A truck had broken down, a frequent occurrence. Repairs were under way on the spot. The truckers had little choice, and a mechanical failure was yet another excuse for a social occasion.

Luis saw a pair of soles sticking out from beneath the vehicle. Three men presumably lending moral aid to the supine mechanic were sitting on the truck bed with feet dangling—talking, laughing, smoking cigarettes.

Luis was familiar with the highway. While he thought the dead rig might be screening a NO PASSING sign, he would not bet on it. He accelerated around the truck. The roadway rose and curved slightly. A Chrysler Cordoba with black-tinted windows, fog lamps, and ship's-prow hood ornament appeared out of nowhere. Luis swerved into his own lane.

Ricky opened his eyes and stammered, "Luis, why do you ignore 'No Passing' signs while I am in your car? You want to kill me, please shoot me. It is not so messy."

"I could not see the sign from my angle. You should have alerted me. María López was a prostitute?"

"Blatant prostitution is uncommon in the Hotel Zone," Ricky said. "In the seedier Cancún City bars, sure, you can purchase sex. There or to go. Bargain pussy. But as they say, let the buyer beware.

"María López, on the other hand, was exquisitely exclusive. According to the police, she took appointments and credit cards. You rented her luscious body for the entire night in a luxury suite—no hand jobs under a table or quickies on a stinking mattress, no sir—and you paid plenty."

"Why are you and the police so convinced that it was a Gilbert killing?"

"Easy, Luis. The sacrificial flint knife was buried in her chest. The same knife. A knife with a broken tip."

In the late 1960s a Mexico City computer selected a skinny, 7-shaped island named Cancún as the site for building a resort-from-scratch second to none. At the time, it was occupied by a hundred squatters. Upward of a million people visit it annually today.

As the island high-rises went up, Cancún City, adjacent on the mainland, grew too, though lower to the ground and uglier. Construction workers such as Luis Balam built it and lived in it. Now those carpenters and masons and electricians were long gone, replaced by cab drivers, bartenders, and chambermaids. The place had become Cancún Island's bedroom and market. It was lively, loud, and lowbrow. Cancún City was old Mexico, circa 1977.

Cancún City's main street was Avenida Tulum. Other downdown streets were named in honor of Yucatán's grandest ancient cities: Cobá, Uxmal, Bonampak, Chichén Itzá, Palenque. Ricardo Martínez Rodríguez's law office was above a bar in a cement building located blocks from any reference to glorious history. Low overhead was an advantage, Ricky often pointed out, as was the proximity of doctors willing to validate Ricky's calamitous diagnoses of his injured clients.

They walked up alley stairs. Ricky unlocked his office door and said, "Before you interview Proctor Smith, we can review my files. I save clippings on every criminal and civil activity our newspapers are permitted to print. You can never be certain what will fall in your lap. If you are prepared in advance, you will make a favorable impression on prospective clients."

Luis followed. They entered a single room containing one table, one filing cabinet, three folding chairs, and a framed portrait of Lázaro Cárdenas, a revered statesman and President of the United Mexican States in the 1930s. Castanets and guitars serenaded them from the jukebox of the bar below.

Luis said, "Press censorship being what it is, your Gilbert file has to be thin."

"Thin but meaty," Ricky corrected, withdrawing a folder, gesturing for Luis to sit. "It contains the essentials."

Ricky, licking fingertips, leafed through his clippings, narrating, "Janie Foster. Saturday, March seventh. A tourist from Portland, Oregon, which is in the Arctic regions. She was a secretary, on vacation with a secretary friend. Her roommate was being seriously wooed in the disco of their hotel, the InterPresidential. Janie Foster was drowsy and went up to bed. She never awakened.

"Judy Jacobson. Thursday, the ninth of April. A timeshare condominium saleslady. I hate to defile the dead with cynical commentary, Luis, but time-share-condo agents outnumber beach peddlers selling junk silver out of valises. She met her end in a room at the Paradise Plaza Hotel. Speculation is that she was awaiting a lover. The identity of this alleged stud is unknown.

"Alison Hall. Sunday, May ten. A Dallas-based flight attendant. She was staying at the Maya InterPresidential, not to be confused with Janie Foster's InterPresidential. An autopsy produced a flint chip, a knife tip that preliminary, unscientific observation indicates is a match for the knife that ended the life of María López. A breakthrough clue and a death warrant for Proctor Smith."

"Common denominators," Luis said, thinking out loud.

Ricky shrugged. "That is why you are here. I lack the detective mind. Crime solving is a quasi-mathematical process and I am not a logical thinker. I excel at cases where, for instance, my client, riding a motorbike, is clobbered in an intersection by a North American tourist in a rental car. We reach him quickly, while he is wetting his pants and generating mental pictures of life imprisonment in a filthy Mexican jail. We are flexible. He can avoid insurance and police hassles by settling. My client and I split. Traveler's checks accepted."

"That sounds like mathematical precision to me, Ricky. Were the murdered women raped?"

"Presumably," Ricky answered. "Rape is not a subject for a family newspaper. Rape is not stated in the pieces."

"Who owns the hotels?"

"Three of four are owned by the Estrada family. The Paradise Plaza has an absentee Mexico City owner. How could that possibly be important?"

It was Luis's turn to shrug. "What is and what is not important? What are our goals?"

"I would say to get to the truth, but I am a cynic, so I will not say that. Our goal, until we are given specific instructions by the Tropical Language Scholars lawyer, Ringner, is to conduct an investigation and keep track of our hours. Billable hours. That is a term taught in law schools worldwide, Luis. It has a harmonious ring."

"The victims were similar in appearance," Luis said. "People who speak of Gilbert and know few facts know they looked alike."

"There are no photographs in my clippings. The North American tabloids published them and, yes, everybody says there were similarities. They would not have been immediately mistaken for sisters, but each was slim and dark and gorgeous."

"Proctor Smith?" Luis said.

"A man of very few words. He already understands how to remain silent. Perhaps you can extract information. My line of questioning apparently bored him. He opened his Bible and read, moving his lips in prayer, as if I were not in the cell. He has difficulties, sure, but is there ever a valid excuse for bad manners?"

String and vocal music wafted through the floor. "La Bamba." A neighborhood mariachi trio was in the bar serenading tourists, five United States dollars per tune. They always requested "La Bamba," Luis thought. Always.

Ricky Martínez grimaced and jabbed his thumbs downward. "I am billing Tropical Language Scholars the instant they will entertain an invoice. And do you know what I am investing my fee on, Luis? The thickest carpeting sold in the Yucatán Peninsula."

CHAPTER FOUR

uis," said Hector Salgado Reyes, "why do evangelicals not fuck standing up?"

Luis Balam sat down, shook his head, and awaited Hector's punch line.

"Because," Hector said, laughing, "God might think they were dancing."

Inspector Hector Salgado Reyes of the Quintana Roo State Judicial Police was Luis's friend and mentor. He had been his supervisor at the traffic police during the trouble. Hector had attempted to save his best and favorite young officer from Mexico City's clout and his own zeal. He barely preserved his own career, let alone an imminent transfer to the state judicial police, in essence a promotion.

"Cheer up, Luis. Smile. This is a happy day. Gilbert is in custody."

"Hector, can I talk to him?"

"You can. I will arrange it. Your lawyer friend who cannot keep his dick zippered inside his trousers or his bills paid, he said you would be coming. Whatever your cause is, it is fruitless, you know."

Hector was dressed like Luis, in slacks, white shirt, and sandals. He eschewed the military-style uniform favored by his peers. Hector was forty-five years old, as round as he was tall, and half bald. Epaulets and khaki would have made him resemble a character in an operetta. He could be rude and vulgar, but he was kind and fair. He was a relatively honest cop, though with seven children he could not afford to be pristine.

Luis said, "Ricky is on retainer to Proctor Smith's missionary organization. They requested an investigation. Ricky bills them and we both get paid."

"Ricky Martínez and his golden clients," Hector said, clucking his tongue. "Ricky would buy a sweepstakes ticket and be thunderously disappointed if he did not win. Ricky has no grasp on reality. Tropical Language Scholars will recognize the futility when they learn the facts. Ricky will bill one day of fees, two at the maximum."

"Ricky concedes that the case is cut-and-dried."

"It is, Luis. Oh yes. You are a private detective and former policeman. You have heard of the smoking gun syndrome? There it is, this maniac evangelical running down a Club Estrada hallway with blood on his hands. His fingerprints are surely on the knife. Forensic people are driving up from Chetumal to do the laboratory work. Then the evidence will go to Mexico City for verification. We are handling this case by the book."

Hector opened his center desk drawer and produced a knife in a plastic bag. The blade had been chipped into lethal form by a harder stone. The hilt was wrapped in leather the color of chocolate.

Hector dangled it by a corner of the bag. "Notice the

tip. It is flat, blunt. The missing sharp tip, the triangular point fashioned by the craftsman a thousand years ago, is in a separate evidence bag, stored with the file on Miss Alison Hall.

"How many Maya priests, I wonder, plunged this exact knife into how many sacrificial chests and extracted how many beating hearts?

"Hector, is this your way of saying the knife is genuine?"

Hector Salgado Reyes wagged a finger. "Touchy, touchy, Luis. You know exceedingly well that I am not making a racial slur. No epithets will ever leave the lips of this half-caste fat boy. In fact, I wish we could deal with criminals similarly. Haul them to Chichén Itzá and up Kukulcán, that great pyramid the tourists adore, lay them flat, cut out *their* beating hearts. Make examples of the worthless swine. It would cut down on pickpocketing, which, Luis, just between you and me, is becoming a headache."

Luis smiled and said, "You could not have authenticated it so soon."

"We could, and did, through sheer luck. An assistant curator at the National Museum of Anthropology in Mexico City is vacationing at the Club Estrada. He was attracted by the furor. He arrived on the scene approximately when I did. He verified that the knife buried in the bosom of the poor López woman, this knife, is authentic, not a replica. A fellow by the name of Figueroa. He will be in Cancún for the remainder of this week and the next."

"Ricky says she was a prostitute."

Hector spread his hands and cackled. "We have no whores in Cancún, Luis. Just ask the tourism authorities.

Boys and girls visit us together to sun, eat, disco, drink, and fuck. Sometimes they are married. Boys and girls visit Cancún separately to sun, eat, drink, meet each other in a disco, and fuck. Cancún is not Tijuana, you know. It is not Mexicali. It is not Ciudad Juárez."

"María López was not a prostitute?"

"María López was a prostitute," Hector said. "She was a Cancún Hotel Zone quality prostitute. A gringo with money who could not score on his own manly merits would eternally cherish María López as a Cancún moment."

"You knew María López, Hector?"

"No, no, no. Admittedly, some of my men were passingly acquainted. Prostitution is tricky in Cancún, Luis. Yes, we have a small red-light district, but the politicians cannot decide whether it should be legal or illegal. It tarnishes the finish of the sole Mexican vacation destination where a sissy-boweled gringo can safely drink the water."

Hector was a poor farm boy, a peasant, from Oaxaca State on the south Pacific coast. He had completed the six obligatory years of grammar school and drifted from a variety of jobs into police work.

"This passing acquaintanceship?" Luis asked.

"Really, what is it you are trying to accomplish? You cannot exonerate this shit-eating dog of a Bible thumper, you know. My God, that knife was implicating your people, one of your people, in the minds of a growing number."

"My men never screwed the girl, if that is what you are implying. Not that they would not have loved to, but a girl like that . . ." Hector kissed his fingertips. "A special quality of merchandise."

"As I stated, billable hours."

Hector laughed and said, "Ah, Ricky. Such a life."

In Hector Salgado's laughter was a sharp trace of bitterness. Law school, let alone high school and college, was impossibly beyond his means. Hector was one-half Zapotec Indian. Thus an unspoken affinity between him and Luis: each had made his own way. Hector understood the law better than anybody Luis knew, far better than Ricky. He could recite the Constitution of the United Mexican States verbatim, and had won countless barroom bets by reciting sections on demand. His self-taught vocabulary was also exceptional, and zestfully overused. Benito Juárez was Hector's idol. A pure-blooded Zapotec, Juárez served in the mid-1800s as Mexico's only Indian President.

"Agreed, María López was special, elite in her profession," Luis said. "How?"

"She was no cantina slut, fat-assed and miniskirted. She dressed old-fashionedly and formally. She wore flowing skirts and fluffy white blouses pinned at the neck by cameo brooches, what ladies might wear once a year to a traditional festival. Or what the heroines in Mexico City television soap operas wear. Her hair was—how can I describe it?—long and curled at the ends, out of a 1940s movie. She worked the discos and exclusive lounges where people spend wads of money to dress however they choose, so she did not stand out like a freak.

"Additionally, María was exceedingly lovely and saucy. She was petite and she was stacked. She had a caustic tongue. She could chop a man to a smaller size without chasing him away. He would sit there and take it, drooling, begging for more. She was, was, was—a conception. Is that what I mean to say, Luis?"

"An image? A facade?"

"Yes, a delectable three-dimensional facade. She was the hot-blooded Latin señorita in her most totally, extravagantly, unbearably lustful, yet prim and composed form. Picture an aristocratic nymphomaniac. A gringo wet dream. This is the image they were buying. She reminds me of an old-time actress whose name eludes me."

"How much?"

"My men claim three hundred dollars per night, including room, which cost her a hundred." Hector crossed himself. "María López had round heels, but she is dead and I can idealize her if I want, so long as I do not tell my wife."

"She had nothing in common with the three other Gilbert victims?"

"No, in spite of her origin remaining a mystery, she did not, nor did the victims share common backgrounds."

"They were slim, dark, and pretty," Luis said.

"Appearances, yes. Lifestyles, no. Deaths, yes. They died alone in their rooms."

"Were they lured up to them?"

"A pattern? A sinister rascal seen with them in public shortly prior to their murders? No, Luis. The last people to see Foster, Jacobson, and Hall alive were friends or associates. Different people. There is no known connection amongst the three and those close to them. Nobody knew anybody. They went to their rooms and were killed. Jacobson was rumored to be awaiting a tryst. We explored the rumor exhaustively. It did not pan out."

"Signs of forcible entry?"

"None. Except for last night, their doors were locked. That is not significant. As you are aware, a proficient burglar can be in and out of a home without disturbing the dust kittens. This information was reported in North American and Mexico City tabloids. You can buy those things in Cancún. You have not kept current on your reading?"

"No."

"A pity. I love their stories. Who in Hollywood is vene-really diseased. Two-headed babies. Homosexual Martians. They cover the spectrum. The copy is overwhelmingly silly, but grisly crime, ah, they do an excellent journalistic job. They are artists of psychosis and gore. A private detective like yourself, Luis, shame on you, you should be better informed."

Homosexual Martians. Luis thought of Dave Shingles. "Proctor Smith?"

"An odd rustic sort of man, typical of his colleagues. Uncommunicative is an understatement."

"What are your plans for him, Hector?"

"Not *my* plans. Gilbert is no simple, routine criminal, you know, some asshole car poacher." He jabbed a beefy thumb at the lazing ceiling fan above his desk. "The big guys, my bosses in Cancún, Chetumal, and, hell, Luis, it is inevitable, the decisions will be made in Mexico City.

"Evangelical missionaries, under Article Twenty-four of the Constitution, are free as human beings to embrace the faith of their choice. They must, nevertheless, practice their dogma strictly within a place of public worship. That is the law. In other words, it is illegal to peddle their religion on the streets and door to door. They flaut our laws. In our liberal, tolerant climate, we essentially shut our eyes to the violations.

"Proctor Smith wandered freely, preaching his gospel with no harassment from my men. Tropical Language Scholars is a leader in its field. They have pursued their pseudointellectual goals for decades in the torrid regions. In Africa, or was it New Guinea, somewhere like that, one of them was once upon a time eaten. Like them or not, they have earned their stripes, and on a minuscule budget.

"Bible translation of Indian languages is their ploy. Yet a substantial minority of these zealots cannot read a road sign without moving their lips. Luis, you have witnessed them in action. They do not care if they tear apart a family. The conversion of the heathen soul is paramount. Forgive me for raising the issue. Your first wife deserted you for an evangelical convert. Proctor Smith passed amongst us unseen, invisible. Yea and verily, Luis. Anonymity is the protective coloration of the serial killer."

"Were all the killings committed at night?"

"Yes. Between eight P.M. and midnight."

"Three of four hotels are owned by the Estradas."

Hector Salgado Reyes moved his head side to side slowly. "I would love to put Raúl, the junior, away too, but do not get strange ideas. Proctor Smith is Gilbert. Period. The knife, Luis, the goddamn knife. We Indians are convenient scapegoats. I worried that we might be placed in the situation of defending Maya villages from mindless vigilantism."

"I worried too." Luis stood. "May I see him now, Hector?"

"You may. You have not seen our jail, have you? It is a Cancún jail, for Mexicans who commit petty crimes and for drunken Anglos who commit indiscretions, urinating off hotel balconies and whatnot. It is a nice jail, not the stereotype. Who knows? One day, it may be written up in *Fodor's*."

"I can hardly wait. How is the food?"

"Not gastronomically extraordinary," Hector replied. "Do not disrupt your schedule in order to stay for dinner. And, Luis, if you have some crazed notion of proving Mr. Smith innocent, do your detecting swiftly."

"Why?"

"Article Twenty, Clause Six, entitles a defendant to a public trial in the district where the crime was committed. Whether this applies to foreigners as well as citizens is a nebulous area. Regardless, our public prosecutor has already conferred with his counterparts in the capital."

"They want Proctor Smith out of Cancún?" Luis asked.

"They do. Oh how they do! Smith is a festering sore. Incarcerated or not, he is a pustulating specter. His presence mocks our paradise. We want our gringos and their hard currency to flock back to us."

"Smith has to agree to a change of venue?"

"He does. A deal is being contemplated."

"Let me guess," Luis said. "The death penalty."

Hector nodded. "Article Twenty-two. There is flexibility. They can file for capital punishment or waive it. If Smith agrees to trial in Mexico City or, preferably, a remote state, the prosecutors will grant him his life." Hector wrinkled his nose. "A finer deal than that dirty, sick, perverted bastard gave those four girls."

"Proctor Smith and I will talk fast."

Hector snapped his fingers. "Oh. This is inconsequential, but it is bizarre and the general public, including the tabloids, are unaware."

"Is it useful to me?"

"No, but it is exclusive, confidential information. Proctor Smith raped Janie Foster. He did not rape the others and no semen discharges were found at the second, third, and fourth crime scenes. If he confesses to you, ask him why, or rather why not, and tell me. This guy, Luis, is weird, even for a lunatic killer."

CHAPTER FIVE

n the sense that it was no primitive hellhole, the Cancún City jail was as Hector had advertised. It appeared clean, but it did not smell as clean as it looked. Luis was escorted along a corridor separating communal cells, through a closed door to a block of individual cells. Proctor Smith, the most notorious prisoner in the jail's short history, was the sole guest.

Three officers were on watch. Their superiors were playing the probabilities that no more than two of three would simultaneously sleep on duty. No need to worry, Luis observed. They were wide awake, as if on intravenous caffeine. Should Gilbert escape or slash his wrists, they could not hide from official wrath short of booking passage with Dave Shingles on his flying saucer.

A guard unlocked Smith's cell. He did not speak, nor did his cohorts. They did not approve of the complications of a visitor, especially an Indian whose professional credentials consisted of a permission note scribbled by Inspector Salgado.

They slammed the iron door behind Luis and stood their ground. A considerably higher authority would have to approve confidentiality, and in typewritten triplicate.

Proctor Smith sat on a steel bunk, head lowered, hands dangling from his thighs, hands the size of baseball gloves. He was indeed a large man, a tall Caucasian of roughly forty. He was broad without excessive fat. His skin was pinkish and freckled, and he wore his reddish-gray hair in a brush cut.

Smith looked up at his leisure. Luis did not take offense; prisoners were stripped of every possession but time. Thick horn-rimmed glasses magnified Smith's eyes, but Luis could not read anything in them except unnatural size. Proctor Smith broadcast no particular emotion.

"Luis Balam," Luis said. "Ricardo Martínez Rodríguez, your Cancún lawyer, asked me to come by and interview you."

"Balam," Smith said. "That's 'jaguar,' isn't it?"

"In Yucatec, yes."

Smith ran a baseball mitt through severely cropped hair. "This language of yours, Brother Balam, it's a challenge to translate the Scriptures into."

"Then why bother?" The instant after Luis said it, he wished he hadn't. A theological debate was not his intention.

Amazement further magnified Proctor Smith's eyes. "Because hardly any Indians speak and read Spanish too good, and English at all, is how come we bother. We got to bring the Gospel to you in your own tongue. God's word is sweet in every language."

Well, Luis thought, unlike Ricky and Hector, at least I have captured his attention. He said, "I am Maya, we are Maya."

"That's what I said."

"You said Indian. That is like me calling you gringo. I am Maya."

Smith ignored the rebuke. "Where'd you learn English so good?"

"In the seventies I worked construction at Cancún. The foremen and architects were Mexican, with a scattering of Americans and Europeans."

"Mexican. You said Mexican like you aren't."

Luis's interview had degraded into free-floating conversation. A missionary gambit? Careful, he told himself, or you will be the interviewee. "Yucatán people are nominal Mexicans. Our customs, our food, the terrain, everything is different. Moctezuma rolled over for Cortés in short order. We have never conceded conquest by Spain, Mexico City, the Church, anybody. Quintana Roo has been a state for less than twenty years."

"Yeah, you're tough little monkeys. No argument there. I been witnessing for the Lord in Yucatán for two years now. I get the feel of isolation. I get hostility vibes. Everybody's poor as poor can be, so it's double sad that so few of you have accepted the Lord Jesus Christ. You read English as good as you speak it?"

Luis shrugged. "I read English fairly well."

"You learned on the Bible?"

"English-language magazines, newspapers, and the 1974 World Almanac. An American mechanical contractor befriended me. I worked hard for him. In return, in the evenings, he taught me English. The magazines and newspapers were mailed to him from his home. They came and went. The almanac was constant, automatic in our daily study. I drilled on that almanac. I learned the world around me while I learned English."

"He didn't do you any favors. He could of done you a mighty service schooling you on the Bible. The world's a cesspool," Proctor Smith said. "A cesspool of sin."

"It is if you have your head down and your nostrils twitching," Luis said. "The almanac was not entirely bad news. Willie Stargell led the major leagues in home runs in 1973. Forty-four. *The Godfather* won Best Picture in 1972. Emission control devices began to reduce auto air pollution. Watergate burglars went on trial."

"You memorized that stuff?"

"It won't go away. I couldn't forget it if I wanted to. Same as you and Bible verses."

"Hearken. Behold, there went out a sower to sow. Your attitude is my answer, but I gotta ask: Has anyone sown their faith in you, Brother Balam?"

"No. I am a secular humanist." The definition of "secular humanist" eluded Luis, but he raised it like a shield whenever missionaries encroached. Evangelicals loathed secular humanists. They were demons as despised as Satan and the Pope.

Smith winced imperceptibly. "Brother, have you not faith in any God?"

Luis said, "My forebears made no distinction between the natural and the supernatural. We worshipped the earth, the sky, the stars. We worshipped maize. We worshipped the rain that made the maize grow. We worshipped time. Our calendar was not devised for agriculture alone, just to guide us in planting. Every day was sacred. The supernatural guided all aspects of our lives.

"The Spaniards came along and told us that we were atheistic savages. They deplored human sacrifice. Never mind that their countrymen were burning heretics alive. They tortured and murdered the paganism out of us and taught us the joy of worshipping the Blessed Virgin Mary, God, and Jesus.

"Four hundred years later, you people are telling us to worship them in reverse order. It's ironic, the whole chain of religions we have lived with and under. If there is a single God, as you insist, He is chasing His own tail. Don't you see the irony?"

Smith did not exhibit a knack for irony. He ignored the question and said, "The religions you people been subjected to throughout the centuries, the blending, the syncretism, it's a miracle the Gospel reaches any of you, the confusion you gotta hold in your hearts, which mixed with this liberation theology some of these radical priests in Central America spout, it's the Lord's mercy the communists didn't march right into Mexico like they did Nicaragua and those other countries around here.

"Whosoever therefore resisteth the power, resisteth the ordinance of God; and they that resist shall receive to themselves damnation. That's what you poor folk got in store unless we can bring the Word and unless you receive the Lord Jesus Christ into your lives."

Smith's tangential rambling thoroughly confused Luis. The missionary was exciting himself, speaking animatedly, exaggerating his rural North American accent. "Communists" was "comma-nists." Words were flooding together as if jabbered by a street peddler in agitated Spanish.

"Where are you from?" Luis asked.

"Oklahoma."

"Are you Gilbert, Mr. Smith? Did you murder María López and the three other women?"

Proctor Smith smiled tightly and studied his feet. "Mr. Balam Jaguar, thou shalt not kill. Heathens like yourself, you've had the Commandments repeated to you on occasion, haven't you?"

"I have. What were you doing at the Club Estrada last night?"

"Wait a second. Whoa! Things are moving awful sudden for a country boy like me. Let's back up and talk about how come I ought to be talking to you? What's it gonna do for me?"

"Tropical Language Scholars, Incorporated, desires an independent investigation. They are sending a Texas lawyer to explain their objectives. Meanwhile, it is in your interest to establish the facts, your version, from your viewpoint."

"I'm an embarrassment," Smith said. A statement or a question, both or neither.

"Delivery of the savages to Jesus would not be aided if a language translator were tried and convicted of multiple murders."

Proctor Smith looked at Luis with outsized eyes. "I know

it's not Christian of me, Brother Jaguar, but I don't much care for you either."

Luis shrugged. "Friendship's unnecessary. Mutual self-interest is sufficient."

"Okay. Deal. Folks think that 'cuz you're with the Lord you can't park a bicycle straight. Believe me, we got our pragmatic side. I'm not ready to go up in front of a firing squad. I ain't ready yet to meet Sweet Jesus up close and personal."

"You were on the second floor of Club Estrada last night. Why?"

"The villages is our primary turf, but I witness for the Lord in the Hotel Zone whenever I got a spare minute, strolling in the lobbies and on the beach, grinnin' and chinnin', generally availing myself to brothers and sisters whose hearts are burdened. You Indians in the villages, ye know not what ye do. I'm bringing the Lord into a vacuum. These Americans flying to Cancún to debauch and dissipate and give themselves unto carnality, they're steeped in sin and they surely don't give a hoot.

"Sometimes, though, they come to the conclusion that they've had a fill of the sinful lives they're leading. A situation like this, it can bring the wickedness and the misery that goes along with it to a head. Jesus called on me. He beseeched me to be there when a tortured soul cries out. I do what I can do."

Luis suppressed a sigh. "Mr. Smith, what *specifically* were you doing at the Club Estrada? Retrace your steps. Where, when."

"Well, I didn't exactly keep track. I go to Cancún Island,

the Hotel Zone, I usually do one hotel at a time. Last night was the Estrada. When, I couldn't rightly say. You Mexicans, time is a foreign concept to you. Nobody's ever on time. The word 'appointment,' I don't reckon it's in the Spanish-language vocabulary. I gave up wearing a watch.

"What I did, I parked the car, went in, hung around the lobby, went up the elevator, walked the halls, kind of made a circuit, just being there for anybody needing to talk. I got leaflets I take around too, maps of the road to Salvation, you could say."

"How was business?"

"Not good," Smith said. "The last things folks are thinking about when they come to Cancún is their immortal souls. I guess I can't entirely blame them. They save their money yearlong and do what they been looking forward to doing, irregardless how sinful.

"Satan, he's got a strong pull in these parts. The Stinko Prince, he got the Yucatán franchise. Cancún City and Cancún Island, they're Sodom and Gomorrah. There's not an iota of difference so far as I'm concerned."

Luis said, "Did you talk to anyone long enough that they would remember you?"

Smith smiled wanly. "Nope. I guess I look like what I am. Most of them, they look straight through you and trot on by."

"Hotel managers cannot be greatly pleased to have you on their property."

"Oh, you're so right." Smith chuckled. "They let me know about it too if a guest complains."

"Last night?"

"No. I couldn't of been in the Estrada for twenty minutes when I"—Smith gulped and cleared his throat—"when I come upon the body, the dead girl."

"María López. Were you acquainted with her?"

"Never seen her before in my life. I was walking down the hall and I heard this loud moaning inside this room. I knocked on the door. The door came open. It was ajar. The moaning was extra-loud then. I knocked again. The moaning stopped. I went in and there was a pretty Mexican girl on the bed. Her chest was covered with blood and an old stone knife was sticking in it. It was dark, but some light was coming in from the hall. She had on a fluffy dress and her eyes were staring wide, up at the ceiling, and she was soaked bloody. Lord have mercy, she'd just died."

Luis studied the missionary. He seemed sincerely shaken by recollection. "What did you do?"

"I went to her to see if she was alive. I'm no doctor, but I took first aid in high school. No pulse, no heartbeat. She was as dead as a doornail. The room lights came on. Folks in the doorway were pointing and screaming at me. I panicked. I ain't proud of it, but I did. I ran right through 'em. I'm a big fella, I reckon you noticed. They ganged up on me out in the hall and called the police. You're clued in on the rest."

"Did you kill her?" Luis asked. "Did you? Did you kill Janie Foster? Did you kill Judy Jacobson? Did you kill Alison Hall?"

"I answered that question before."

"Not directly."

"Strike me dead with a bolt of lightning and float me adrift on the River Styx without a paddle, Mr. Balam, I don't take human lives. Let me into your heart and through Jesus I'll give you everlasting life. No. No sir."

His denial was typically flatulent, but borderline believable. "Can you provide alibis on the dates the other three women were murdered?"

"My wife Ellen, her and me have a small apartment in Cancún City. Can Ellen be my alibi?"

"No. She has a vested interest. We need unbiased strangers. In your case, frankly, many unbiased strangers."

"Well, I reckon that's a zero. Me and Ellen, we're it for Tropical Language Scholars in northern Quintana Roo. They set a budget and turn us loose with a long leash. We're on our own, Ellen and me.

"Say, speaking of preaching, this prosecutor fella dropped on by an hour ago. He had on a spiffy suit and he was perfumed and pomaded to the nines. He was pushing me to sign this piece of paper to okay moving my trial. A hard sell, Brother Balam. I thought *I* was a bulldog."

"Did you sign?"

"Nope. He was talking Mexico City or Guadalajara or Tampico or Veracruz. I couldn't pin him down which. He said I'd be doing myself a huge favor. I asked how come. He insinuated that whether I got the death penalty or not was up to me. Me, Gilbert.

"Me and Ellen, we don't have the money for her to chase me around Mexico while they make a circus out of me. Tropical Language Scholars, they figure I'm dead-to-rights guilty, they'll bail out like I'm an airplane what caught on fire. We sold our farm when the Lord asked us to do His work. That money's already gone. Like I told the dandy, I'm between a

rock and a hard place. I got some serious thinking and praying to do before I sign anything."

"Good. The public prosecutor will return. The political
pressure on him is enormous. Do not cause him to lose face
with an absolute refusal. Be vague. He understands vague.
He lives by vague.

"Before I leave you, what else have you not told me that
will benefit the investigation?"

"Nothing."

"Nothing" was too snappy, too abrupt for the leaden missionary. Luis knew he was lying, concealing information.

But what?

CHAPTER SIX

t is written that ten centuries ago a mythic Toltec ruler named Quetzalcoatl crashed down from Mexico into northern Yucatán to assimilate the Maya. Quetzalcoatl, meaning "Plumed Serpent," established his reign at Chichén Itzá. Quetzalcoatl became Kukulcán to the Maya. Kukulcán was said to have been wise, gentle, and charismatic. But was he real? God, king, or god-king?

Kukulcán Boulevard was Cancún Island's main and only drag. It bisected hotels and ribbons of sand that could be mistaken for granulated sugar. Cancún was too slender for a second thoroughfare.

Driving on the demigod's namesake, Luis wondered again what he/He would think of Cancún. Be he mortal, Kukulcán would be spinning in his grave. Be He a deity, the feathered snake would be pacing above the clouds, plotting vengeance. That is, if He hadn't already taken His vengeance in the forms of Gilbert the storm and Gilbert the psychopath.

Luis wondered again what he himself thought of Cancún. Yes, the resort was his ticket out of the cornfields. It was also

47

his introduction to crime and commerce, a disgraced police career, and a tent in which he and his babies bargained the price of beads with strange life-forms such as Phoenix stockbrokers and ophthalmologists from Tampa. Good or bad? he debated for the thousandth time, coming to the same nebulous conclusion.

Club Estrada, a latter-day pyramid of stucco, glass, and view decks, stood on the southerly, less developed stretch of the island. Straight through the lobby was a disco boasting the latest electronic glitz, to the right a coffee shop selling tacos made of American cheese and iceberg lettuce, to the left an arcade of boutiques and time-share realtors.

Behind the front desk was an office. A squat, pockmarked man spotted Luis and strode into the lobby. "Balam, my plate is full of problems today. You walk in and it spills over."

Enrique (Bud) Rojas was manager of the Club Estrada. Rojas and Luis went back to Cancún antiquity, the late 1970s, when everybody knew everybody. Rojas's first Cancún job was bellboy at a newly completed hotel Luis had worked on as a laborer and electrician's helper. They were acquaintances in the least affectionate definition of the term. Hector Salgado Reyes referred to Rojas as a Polyester Asshole. Luis could not disagree.

A necktie in Yucatán was as rare as a snowdrift, but Luis had never seen Rojas without one. The tie transformed him into a Business Executive. He preferred paisley and neon atop dark dress shirts, above doubleknit slacks and wingtip oxfords. Rojas, with his throbbing attire and lunar complexion, looked to Luis like a minor player in a gangster film, an extraneous thug who is machine-gunned out of the script early.

"Bud," Luis said, gesturing vertically, "for your sake, I hope the air-conditioning never fails. You are head to toe in man-made fibers. You will drown in sweat."

"Funny," said an unamused Rojas. "I have a million priorities. None include you. In case you have not heard—"

"I have heard, Bud," Luis interrupted, thrusting a note from Hector at him. Rojas was Enrique to Mexicans he considered equals, Mr. Rojas to the Maya who laundered bedsheets and scrubbed pots in the kitchen, and Bud to North Americans. "Bud" was the north–south linkage, a validation that Cancún water was truly potable. Rojas would forever be Bud to Luis.

"This is garbage," Rojas said, crumpling the note and thrusting it back at Luis. "They have Gilbert. A missionary, no less. I am overjoyed, but why did it have to happen at my hotel? The police are investigating an open-and-shut case. I will not have some civilian detective snooping in my hotel."

Luis grasped the note and Rojas's fingers. He squeezed and pulled the manager close. He reeked of cologne and mint. Rojas's mouth opened, but he did not make a sound. Machismo forbade a cry, a whimper.

Luis released him, retaining the note. "Sorry, Bud. The paper must have stuck to your hand. I had to tug hard. Now listen to me. Inspector Salgado authorized me to inspect the room. I will not disturb your guests."

Rojas flexed his hand gingerly, slowly, looking at it, testing the joints. "You have twenty minutes," he said, his voice an octave higher.

"That is extremely generous, Bud. Thank you," Luis said, returning to Rojas a fraction of his lost face.

"You no longer are a policeman for Salgado. Mr. Estrada saw to that. You have a client?" Rojas's face was contorted, a grimace gone to a smirk. Not a handsome sight.

Luis answered evenly, "I have a client. How is the junior? Is he behaving?"

"I am a compassionate man, Balam. I will not repeat your insult to Mr. Estrada. He is too busy at Puerto Estrada to be concerned with the likes of you. His life functions on a massive scale. He put you in your place once. He can do it again, as easily as he can yawn."

"Yes, probably. The junior is an experienced yawner," Luis said, glancing at a wall clock. "Is our pleasant conversation counting in my allotted twenty minutes?"

"It should be. Who is your client?"

"Yes," Luis replied, "I have a client. Did you know María López, the prostitute?"

"I resent the insinuation. I do not condone prostitution. Prostitutes are thrown out of the Cancún Club Estrada and every hotel in the Estrada Group. This woman comported herself as a high-class barfly, so I have been informed by my staff. She was clever. Nobody witnessed money transactions. I do not normally work nights. I was not present at the time of the murder.

"My bartenders and cocktail waitresses were familiar with her, but they regarded her as an amateur. Do not interview them, Balam. Mr. Estrada and I have ordered them to decline comment to anybody but the authorities. For your information, López was a beautiful tramp with an unladylike mouth and elegant clothes. She drew horny gringos like flies. Promiscuity is not illegal, you know. Pickups in the lounge, casual encounters that lead to bed, do not violate hotel policy."

"She rented a room from you to turn her tricks and it did not occur to you or your idol, Estrada Estrada, that she was a professional?"

"Goddamn you, Balam, the Gilbert case is solved! My business is off sixty percent thanks to that lunatic. I want him forgotten, and every day a cop or a detective is in the Estrada is a reminder of Gilbert. Prospective guests will do an about-face and check in at the competition. God knows, there are vacancies."

Luis did not reply. He was by then walking up the spiral stairway of lush carpeting and wrought-iron railing. Enrique (Bud) Rojas, he thought. General Manager and Executive Director, Club Estrada, Estrada Hotel and Leisure Group; Kukulcán Boulevard, Cancún, Q. Roo, Mexico.

That's what was printed on his business cards. Rojas distributed them extravagantly. They impressed equals in the restaurant and hotel trade, and intimidated lessers. He gave them out like candy to ladies, but could not for the life of him get laid without paying. Upward mobility did not compensate for an ugly appearance and an uglier personality. The man's persona was darker than his gangster shirt.

Luis conceded envy, envy that impelled him to hurt the hotel manager. He had cheated him with his surprise grip, clamping harder and harder while entertaining a fantasy that the Polyester Asshole's knuckles were grinding into calcium dust. He felt badly. He felt tiny. He felt like a bully, a piece of garbage. There was nothing lower than a bully. The feeling would soon pass, however; it would not invade his dreams. He did not like himself at the moment, but he liked Rojas less.

He and Rojas broke in at the outset of the Cancún boom weeks apart. Rojas was a mestizo—an automatic edge on a Maya, yes—but his circumstances were as impoverished. He had had a father for as long as it took the sperm to splash his mother's egg. Mother, six siblings, and Enrique eked a living weaving hammocks and selling them on the streets and in the markets of Mérida.

Rojas had clawed inexorably upward. A dozen hotels. Bellboy to bell captain to night manager to assistant general manager to big boss. Luis had climbed, fallen, and was indefinitely scuttling sideways, searching for "up" without an especially keen sense of direction.

Bud. Stupid nickname. Self-serving, ludicrous, no connection whatsoever with Mexico proper or Yucatán. Bud: the name of a St. Louis beer, a retired Oklahoma University football coach, a prepubescent blossom. Rojas, he yearns so fervently to be a bigshot admired by North Americans, he should bleach his hair blond and drive a German car while talking on a telephone.

Names. Raúl Estrada Estrada. In Mexico a man's surname is his middle name, his last name his mother's maiden name. Most men hung on to all three. Others carried the last as an initial. Some, like Luis, dropped it altogether. Luis loved his mother as much as any man, but the appendage seemed an affectation. Excessive Mexican-ness.

Psychologists, attempting to explain the endemic infidelity and abusiveness of the macho Mexican male, asserted that he deemed just two women as worthy and pure: the Virgin Mary and his own mother. The rest were whores. Tar me not with that brush, Luis thought.

Ah, Estrada Estrada. Before Luis died, he would have to ask the junior if his father had married his sister. He would not have otherwise lived a complete life.

The state judicial police officer guarding the murder room was seated in a wooden chair tilted on its hind legs, leaning against the door. He looked drowsy, but Luis's approach brought him out of his torpor and his chair. Luis knew that during these episodes he wore his self-defeating poison on his face and in his body language. He came across as morose and menacing, and passersby gave him space.

Ashamed of himself, Luis forced a smile and damped the jerkiness in his gait. He asked the officer how he was, and presented Hector's note.

"Uh, fine. You are a—what kind of detective?"

"Private, independent, civilian. Whichever."

"You cannot disturb or touch anything."

Luis nodded. "I have been preceded, I take it."

"Brass from here, there, and places I never knew existed. Police, prosecutors, specialists, journalists who paid off the right people. They are not half that speedy in the cops-and-robbers movies. Gilbert, he has lit a fire under everyone." The policeman unlocked the door. "What are you going to do?"

"Search for mystery clues."

Both men laughed.

Luis entered. Unless you paid for a suite, Cancún hotels

rented you a bedroom, a bath, and sliders leading to a small deck and the ubiquitous view of the inland lagoon or the eastward Caribbean. Not that this room was cheap. Rojas and the junior were raking it in. As Hector had said, a hundred dollars a night. Minimum.

The bedcovers were pulled aside. The linen was blood-drenched. Luis went into the bathroom. Toilet, sink, shower, empty medicine cabinet. Besides the bed, the bedroom was furnished with a color television, on a swivel mount, and a dresser.

He hooked his pinkie and slid each of the drawers toward him. In Luis's interpretation, he was not disturbing and/or touching anything so long as he didn't deposit fingerprints and get caught. The drawers were empty.

He nudged apart the sliders with a sandaled toe. The deck held three people standing or two sitting. There wasn't anything out there either except the view. The weather was overcast and breezy. The sea looked like angry dishwater.

He shut the door and performed a slow-motion pirouette. The room was a shell. No possessions, no loose articles, not a cable TV schedule, not a complimentary bar of soap. This was López's temporary workplace, not her home. Had María left behind anything but the liters of blood sopped into the mattress, Luis knew, the artifacts would have been scavenged by prior investigators, prosecutors, newshounds, and freelance voyeurs. Souvenirs rather than evidence, he thought. They already had their Gilbert.

He closed his eyes and conjured up last night. María López, in a high-necked dress, sitting up in bed, maybe reading a Victorian romance novel. Who's there? Me, my little tamale. Trick coming in, María coquettish, he gallant.

A charade of seduction—spunky María fending him off, the Yanqui stud tanked on an evening of margaritas eventually prevailing, a denouement with María crying out in prolonged orgasm.

Luis recognized several slight problems in his illustration. No romantic trick had shown up. Gilbert had. Proctor Smith had. Whether they were separate or the same, it hadn't been an ordinary evening for María López. How had Gilbert gained entry?

Luis opened the door. The guard stood.

"Relax," Luis said. "I am testing."

Luis released the door. The tensioner whooshed, pulling it shut. The deadbolt latched with a baritone clack.

So. How did he or they gain entry? This apparatus was standard in Cancún luxury hotels, where guests were affluent and had belongings worth stealing. Proctor Smith said the door was ajar.

Luis again opened the door and released it.

Whoosh, clack.

Maybe María López had wedged folded paper under the door to hold it ajar. She could not have been primly in bed reading a Victorian romance novel if she had to let her trick in. Maybe she hadn't.

Luis went into the hallway and watched the door go whoosh-clack. "A crazy world we live in," he said.

"Crazier and crazier," the guard said, frowning.

"Do you normally patrol the Hotel Zone?"

"Normally. Who can guess how long I will be confined to this duty." A pear-shaped man, he rubbed ample buttocks. "This chair is like iron."

"Did you ever run across María López?"

The guard looked at him.

Luis gave him two thousand pesos. The guard wrinkled his nose. Luis improved the aroma of the bribe by layering it with an identical banknote. The guard pocketed the currency and said, "Not personally. Some of the guys did. They put moves on her, but she was untouchable. She was in the major leagues, the first division. She paid off the hotel managers. They paid our shift commanders. A little bit trickled down to us."

"How long had she been operating in the Hotel Zone?"

"Three or four months. Nobody knows where she came from."

"When are they releasing the room to the hotel to rent?"

"To take off the police hold, somebody has to make a decision," the guard said sadly. "I may retire in this hallway."

Luis patted his shoulder sympathetically and advised, "Next shift, bring a pillow for your butt."

CHAPTER SEVEN

*T*he rain came at sundown and like a waterfall. Pavements steamed, lights flickered, and thunder boomed like war. Lightning converted the sky into a video game. The air smelled of ozone, of sewers not up to the overflow.

Luis Balam took refuge in a workingman's bar and waited it out. He was on the western fringe of Cancún City, ten kilometers or a million from the discos, American-cheese tacos, and prefabricated pyramids.

Luis sipped a León Negra and watched the second floor of a cement-block apartment house across the street, third window from the left. He couldn't see the entrance from this angle, but unless the weather knocked out the apartment building's electricity, he would be able to see when Ellen Smith arrived home.

Luis had obtained the address from Hector. He presumed she was visiting Proctor. The rain began to abate. Yucatán storms were as fleeting as they were ferocious. A two-León deluge, Luis gauged. He ordered a refill and paid the bartender with a five-thousand-peso coin.

The bartender held it up to a bare light bulb above the register and squinted.

"Problem?" Luis asked. "I doubt if it is counterfeit. They haven't minted in silver since the peso had value."

"No, not that, not what you are thinking," the bartender said. "I am a numismatist. I collect coins and this is a fiftieth-anniversary commemorative, 1938–1988. The nationalization of the oil fields by President Cárdenas. The British and American oil barons, he tweated their stuck-up noses!"

And it was a national holiday too, Luis thought. If we have an opportunity to tweak a First World Anglo-Saxon nose, we tweak. "So, does that mean you are paying me for it?"

The bartender closed his hand on the coin. "No way. Of course not. It is worthless now. I am speculating, thinking of the future."

"I envy anybody who thinks further ahead than the present. A free beer? We will drink a toast to Pemex and the patriotic gasoline they sell."

"Hah!"

"Of course not," Luis said. The rain stopped. Mrs. Ellen Smith's light went on. Well, maybe a one-and-a-half-León deluge. Bottom's up. Luis drained the bottle and went to the apartment house.

There were eight units, four down and four up. The structure was nameless and new-old, built within a decade but aging fast, subtly crumbling and mildewing in corners and in the substructure, victim of tropical humidity and graft. P. Smith was upstairs, in number 6.

A plain woman Proctor Smith's age answered Luis's

knock. She was shapeless in a flowered print dress, somewhere between skinny and fat. Straight brown hair hung to her shoulders. Luis focused on her eyes. They didn't match their package. They were remarkably clear and vibrant, a warm green.

Luis confirmed that she was Ellen Smith and introduced himself.

"Proctor mentioned you. My, Tropical Language Scholars already hiring lawyers and a private detective," she said, stepping aside and ushering him in. "That's the only promising note in this horrid mess."

Luis sat on a sofa that creaked. The furnishings were spare and cheap. Spindly dinette set. Folding chairs. Cardboard end tables topped with gaudy ceramic lamps of the sort peddled at Cancún City markets. Pine bookcase crammed with Bibles and religious volumes. The umbrella that had kept her reasonably dry was in a corner, airing.

"As you can see, Mr. Balam, the Lord's work isn't lucrative. Were you waiting long for me?"

Luis flushed at being nabbed checking, appraising. "Not too long, ma'am. I was across the street."

"My name is Ellen. As you might've guessed, I was gone to the jail. You have alcohol on your breath."

Her tone was matter-of-fact. She was not admonishing him, but he was nevertheless compelled to make excuses. "I ducked in out of the rain and drank a bottle of León Negra. Brewed in Mérida, it is the tastiest beer in the world. How is your husband?"

She fluttered a hand. "Don't fret. I've read my share of detective novels. Private eyes are *supposed* to be drinkers.

Proctor is getting along as well as can be expected. They're not abusing him. We thank the Lord for that. I'm going to have to ask you a question before we continue, Mr. Balam. Do you believe Proctor is innocent or guilty?"

"No opinion yet," Luis said.

"Well, you're honest. I'd be suspecting your skills and integrity if you came right out this early in the situation and said you thought he was innocent. The cards are stacked against my Proctor. We have to be realistic."

Luis recited the dates of the Janie Foster, Judy Jacobson, and Alison Hall killings and said, "Mr. Smith listed you as his alibi for those nights."

"Not good enough, is it?"

"No."

"Well, I'm positively certain Proctor and I were together those dates, but I don't keep a journal or a diary."

"Mr. Smith sometimes went alone to the Hotel Zone to preach," Luis reminded her.

"He may have on those days, but I wouldn't testify to it. We're a team usually, out in the villages or the small towns along the highway. Proctor couldn't focus on the villagers and forget the tourists. He had to save everyone. Regardless, without a third party, my corroboration doesn't mean a hill of beans. You said as much to Proctor, and my rational mind says I can't dispute them thinking they've arrested their Gilbert."

"You and Mr. Smith farmed in the United State of Oklahoma, Mr. Smith said."

"We grew hay and peanuts. We were childless, although I won't palm our childlessness off as the reason why our lives were empty. There were forces far more profound. One night, we went to the fieldhouse to hear an evangelist speak. I can't for the dickens remember his name, but he was talking right to us. When he called out for the folks who were rededicating their lives to the Lord Jesus Christ to step forward and be counted, Proctor and I looked at each other and up we went, and we've never looked backward. Jesus said to reach out and save the poor people in the hot countries who had not heard His word, the Good News. We contacted Tropical Language Scholars, sold the farm, and here we are. There are language studies to be done and souls to save from eternal damnation. Your people aren't receptive. The Lord has given us a challenge."

"The farm was profitable?"

"We scraped by. You can't make a comfortable living in the States farming unless you're a gigantic agribusiness. The socialists and crooks and democrats in Washington skin you alive if you're not. Well, we weren't full-time farmers, so the droughts and subsidy cutbacks and shenanigans on the commodities floors didn't affect us boom or bust, like they did some folks. I'm degreed from Oklahoma State University in education. I taught junior high.

"Proctor held a variety of jobs. He could've been the top diesel mechanic in four counties if he'd stuck with it. He was always restless and searching till the Lord Jesus Christ came into our lives. Proctor's masterful with his hands. He was partners in a cabinet shop that specialized in kitchen cupboards. They did varnished oak that'd make you weep, it was so lovely.

"We were kind of out in the sticks, so there wasn't a

selection of jobs—regardless how talented you were at what you did. Locksmithing, it was his major talent. I'd've never thought it, a trade requiring finesse and a light touch. You've seen Proctor. He's a big fella and his hands are mammoth."

"Locksmithing?"

"He filled out a coupon for one of those correspondence courses and bought their program. Proctor became so good at it they'd call him with problems nobody else could handle. It got to be a bother. Drunks phoned Proctor from taverns in the middle of the night. They'd locked their keys in their cars."

"Locksmithing," Luis repeated, thinking about the María López death room, the door that was ajar but couldn't have been. A mystery was becoming a theory, and the scenario was not in Proctor Smith's favor. "Your husband should not volunteer his locksmithing background to the authorities."

Ellen Smith brought steaming cups of tea. She had been in and out of the kitchen, preparing the tea while jabbering, and Luis, a detective, hadn't noticed. "He's not saying anything to them, but that's a valid point. I'll pass it on when I see him tomorrow. Proctor's ability to enter locked rooms, well, that would be the icing on the cake, wouldn't it? They'd railroad him without thinking twice."

Luis nodded.

"Not that they won't anyhow," she said, her voice cracking.

"I am sorry for your sadness, Mrs. Smith, ma'am, Ellen, but I must ask you this. Is your husband a liar? I am not implying he is lying about the killing. I'm referring to little, habitual, everyday lies."

Ellen Smith's reddening eyes widened. "My, you're not beating around the bush. Proctor's a man of God. Man falls short of the glory of God. Proctor is a mortal. He has feet of clay."

While Luis's comprehension of English was superb, he had not entirely mastered obfuscation. "Is your answer yes?"

"Little white lies that couldn't be disproved, I suppose. If I told you I never fibbed, that would be a whopper. Let he who is without sin cast the first stone."

"Has he ever struck you?"

"The day my man hits me is the day I pack my bags," Ellen Smith said firmly. "I think I see what you're driving at. Take your measure of the man through his mate and best friend. Have I swayed you in either direction?"

"No," Luis answered, sipping hot tea, which was not compatible with cold León. Luis Balam the detective wanted to ask Ellen Smith when she had last had sex with Proctor Smith. What did homicidal perverts and/or evangelical fanatics do to their wives in bed?

Luis Balam the man settled for, "Is there a single, solitary shred of information I should know that could be important to the investigation? Absolutely anything whatsoever."

"No," Ellen Smith said. "I wish there were. I wish it were the final pages of a paperback detective novel and I could reveal the true killer."

Luis finished his tea and got up. "I'll investigate open-minded. I promise you."

Ellen stood. "A person can't ask for more. I'm satisfied you'll do your utmost, Mr. Balam."

"Luis."

"Luis, Proctor says you and he had some friction."

"We are different types of people."

"Proctor says you wear your atheism on your sleeve."

Luis smiled.

Ellen escorted him to the door, her arm around his shoulders, saying, "Proctor tends to be a zealot. His heart is in the right place, but he can grate on people. I learned early on that you can't lead everybody by the nose down the road to Salvation."

"I will be impartial."

"You don't know Proctor. I do," Ellen said, looking at him. "Like most men, he hides his feelings. You can't fathom how scared he really is. He's terrified."

Esther and Rosa were closing Black Coral for the day, packing trays of merchandise into suitcases. Abandoned luggage gravitated from Cancún Island hotels to Cancún City markets. Tourists were hustled into upgrading at tony shops and Luis had picked up the shabby yet roomy discards for a pittance.

"Father," Esther said. "Your usual timing. We finish bundling up the stock. You drive in."

"My luck is holding."

"Father," Rosa said. "I sold the grotesque ring for eighty dollars, the price marked on the tag."

"The silver monstrosity with the triangular turquoise stone?" Luis asked, eyebrows lifting. "I figured I had made such a great deal by paying twenty. I thought I would have to wear it myself to be rid of the thing."

"Yes!" Rosa said gleefully.

"Esther, what is the matter?"

"Nothing, Father."

"Nothing? Your lovely face turns to a block of stone and you say 'Nothing'?"

"She lied to the customer," Esther said hesitantly.

Rosa glared at her sister, then said to her father, "He kept going 'native craftsmanship.' Whatever he bought, it had to be 'native craftsmanship.' Mexican and North American tribes in Arizona and New Mexico, up north where they mine silver and turquoise, they specialize in it. This piece, it came from Sonora State. It was 'native craftsmanship.' "

"Rosa told the man that the ring was made in our village. By a ninety-year-old craftsman who fought in the Revolution and knew Emiliano Zapata and Pancho Villa."

"Is it my fault he was ignorant?" Rosa screamed at Esther.

"Stop!" Luis said, clapping his hands. "Rosa, you do not lie to customers. You can overcharge fools if they do not choose to dicker. All the guidebooks advise them on the subject. If they are too rich or stupid, we have a windfall. But you do not lie. Is that clear?"

Rosa said, "Yes, Father."

"Esther, you are the older sister. You are in charge while I am gone. You should have taken her aside before the idiot paid."

"Yes, Father."

"Come on," he said, hefting a suitcase and smiling from ear to ear, to say that he was not angry and that the quarrel was done and forgotten. "We are going home while you listen to a story."

■　■　■

This VW Beetle, Luis thought, bumping along the rutted dirt road to Ho-Keh village, this car is a bottomless maw. Mexico City cabbies were renowned for stuffing six passengers and baggage into a Beetle. Loaded as the car was with his daughters and the valises of rattling beads, Luis could still see out half the windows. Only Mexico continued to manufacture the Beetle. Until automotive technology improved to Beetle level, he firmly believed, they should not cease production.

"Father, is Proctor Smith guilty?" Esther asked.

"I was wavering. Yes, no, yes, no. The locksmith revelation leans me to yes."

"He is Gilbert," Rosa pronounced. "Dead meat."

"I vote for guilty too, Father. You speak as if you like his wife," Esther said.

"Nice lady," Luis agreed. "Why she married him is a mystery."

"What do you do next, Father?" Esther asked.

"Go into Cancún tomorrow to Ricky's. The missionary lawyer from Dallas, Texas, is due momentarily. They can decide."

Ho-Keh was a village of fifteen homes. One was occupied by Luis and his daughters, another by his father and mother. Ho-Keh was Yucatec Maya for "Five Deer." The story had been relayed verbally from generation to generation that unknown ancestors at an unknown point in time had walked into a clearing and spooked five deer into the brush. There were few better reasons for establishing a village than plentiful game, so Ho-Keh had stuck.

Luis stopped at their house. It was traditional Maya construction, elongated and stucco, with a steep thatch roof. Only the electrical line drooping from pole to meter on the side of the house denoted the century.

The interior, one room, was furnished with wooden tables and chairs, lamps, a radio, a metal tub for bathing, and three hammocks. Rural electrification was a Mexico City modernization priority. Running water and schools and sewage facilities could wait.

Luis nestled into his hammock, comparing the amenities of Ellen Smith's modest home to his. She had an indoor stove, bathroom, and running water; he did not. He had his two babies; she had an enigma in jail. No contest.

Rosa spoke to her father. She asked if he would like a warm drink, something to help him relax and sleep. Luis did not reply. He was already snoring.

CHAPTER EIGHT

W. (Lard) Ringner, attorney at law per an embossed business card, cut a piece of his luncheon-special New York strip steak. He chewed thoughtfully, set fork and knife on his plate, gulped bourbon on the rocks, smacked his lips, joined thumb and index finger in a circle, and said, "I give it two and a half stars. I'm scoring on a Dallas steakhouse scale, mind you, so if the chef's overhearing, providing he *spreckens da inglés*, he shouldn't have diddly cause to be insulted."

Hector Salgado Reyes was having the Hungry Hombre sixteen-ounce dinner sirloin with double fries. He smiled faintly and indulgently. Ricardo Martínez Rodríguez had ordered the smallest London broil and a green salad. He beamed obsequiously. Luis Balam, who knew an assistant chef, had wangled a plate of black beans and tortillas. He stared.

They were eating lunch at the Crazy Cow, a Hotel Zone restaurant that specialized in imported beefsteak. A leering bovine, neon and manic, USDA PRIME branded on his succulent flank, formed the marquee. Because the peso was thirty-two hundred to a dollar and galumphing downhill at the rate of one per day, prices were (as on most Mexican menus) written in pencil. The paper under these outrageous digits was fuzzy from repeated erasures.

Luis had gone into Ricky's office that morning as Ricky was scurrying out to meet Ringner at the airport. His lady friend at the telephone company had personally delivered a fax from the attorney, a cryptic message stating flight arrival number and time, and the instruction to "arrange lunch, my treat, for all principals, no taco stands, no Tex-Mex, thank you very much, but if you have a joint that broils beef so tender you can cut it with a dirty look, I'll be eternally beholden." At Ricky's request, Luis made reservations. He also invited Hector, a bona fide principal if there ever was one, a man who dreamed of free lunches.

"Dallas–Fort Worth International Airport is a two-hour hop from Cancún and I've never taken the pleasure of a visit before," Ringner continued. "That's an oversight I can blame partly on Mrs. Ringner. She's a skier. Gives her an excuse to spend three grand a year on outfits so she can snap on a pair of sticks, go fifty feet and fall on her keister. She says, 'Ring, Dallas is as hot as a popcorn fart two thirds of the year—we take a vacation, we're gonna get *cold.*'

"Yankees, conversely, they head south in the winter, come home with second-degree sunburn, and everybody's so drop-dead jealous they can't stand it. This attorney buddy of mine, he went to New Zealand two Julys ago, did the heli-copter skiing thing where they drop you at the summit, feed you a gourmet meal, and see you later at the bottom. Bubba has self-confidence coming out of his pores, professional and athletic. He played outside linebacker for an Aggie Cotton Bowl team. In this situation, confidence was his undoing. He took on a slope about ten degrees steeper than vertical. By the time they dug him out and choppered him to the hospital, it was two late to save three toes on his left foot.

"He comes home and it's one-oh-five in the shade and Bubba's recuperating from *frostbite*. He couldn't buy a drink at the club till Labor Day, I kid you not."

Ringner's rapid-fire anecdote overloaded Ricky's and Hector's English proficiency. They stared.

Luis smiled broadly and bluffed. "Ironic."

Ringner glanced quizzically at his guests, a trio of loco Mexicanos. He resumed eating. Hector and Ricky eagerly followed his example.

Luis ate too, sizing up the lawyer. Ringner was trim and natty, gray of eye, strong of jaw, and red of nose, a handsome, sideburned man of approximately thirty-five. He wore an open-neck white shirt, a ten-gallon hat, and ornately tooled boots. Three empty bourbon tumblers formed an arc around his plate.

Luis's first impression was of a Southern tourist in formal attire. A cartoon North American. Further examination persuaded him otherwise. Ringner was no good ol' boy cliché. He had controlled the luncheon meeting from the outset. Hector was feeding his face on prompt and Ricky was gaga. W. W. (Lard) Ringner, he thought: competent, immoderate, possibly dangerous.

After they'd finished eating and fresh drinks were brought, Ringner said, "I might as well go right to the nitty-gritty, gents. You're intelligent guys. I knew that from the git-go. Shouldn't knock you over with a feather when I say that the bottom line is damage control."

"I comprehend damage control," Hector said. "Your missionary bosses want the mess cleaned up exceptionally soon. They endeavor to avoid extended humiliation."

Ringner winked at him. "Give the man a cigar."

"Excuse me for seeming negative, Mr. Ringner," Hector continued. "But a North American saying occurs to me: Up shit creek without a paddle. That is Mr. Proctor Smith, and his canoe is leaking. Therefore, I think, damage control will be rather difficult."

"Our independent investigation is not completed, sir," Ricky broke in. "There could be developments."

Hector folded his arms across a considerable chest and laughed. "Developments! The lawyer is chasing fees. Proctor Smith is Gilbert. You are, my friend—another proverb, forgive me—flogging a dead burro."

"I know where you're coming from, Inspector," Ringner said. "Smith is a definite problem, a definite liability. I'm not especially savvy on Mexican law. It's based on the Napoleonic Code, isn't it?"

"Yes sir," Ricky said, blushing at Hector's insult.

"Essentially guilty until proved innocent?" Ringner asked. "The vice versa of ours?"

"Correct," Hector said. "Prosecutors and investigators present evidence and testimony. A judge decides and hands down the sentence. There are advantages and disadvantages to the defendant. A Cancún jury of Mr. Smith's peers would bring to the courtroom rope and a footstool. We have a bail system, yes, but it is inapplicable to capital crimes."

"Counselor?" Ringner asked Ricky.

Ricky, refusing to concede Hector's superior legal knowledge, said, "A writ of *amparo,* perhaps, can be obtained."

"A who?" Ringner lit a long black cigarette.

"Article one-zero-seven, Section One, of the Constitution of the United Mexican States," Hector said.

"*Amparo* is similar to your appeal system, sir," Ricky explained. "*Amparo* protects a defendant after a trial if a retrial is appropriate. Or during acts in a trial that unfairly prejudice a defendant. False arrest, cruel and unusual punishment, violation of rights, and so on."

"That's shaky in this situation, right?" Ringner asked Hector.

"Impossible. You could obtain a sentencing delay for Gilbert—"

"Smith," Ringner corrected. "The alleged Gilbert."

Hector smiled. "My apologies. A delay of the inevitable. Little else."

"Jungle drums tell me the prosecutors are anxious to ship Smith to the boonies for trial." Ringner leaned back, blowing a smoke ring.

"Gilbert has hurt merchants and hosts," Hector said. "Look around. Cancún's finest beef, and two tables in three are vacant."

"I read the papers. I've stayed up to speed on this thing. I can empathize how Gilbert's put Cancún through the wringer."

"Five-headed calves," Hector said. "Abominable snowmen. Hollywood starlet gangbangs. Are they not grand?"

"Hey, I think I saw that issue. Anyhow, where I'm coming from, where I *have* to be coming from, is my client's perspective. I'll be honest with you gents." Ringner leaned forward and lowered his voice. "Confidentially, I'm not too peachy-keen fond of the product Tropical Language Scholars is peddling. Their critics contend that fundamentalist missionaries are a major social problem in the Third World, and between you and me and the gatepost, I'm inclined to concur. Quote me, I'll swear you're lying, so help me God."

"Why do you practice law for them?" Luis asked. "Why do you take their money?"

Ringner looked at Luis, organized his words, and said, "Standards of morality? They have theirs, you have yours, I have mine. I get so goddamn sick of having ethics interpreted and rammed down my throat by every swinging dick who climbs a soapbox. Okay, do you have any idea how many attorneys there are in America?"

"No."

"Do you have any idea how many attorneys are cranked out of law schools every year? Baby shysters with tiny, sharp teeth."

Luis shook his head no.

"I don't either, but if you lined their sheepskins end to end, they'd stretch to Jupiter."

"You're a bright man. Your teeth are sharp and not tiny."

"Luis," Hector said softly, "don't start anything. The gentleman bought us a splendid lunch. Let him speak his piece. Shut the fuck up. Please?"

Luis repressed a smile and nodded yes.

Ringner sighed, took a generous gulp of bourbon, and

said, "Thank you, Inspector. Thank you, Mr. Balam. With the exception of the inspector, we're here because we're going to be paid money for performing a service. Capitalism in progress. Somebody's got to come out of this thing smelling like a rose.

"I frankly flat out need the bucks. I have a so-so practice and pretenses to maintain, peace to keep on the home front. An expensive lifestyle is a curse, boys. It's like a six-hundred-pound albatross hanging around your neck.

"And correct me if I'm off the beam, but Proctor Smith is entitled to due process and an adequate defense, such as it might be. I rest my case.

"On to damage control. Before we got sidetracked, we were discussing damage control. My clients, their frontline people, they have this image problem. I'm addressing the topic generically. The missionaries we're subjected to in the States: your New Age crystal guru-geeks, your slicky-boy televangelists, your door-to-door Jesus drummers, your campus dorks for Christ, your shaved-head airport loonies, your sidewalk Armageddonists, you name it. The image is negative with a capital *N*.

"Tropical Language Scholars has to date been free of major-league predicaments. Oh, they've gotten into binds. No denying it. Boys will be boys. This gent in Guatemala was translating something besides the Bible to indigenous populations of the teenaged-girl persuasion. I think it was the *Kama Sutra*, the illustrated edition. TLS donated a generator to the village, and the situation died a merciful death. A cocaine brouhaha in Bolivia. Pitifully small-time—coca leaves, actually. A middleman setup to finance Spanish-language Sunday school materials.

"Inconsequential bushwa like that. When you compare it to Jonestown and the multimillionaire TV preachers with their tax dodges and perpetual hard-ons, TLS's indiscretions haven't amounted to zip. TLS is basically small potatoes. They'll go into the boonies on a joke of a budget and take their saved souls one godless savage at a crack.

"That's out the window now, gents. My clients are center stage. Gilbert's aimed the spotlight at them and they're shitting bricks. The reverends are diving under tables. I'm the nearest facsimile to a TLS holy man you're gonna see.

"Okay, talk to me about Gilbert. He stabbed those gals with an old Mayan Indian knife they did virgins in with, right? He's one innovative fruitcake."

"Yes," Hector said. "A Maya sacrificial flint knife. It has been verified."

Ringner took a drink and said, "Gilbert sacrificing nonvirgins. The Freudians will have a field day. Damage control. Moving the venue to quiet things down, is that a problem?"

"Our client is determined to remain in Cancún for trial, sir," Ricky said.

"Who's talked to him?" Ringner asked.

"We three have, separately," Hector replied. "The lawyer and I, to us he would not say shit if he had a mouthful. He responded to Luis."

"What can you give me?" Ringner asked Luis.

Locksmithing? A loyal wife? Luis's ambivalence? Luis gave him, "Smith is adamant that he is innocent."

"Super. Hunky-dory," Ringner said. "Pleading innocence, that just proves he isn't crazy. I'll go see him, explain the facts of life."

Ringner snapped his fingers. *"Garçon, el checko, por favor.* We'll smoke and joke, Smith and me, one to one. Trust me, I'll penetrate his thick, godly skull. Plea bargaining, the benefits thereof, it's a universal language. Save thine ass.

"Meanwhile, Mr. Balam and Mr. Martínez, you guys snoop and be on stand-by, all right? We'll go through the motions. We'll have to afford Smith that. TLS insists and so do I. Inspector Salgado, I definitely appreciate your joining us."

Hector belched softly, ordered cherry cheesecake and another beer in Spanish before the waiter finished totaling the check, and said, "The pleasure belongs to me. We will be adversaries henceforward, I regretfully suppose."

Ringner again circled thumb and forefinger. "We're moving ahead. I can't bitch when we're making positive yardage. Gents, any recommendations?"

Ringner laid three crisp fifty-dollar bills on the waiter's check tray and said, "I see you're not raising your hands. Okay, it was a tough question. I guess we hang loose and play it by ear."

Luis said to Ringner, "Any recommendations from you?"

Ringner hesitated in mid-swig, then replied, "I was going to tuck this tidbit tight to the vest, but, okay, why not? Proctor Smith has been under a cloud at Tropical Language Scholars lately."

"For assaulting young ladies?" Hector asked.

"No, no. For assaulting his expense account. Possible, alleged, suspected embezzlement. He was basically nickel and diming them on cash advances for supplies and utilities and gasoline, petty things that add up and he couldn't justify. They'd demand receipts and Smith would comply, at his own pace, with half-assed forgeries. If they weren't so cheap, they'd hire a handwriting expert. I recommended they do it months ago. I think they'd've had Proctor Smith by the short hairs."

"Adding up to how much?" Luis asked, picturing Ellen Smith's sterile, dignified poverty.

"Chicken feed. Two to three to four hundred a month. The bean counters at TLS, praise the Lord, they could press blood out of George Washington's engraving."

W. W. (Lard) Ringner's jargon had finally lost Luis. "Four hundred dollars per month?"

"Yeah, max. Allegedly. The prices I've seen in Cancún, Neiman-Marcus ought to open an outlet. Lunch at this place, a stroll through one of these cutesy malls, and four hundred bucks could sift through your pockets, you wouldn't even feel it. Food for thought. Enough said."

Ringner stood and slapped a flat stomach. " 'No lard,' somebody'd've said by now back home, 'you're not packing a spare tire.' But that's the States, the You Ess of Eh. Kids don't pick up on it, but an older guy, in his fifties, he'd peg the nickname in a minute. I'll run through it in case you're asked.

"What it is, my daddy and favorite uncle whipped it on me when I was a pup. It's not, like I said, weight, obviously. It's a semantic thing, a flip-flop."

"Ring Lardner. Short-story writer and journalist, 1885–1933."

Ringner sat down and said, "Jesus H. Christ, Tonto, how'd you pull that out of your hat?"

Tonto? "World Almanac, 1974, page 365."

"That's what, not how. May I ask?"

Luis was enjoying Ringner's flummoxed expression, his competent handsome jaw drooping. "No."

"Okay. The world's full of surprises, I kid you not," Ringner said. "We'll do our jobs and live happily ever after. Mr. Martínez will be the liaison. I'll be in the background. This is a Mexican situation, you know. In the long run, pardon the hell out of the pun, a Mexican standoff."

"A rude question, please, Mr. Ringner," Hector said. "You work for the evangelicals for money, yes. You are candidly straightforward and I, a man not unfamiliar with the aspects of greed, applaud you. The question. How come the Bible-thumping dogs hired you?"

"I'm good," Ringner said. "I'm good, but I'm not great. They won't pay for great, but they'll spring for good. In this situation, good'll do. Proctor Smith, let's face it, whatever we do, he's shit out of luck.

"You know what Tropical Language Scholars' first choice was when they were screening to hire a general counsel? I heard this through a reliable grapevine."

"What?" Luis asked politely.

"A Jew. A Jew lawyer. That's how their prejudiced little brains click. Jew lawyers are the smartest and dirtiest and shiftiest according to their stereotype."

"You are not Jewish?" Luis asked.

Ringner laughed, lifted his glass, and sucked the patina of whiskey from the ice cubes. "Hell no! I'm a lapsed Pentecostal, but I am good. They didn't, they couldn't, have their Jew. They took a bulldog instead, a midpriced bulldog. Me. How could they have a Jew? How could they?"

"How could they?" Luis repeated, not understanding the question or whether it was a question.

"They couldn't. They flat couldn't," Ringner said earnestly. "The Jews allegedly whacked out their Savior. If that isn't conflict of interest, I don't know what is."

CHAPTER NINE

*L*uis Balam considered a business friend one who would accept a smaller-than-average bribe. Ignacio, a bus driver, was such a friend. He drove tour coaches out of the Hotel Zone to Chichén Itzá, Tulum, and Cobá. Occasionally, due to illness or turnover, there were temporary spots for guides. While yesterday's Tulum visitors had perused the exotic treasures at Black Coral, Ignacio collected his gratuity from Rosa and reminded her with a wink that today was payday. Rosa knew the code. She paid Ignacio extra and informed her father upon his return that tomorrow's Cobá run was his.

And it was. "Payday" referred to Paco, Ignacio's regular guide. Paco was a payday binge drinker. The day after, he was consistently too ill to report to work, an acute sufferer of the Corona/Dos Equis/Tecate Flu.

Luis substituted for the ailing Paco wearing navy and light blue, his traffic police issue, cum LUIS nameplate, sans patches and hardware. Unlike scrounging up a group at the Tulum wall, bus guiding required formality. Blue on blue and slicked-down hair sufficed nicely.

Standing at the front of the bus, commenting into the microphone, Luis was a native expert who respected dress codes. He was serious and neat, a justification of the ticket price.

Cobá groups were tough. They were challenging and fun. Tulum and Chichén Itzá visitors received painless, doorstep Maya culture, pureed and spoon-fed. Physical demands were minimal. Souvenir shopping and refreshments awaited at convenient proximity.

Cobá sprawled and was partially excavated. There would never be the time or money to complete the project. You could walk ten kilometers and not cover everything. There were no beverages and T-shirt vendors at site destinations. Cobá was inland, remote, and excruciatingly hot and humid.

Cobá visitors were up to it. Young and old, male and female, the bulk were fit and lean. They carried binoculars and field guides. They ate trail mix and did not smoke cigarettes. They spoke to one another about vanishing rain forests.

Luis spoke of Cobá—Maya for "Wind-Ruffled Waters"— a reference to its five lakes and the rarity of bodies of water in Yucatán larger than a sinkhole well. He spoke to ten people, down from a pre-Gilbert average of twenty-five. He spoke blah-blah-blah of Cobá's six thousand buildings, its dominance during the Maya Classic Period, a city-state inhabited by fifty thousand people—a people fourteen hundred years older than we on this bus. He spoke of traces of ancient roads, some as long as one hundred kilometers. He spoke of flora and fauna, of motmots and iguanas, of the color spectrum of butterflies, and of wild citrus trees.

The riders responded. They were enthusiastic and they

asked intelligent questions. They passed Black Coral. Somebody pointed at Luis's crude sign and remarked at the environmental damage done to the reef by coral divers. Luis vaguely agreed and remarked that this particular establishment, one-hundred-percent Maya-owned and -operated, dealt nominally in black coral and in fact specialized in turquoise and silver, and stocked perhaps the finest selection along the Quintana Roo coast.

They turned westward at Tulum and drove forty-five kilometers on a two-lane road straight as a ruler, past isolated villages, to the Cobá parking lot. There were too many structures and monuments to choose from. The group split according to principal interests and rejoined later for the not-to-be-missed site: Nohoch Mul.

Nohoch Mul, or El Castillo, or The Castle, was one hundred forty feet high, twelve stories, the tallest pyramid in northern Yucatán. At the end of a two-kilometer jungle path, the monster loomed without warning. The group made nonverbal sounds of awe, and the suddenness of its appearance never failed to cause a hitch in Luis's breath.

He was content, however, to send his charges to the top on their own, with suggestions of caution. Luis had climbed the one hundred twenty-two limestone blocks before. The steps were flat and fairly uniform, though steep and tiring.

He heard whistling and yelling. He looked up and saw, sitting on the top edge of Nohoch Mul, a young man with glasses and a silly grin. Dave Shingles was waving at him with both hands.

Luis sighed and started upward. A dyspeptic religious

fanatic and alleged serial killer, he thought. A cynical, bigoted, alcoholic Texas lawyer. A flying saucer crank who is revising history. A *Homo sapiens* menagerie. North Americans escaped from a zoo. What craziness will follow?

"Man, this is some view," Shingles said. "On a clear day I'll bet you can see Guatemala."

Luis sat and gazed out at verdant flatness, which was disturbed only by undulations of unexcavated structures. He was in no humor for hyperbole. "No you can't."

"I've been taking the lay of the land," Shingles continued. "And you know what I think?"

"I cannot imagine what you are thinking."

"My date's still correct. The end of the great cycle of the long count is a week from Tuesday."

"When they are coming for true believers?"

"Hey, am I converting you?"

"No," Luis said. "Now listen to me. I may not be an archaeologist or a research professor, but I know something of how my ancestors kept track of time. Your great cycle of the long count, I presume, is the *baktun*, a 144,000-day chunk of time, roughly four hundred years."

"Yep. They say that this, the twelfth *baktun*, began in 1618. The thirteenth will begin in 2012. Well, they're wrong. It's a week from Tuesday, not 2012, and the thirteenth *baktun* isn't beginning in any pertinent manner."

"The saucer men are coming to whisk us to Venus or Mars or Los Angeles. I've heard about Los Angeles."

"What's going to happen exactly, I can't say."

"Intellectual humility?" Luis asked.

"Make fun of me," Shingles replied, squinting at the horizon. "You'll see."

"Nobody has proven the long count has a beginning or an end. My ancestors counted with *baktuns* and smaller units in factors of twenty, millions of years into the past, millions of years into the future."

"Conventional wisdom," Shingles said. "Conventional wisdom sucks. You know what I think?"

"You ask the impossible. Please tell me."

Shingles cocked a thumb over his shoulder. "What do you see?"

Luis did not have to turn around. Nohoch Mul was capped by a squarish temple. Carved above the low doorway was the Descending God. The Bee God. The Diving God. He said, "The upside-down guy. Small world."

"It's not a coincidence," Shingles declared solemnly. "They're coming to Cobá instead of Tulum. There's a fifty-fifty chance, I think."

"Why?"

"No solid reason. Privacy, relatively speaking, is my hunch. Tulum's overrun with tourists."

A nugget of logic, Luis thought.

"Will you come to Cobá? Dawn, a week from Tuesday?" Shingles slapped his stone seat. "This is where I'll be, packed and ready to head out."

"Sorry, no thank you. I'm too busy. Gilbert has me pre-occupied."

"Huh? What's a Gilbert?"

"The Tulum tour group discussed Gilbert at length, near the end of the tour."

"I guess I'd kind of drifted off on my own by then."

Even if he hadn't, Luis thought, he wouldn't know about Gilbert. Some people didn't know: monks, the comatose, a dozen Chinese. If extraterrestrials scooped Dave Shingles off this magnificent rock pile and sucked him into outer space, it would be a family reunion.

Gilbert, and Luis's detective connection to the maniac killer, gushed forth. He narrated Gilbert's crimes chronologically. He described the events leading to Proctor Smith's capture and the evangelical's predicament. He divulged confidential details. The murder weapon, the Maya sacrificial knife, the tip of which had snapped in Alison Hall's rib cage. The political pressure to transfer venue. Presumed sexual abstinence in the second, third, and fourth killings.

Luis couldn't stop himself. Shingles was so peculiar, his opinion might be fresh and original. His position on misogyny would be enlightening, this unquestionable man-virgin. Also, he was a nice, sappy kid and Luis simply had the urge to babble.

"Man, that's disgusting," Shingles said in a quavering voice. "That's sick. I'm killing time. I'll help you on your investigation."

Luis looked at Shingles, whose eyeglasses were misted. Luis said, "Thanks for the offer, but no thanks. Is Proctor Smith Gilbert?"

"I wouldn't risk my life's savings on it, but yeah, he's your killer. You shouldn't cancel your investigation on account of what I say, though. You have to cover the bases."

"Explain why you feel Smith is Gilbert."

"Because God makes people who want to do bad stuff do bad stuff."

Inarticulately profound, Luis thought. "Who is Tonto?"

"The Lone Ranger's faithful Indian companion. Why?"

"No solid reason. None at all."

CHAPTER TEN

*I*gnacio interrupted the return trip to stop at Black Coral. He, too, coincidentally, was familiar with Black Coral's esteem for premier-quality turquoise and silver. Inside the tent, Luis, still the guide, steered Cobá explorers from the offending black coral to said turquoise and silver, not to mention extraordinary bargains in lapis and rose quartz. Rosa and Esther, total strangers to their father, utterly charmed the group. Black Coral had its best day in weeks.

Luis picked up his Volkswagen and drove from the bus company to Ricky's office to check the status of their investigation. Double-parked outside the bar was a sports car, a gold Mercedes-Benz 500SL that blocked the alley-width street for any vehicle heftier than a motor scooter. The car looked new. Passersby and victims of the congestion it created ogled. Nobody complained.

Luis parked behind it, got out, and found himself amused by the contrast; you could buy every terminally ill rental Beetle at Cancún International Airport for the price of this crouching metallic beast.

He had a pretty good idea who it belonged to even before he walked to the driver's door and squinted at the black-tinted window. He couldn't distinguish anything except an immense silhouette behind the wheel.

Luis pointed at the ground and froze like a statue until the occupant responded. Smoked glass eventually purred downward.

"What the hell do you want?"

Luis recognized the speaker. Pancho Villa mustache. Nasty little eyes. Chin that merged into shoulders, a neck somewhere in between. Fat fingers gripping the steering wheel.

He was a big boy, Raúl Estrada Estrada's current chauffeur-bodyguard-pimp. Luis could not recall his name—if he had one—but knew him by reputation as well as sight. A former federal policeman, too rough and venal even for the hated *federales,* he had been tossed off the force.

"Excellent car, boss," Luis said, smiling. "How much did your owner pay for it?"

"Fuck you, Indian. Fuck your mother. Get lost."

Luis stood fast, smile frozen on his face. He was inviting the goon to step out of the car and make him get lost.

"I ought to wipe the sidewalk with that stupid grin."

"Come on and try, fatso," Luis said, knowing he wouldn't. His responsibility was the junior's car. Should it be scratched or the stereo stolen while he was distracted, repairing his damaged pride, he would lose a cushy, lucrative job.

The goon muttered curses at Luis as the window purred

shut. Luis went up the stairs whistling. Estrada was loudly lecturing Ricky. Luis discerned the words "interference" and "disruptive."

"Luis!" Ricardo Martínez Rodríguez said, as if to a rescuer.

"Ricky. New client?"

Raúl Estrada Estrada looked at Luis without a hint of recognition. "This is a private meeting."

"But, Mr. Estrada, Mr. Luis Balam is my independent detective," Ricky said.

Estrada was Luis's age, mid to late thirties, tall, not a strand in his receding and glossy hairline out of place. Mexico City's finest plastic surgeon had fashioned a North American upturn for his prominently downturned Mexican nose. He dressed in the confectionery colors of a professional golfer. Flesh was starting to spill over his beltline. Luis had not seen him lately. The hair loss and spare tire were new. They were happy signs that Estrada was in a preliminary stage of decline.

"Whoever you are, you were intimidating my manager."

Estrada had not acknowledged Luis during the trouble; he had been an abstract irritant, a maddening itch caused by a persistent fungus. So why, Luis thought, should I have an identity now? He sat in a folding chair and said, "I was investigating. I was practicing damage control."

"You are upsetting my people and hurting my business at the hotel," Estrada said, pointing finger and bent thumb at Luis like a cocked pistol.

"Your Mercedes is beautiful. Is it brand-new? I wanted to read the odometer and see if it was, but the glass was too dark and there was something behind the wheel that should be extinct."

Estrada's head swiveled from Luis to Ricky and back. "What is this yak-yak? What does my car have to do with the problem?"

"Luis," Ricky said.

"It was smart to trade in the old Mercedes," Luis told Estrada. "It was repaired, yes, but once you bend the frame, they are never the same again."

"Cars." Estrada spread his arms in despair. "Who cares about cars? You idiots, Gilbert is in jail! We should be rejoicing. You people, you are stirring the pot. My Hotel Zone properties are losing money faster than I can count it. Our enormous investment in the Puerto Estrada destination resort is jeopardized. Keep out of this!"

"Mr. Estrada, sir," Ricky said. "Please understand that we have clients."

Ricky looked ill to Luis, on the verge of deathlike. His eyes were red, his skin waxen. A virus? Luis wondered. Ricky disliked conflict, but the junior's tirade could not have upset him *that* badly.

"You tried to break my manager's hand."

"My friend Bud's hand? No," Luis said. "If I had intended to break Bud's hand, I would have broken Bud's hand."

"Rojas tells it differently. Get out of it and stay out of it. The Gilbert thing is done as far as you are concerned. It is now up to the courts.

"You, an Indian, of all people should cheer. One more Gilbert murder and mobs would be tearing your villages apart, hunting for that sacrificial knife."

"Mr. Martínez is correct to point out our obligation to our client," Luis said. "Proctor Smith is entitled to a defense."

"You stubbornly insist on defending that evangelical nuisance, go ahead. He can have his defense in court. But keep off Estrada property or you will go to court too, for trespassing."

"My investigation is not complete."

"You confine your sorry investigations to situations more befitting your skills, and confine them outside my properties."

"I am not certain I can." Luis affected a sad expression.

"Luis," Ricky pleaded.

"Why not?"

"Mystery clues."

Estrada laughed.

"I found a mystery clue in the López girl's room," Luis lied. "An instrumental clue that the authorities had overlooked."

Estrada hesitated, then asked, "What clue?"

"Sorry. Confidential."

Estrada flicked his wrist in dismissal. "You are behaving like an ass. You have nothing. Smith is guilty."

"Smith guilty of killing López? Quite possibly," Luis admitted. "Smith guilty of killing Foster, Jacobson, and Hall? Quite possibly not. The patterns may not be conforming."

"Conforming patterns." Estrada shook his head. "Bullshit nonsense."

Luis said, "I have not yet ruled out alibis for Proctor Smith on the dates of the first three murders."

"A brilliant detective you have on your payroll," Estrada

said to Ricky, whose elbows were on his desk, his chin cradled in his palms. "Alibis are invented by the guilty."

Ricky managed a weak nod. Morticians had livelier material to work with, Luis observed, saying, "Alibis cannot always be invented. They cannot be reconstructed as easily as a collision-damaged Mercedes-Benz. For instance, Raúl, where were you on March seventh, April ninth, and May tenth?"

Estrada flushed crimson and yelled at Ricky, "Lawyer, I am a generous, forgiving man. I will pretend I did not hear myself being slandered. But you muzzle and leash this ugly little Indian, or you will be in for some kind of grief, you and him both."

Ricardo Martínez Rodríguez winced in pain when Estrada slammed his door. When the junior was down the stairs, Luis advised, "Ricky, go home to bed. A hurricane hits Cancún. Then a madman killer. Now you are spreading the bubonic plague—"

"No, no, no Luis. No disease. I entertained Lard Ringner last night. I showed him Cancún's nightlife."

"Ah."

"I, as you are well aware, am no slouch when it comes to going out and having a good time. I am, in North American tourist vernacular, a party animal. I can drink and carouse and chase pussy with champions."

"True," Luis agreed. "You belong in the hall of fame."

"Yes, I do. Thank you. Oh, but this Ringner . . . Luis, the man is not human. We barhopped the Hotel Zone. Everywhere we went we bumped into Texan tourists. Ringner instinctively recognizes fellow Texans. It is like a Lithuanian recognizing a Lithuanian, I suppose. How they do it, I cannot comprehend. Anyway, Texans love tequila slammers. Are you familiar with the concept?"

"A shot of golden tequila and a splash of Sprite," Luis said. "Slam, slam, slam the jigger on the bar, foaming it, then swallow it in one swig."

"Yes. A pagan gringo ritual they allege we Mexicans invented. Do you recall my lady friend Hortensia, Luis?"

A green-eyed mestiza who worked for a Hotel Zone condo realtor. Luis nodded. "A member of your harem."

"No longer," Ricky said, sighing. "Hortensia is incredibly beautiful. I could love that girl if she were not so shallow. As it is, Hortensia will never speak to me again."

"Because of tequila slammers?"

"Yes, indirectly, they were the culprits. Hortensia brought her friend Carla for Lard. We were enjoying ourselves immensely, Lard and I slammering, the girls nursing theirs, though nevertheless growing tipsy. They are sexually liberated young ladies. The Virgin of Guadalupe does not peer over their shoulders. The night, therefore, was extremely promising.

"Well, I was three slammers beyond my limit before I realized I had reached my limit. I threw up on the table and in my shoes. Lard and the girls dumped me into a taxi and went on partying. Luis, I am ill. I am deathly ill."

Ringner *is* dangerous, Luis thought. "Did you discuss fees?"

"Whenever I broached the subject, he bought a fresh round of slammers."

"Go home, Ricky, before you ruin the shoes presently on your feet."

"Forget my illness. I almost had a heart attack when you insinuated that Mr. Estrada is Gilbert."

"I did not insinuate. I asked him where he was on three specific dates. I was merely using him in my example."

"Whatever the purpose, however much you hope and pray that the despicable junior hangs by his gonads, you cannot think he is Gilbert. You are not being realistic."

"Maybe."

Ricky twisted his thumb on the desktop. "Luis, the man can do this to us. He can squash us like bugs. Your timing was not good. His outburst of temper was running its course. I was placating him. In the long run, we would have come to a satisfactory arrangement."

"Ricky, you have clients."

"Luis, your glaring weakness is your inability to detect shades of gray in situations."

"You cannot take his money," Luis said.

"He would not have been placing me on retainer to essentially toss Proctor Smith to the wolves. After all, the wolves are already ripping and tearing his flesh. Our hypothetical arrangement would have been predicated, I am presuming, on a less visible, less zealous investigation and defense."

"Sounds good in theory, but"—Luis mimicked Ricky's thumb twisting—"Estrada makes the rules. He can do this to arrangements. You cannot trust him."

"You make sense, as sickening as it may be."

"Has Ringner visited Proctor Smith yet?"

"No," Ricky replied. "He said he would work it into his schedule today, although I have doubts. Carla was discussing parasailing with him and he was rather intrigued. Luis, were you bluffing Estrada about alibis and multiple killers?"

"Yes and no. The idea jumped into my head. It is not impossible. A pattern in the days of the month or days of the week of the four murders is something worth exploring too, as is corroboration of the physical evidence."

"Oh, that scares me, Luis." Ricky moaned. "Days, weeks, and months smack of astrology and ancient lore."

"Not from me," Luis said, standing up. "You have no cause to worry. My feet are on solid ground and my investigation is logical and prosaic. You are looking at a modern man, a scientific detective."

Ricky looked at him skeptically through eyes that seemed in critical need of tourniquets.

"Yes you are, Ricky. In fact, earlier today a man from Mars voted Smith guilty. His logic was compelling, but I am not forsaking the scientific approach on account of it."

"Luis, what are you saying? What are you planning to do next?"

"Corroboration of the physical evidence. Go home, Ricky. Go home."

CHAPTER ELEVEN

The first place you looked for someone at a Hotel Zone hotel was the pool bar, thought Luis Balam the detective. Perhaps this was not a logical and scientific approach, he thought further. But if he were a guest, that is where you would find him, leering at the string bikinis and guzzling cold León Negra.

His "someone" was staying at the Club Estrada, where Luis could never be a guest, let alone welcome in any capacity. His camouflage, therefore, consisted of sunglasses, a LUIS nameplate, and, pilfered from a busing cart at the terrace restaurant, a tray and an order pad. A thousand-peso coin pressed into the hand of a bellhop bought an inquiry and confirmation of Luis's pool-bar hunch. Five hundred additional pesos purchased a description.

Luis Balam the waiter took several drink orders while he searched for Figueroa, the National Museum of Anthropology assistant curator. He conscientiously wrote down the margaritas and the brands of beer requested. He hoped that these customers were not genuinely dehydrated.

The pool bar featured concrete stools molded into its bottom, a hundred brands of beer and booze, and a view of the Caribbean. The bar, a human dock of sorts, was only a quarter occupied. A dozen other people lazed in the pool. No one was actually swimming.

Pool-bar guests appeared to be pleasant and happy. They were having fun. The sparse turnout substantiated the junior's financial complaints. Life, Luis decided, is not always unfair.

Chubby, middle-aged, hairy back, wispy hair on top, rimless eyeglasses. Luis spotted his man seated sideways on a center stool. He was holding a bottle of Corona and watching a broad-hipped woman play and splash with a small boy and girl in the connecting children's pool.

Luis pocketed his nameplate and pad, discarded the tray, squatted at the edge of the water, and stared at Figueroa until he made eye contact. Luis smiled and waved. Figueroa stared back, glasses on, blinking; then glasses raised, blinking. A shy, deliberate man, Luis assessed. He waved again. Figueroa tentatively waded toward him.

"Professor Figueroa?" Luis asked. "Doctor Figueroa, is it?"

Figueroa beamed, flattered. "Well, I do not have an advanced degree, the credentials to teach—"

"You are a curator, a specialist," Luis cut in. "It is not often that I have the privilege of meeting an intellectual. As far as I am concerned, working day to day with our rich history, your credentials exceed those of university academicians."

"They are in abundance," Figueroa said cheerily. "They

obtain their knowledge from books. They would not know archaeology if they tripped on a sectioning string and fell into a pit. I have an archaeological background. I have had dirt under my fingernails. I know what is involved in bringing an object from the earth where it has slept for centuries, identifying it, cataloging it, restoring it, and displaying it in a suitable exhibit. Who are you?"

"Reporter for the *News of Quintana Roo,*" Luis said. *Novedades de Quintana Roo* was the leading newspaper on the coast. "Let me tell you, an interview with a noted curator is a journalistic prize."

"I am sorry. I am on holiday. Story requests on the Museum must be made to the Museum public relations staff in Mexico City. I can give you the name of an excellent person to contact. She will circumvent the red tape. When this is accomplished and if the standard press releases are inadequate—and they frequently are—I would be delighted to respond by telephone or in writing to your areas of interest in which I have expertise."

"No, Professor, not a museum story. I wish to interview you regarding your role in the apprehension of Gilbert. You inspected the weapon with which María López was killed."

"Yes I did. Who are you?"

"The *News,*" Luis said, scribbling beneath 'Budweiser, hold the lime wedge.' "I am the Indian affairs reporter. You told the police that the flint knife impaled in the unfortunate young woman's chest was Maya, not a replica. How old would you estimate it was, Professor?"

"This is a police case. I should not be discussing a police case with a journalist, certainly not a case of this magnitude."

"You do have a point. I would also be interested in your archaeological experiences, in general. That is a harmless topic, I think. What is taken from Mexican soil relates to my native heritage. I believe I could develop a feature article from your comments."

"Teotihuacán," Figueroa said dreamily. "Memories. Those were heady days."

"Teotihuacán, the great imperial capital near Mexico City?" Luis prompted. "When were you there, Professor?"

"Yes. Two thousand years ago it may have been the largest in the world. In the 1960s. I was fresh out of college. Work at Teotihuacán began in the 1920s, but in the sixties it became a full-scale excavation and restoration effort. We were kids. We worked day and night for the sheer love of our glorious task."

"The past lives in you. I see it."

"It feels like yesterday. I had a flair for pottery. Give me a pile of potsherds and I could assemble them when no one else could. To me, the fragments were a series of jigsaw puzzles."

"You cannot teach that talent," Luis observed. "It has to be intuitive. You deserve your distinguished career."

The glow in Figueroa's face died. "Off the record, a career that should have been distinguished. Without money, without connections, talent can propel one only so far."

"Nevertheless, you have the satisfaction of being an authority on the Teotihuacán inhabitants and the Toltecs and Aztecs who succeeded them."

"Yes, in a modest regard I am," Figueroa said immodestly.

"You cannot be expected to know everything, though. You are probably not a Mayanist too."

"No. No I am not."

"So how can you be so positive the murder knife was Maya? Counterfeit replicas of these knives as well as other Maya artifacts are sold for big money. Unscrupulous characters will sell anything a tourist is willing to buy, bona fide or fake, even the endangered black coral," Luis said. "What was your criterion?"

Figueroa shook his head. "We have reentered forbidden territory."

Luis gestured to the stout woman and the small children. "Your family?"

"Yes."

"I have two girls myself. They are older, but they will always be my babies. I think it would be nice to have your family in the photo."

"What photo?"

"For my feature article," Luis replied. "Human interest. I can telephone the *News* and have a staff photographer here in twenty minutes."

"No, no, no! No photographs. No article either. This interview is finished."

"Professor, a hypothetical question. A general question. What would differentiate a genuine flint sacrificial knife from a reproduction?"

"Subtle things a layman could not possibly comprehend."

"Be patient with me and speak slowly. I will do my utmost to comprehend the technical aspects."

"There would be weathering."

"Weathering? Flint does not rust, does it? A knife dredged from the bottom of a *cenote* would be scummy, but good as new as a weapon, would it not? Also, it could be polished and sharpened. What type of weathering?"

Figueroa was not just obstinate, he was frightened. Clutching his Corona, he retreated to his bar stool, backward and slowly, like a ferryboat clumsily maneuvering into a slip. "There is no article. I will deny quotations attributed to me. I will deny this meeting. You and I never met."

"You must have meticulously examined the knife to arrive at your conclusions."

"A police case. No comment."

"Are you absolutely certain it was a Maya knife?"

Figueroa ignored Luis.

"Toltec? Olmec? Mixtec? Zapotec? Made in Taiwan?"

No reply.

"How did you happen to be so fortunately available at the murder scene, Professor?"

No comment, no eye contact, no communication whatsoever.

Figueroa was seated now on his stool, gazing into his beer bottle. His jaw was clenched and the knuckles ringing the bottle were ivory. At a pool bar, Luis mused, you could pee in your pants and nobody would be the wiser. Judging by Figueroa's bearing, a bit of squirming and fidgeting below the water line, he was doing just that.

Why was the knife's provenance so important? Luis

asked himself as he saluted the assistant curator and walked away. Answer: Because of Figueroa's bogus appraisal and his urine in the Club Estrada pool bar.

But why would Figueroa compromise his professional ethics? Why was he so obviously terrorized? Answers: None.

Another Luis-to-Luis question: How could Figueroa afford upward of two hundred U.S. dollars per day for the room alone, plus tourist prices for pool-bar chilled beverages and who knows what else?

Answer: Same as above.

But answer one question, he thought, and you answer them all.

CHAPTER TWELVE

uis," Inspector Hector Salgado Reyes said, "have I told you how precariously shitty your road is? My car bottomed out twenty or thirty times. And dark! I could not see in front of my nose."

A bleary-eyed Luis had answered Hector's gentle, tapping knock. "It is dark, Hector, because it is the middle of the night, and your car is bottoming out because you are driving on the original factory shock absorbers and your car is older than Esther. Speaking of whom—"

Luis turned and saw her outline bolt upright in her hammock. Rosa remained a softly snoring mound. A moth colliding with a lantern would awaken Esther, while Rosa could sleep through a hurricane. Luis signaled Esther that all was well, tamping air with his palms to urge her prone in the hammock and asleep.

Hector wagged a finger, beckoning Luis outside, saying, "My apologies for the intrusion, but this is supremely important."

Luis quietly shut the door behind him. "Important to whom?"

"Such a suspicious man you are, Luis. The amount of cash money you earn in your various enterprises, you should get out of Ho-Keh, get out of this village and live in town. Find a steady girlfriend. These one-night stands you embark upon three times a year, they are a waste of your maleness. Find a nice lady with bazooms who can cook."

"Why should I?"

"Amenities, my boy. Cable television. Streetlights. Plumbing. Legs wrapped around you every night."

Luis knew that Hector was needling him partly in fun and partly to ensure that Luis was fully awake and alert. Hector, his wife Carmen, and their seven children lived in Cancún City in a claustrophobic three-bedroom apartment. Hector had never stolen enough to live as well as his peers, some of whom had villas and ensconced their mistresses in love nests more spacious than Hector's home. Hector did have plumbing and did habitually watch soccer and baseball beamed in from Mexico City, and Michelle Pfeiffer movies on his VCR.

"Overall, however, in the bigger scope of things," Hector said, looking around at the silent blackness, "there is a lot to be said for squatting and taking a crap in the countryside. This implies, therefore, that you own the piece of the countryside you are crapping upon. I fart and my neighbor bangs on the wall and says to stifle the noise."

"Hector," Luis said, "what is going on?"

Hector jabbed a thumb at his car. "Trouble."

Hector's car was a Dodge Dart sedan. Spotlights were

mounted on both front doors. Antennae connected primarily to broken and nonexistent radios bristled from fenders and quarter panels. The trunk was an arsenal of confiscated guns and ammunition. The Dart's glass was of course tinted black.

The automobile terrorized pulled-over speeders, especially North Americans, who invariably drew comparisons to the Mel Gibson *Road Warrior* films. Whether they had exceeded the speed limit or not, Hector seldom received an argument.

"Trouble with the car or trouble within the car?" Luis asked.

"I should be so lucky as to have a howling wheel bearing or a burned valve," Hector said, sighing. "Inside the car."

"Trouble I can assist you with?"

"Please."

"First, Hector, answer a few questions on a matter."

Hector sighed again. "I know you, Luis. This is blackmail. On what matter?"

"Inexpensive blackmail. Figueroa, the assistant curator."

"An odd, jumpy little man. But these intellectuals are inclined to be sissies. What about Figueroa?"

"You told me that through sheer luck he was attracted by the racket and arrived at the scene approximately when you did. Is 'approximately' simultaneous or slightly before or slightly after?"

"A moment before. Not long. He and other hotel guests and employees were creating a bitch of a traffic jam for us. Between those ghouls and the number of my men required to keep Gilbert subdued, you could scarcely navigate."

"Did he inform you then that the knife was authentic?"

"No," Hector said. "He came to the station later in the evening. What are you driving at, Luis?"

"I wish I knew. Did you recognize any of the hotel employees at the scene?"

"No. Bellhops and busboys had ganged up on Smith. There may have been night managers in the vicinity, but I did not see any. I had to send downstairs for management."

"Raúl Estrada Estrada?"

"No such miraculous luck for you, Luis. No, nobody saw him. He was presumably at his Puerto Estrada."

"Figueroa is a guest at the Club Estrada. How can an assistant curator afford to pay rates a majority of North American tourists cannot?"

Hector rubbed thumb against fingers. "In Mexico City anything can happen. It is as crazy there as they profess Los Angeles, California, to be. Maybe he peddles priceless antiquities in the alley behind the National Museum of Anthropology. Who knows?"

"Could you check him out for me, Hector? What he has been doing in Cancún, how he is tossing his money around, and so forth?"

"Yes, yes," Hector agreed impatiently. "Can we progress along to my trouble? Thank you. My trouble is coincidental to your matter. Her name is Denise Lowell. She is the sister of María López."

"Denise Lowell is a North American name. María López was Mexican," Luis said.

"Right and wrong. Yes, Denise Lowell is North American. No, María López was not Mexican. Denise Lowell states that María López's given name was Mary Ann Lowell. She has photographs and documents to prove it. We did not subject her to the ordeal of identifying the remains, but she described her with the personal details of scars and birthmarks that only an intimate could know.

"Trust me, Luis. Denise Lowell is the sister of María López who was"—Hector crossed himself—"Mary Ann Lowell."

"Hector, what is it you are asking me to do?"

"Denise Lowell flew in this evening from a North American city that is unpronounceable in Spanish," Hector said, deflecting Luis's question.

"What city?"

"There is an extra *t* and the usual silent letters that have to drive the poor gringos who have to speak English cuckoo. S-e-a-t-t-l-e. Toss out that stupid, useless second *t* and you should say Seh-awt-leh. Yes? Miss Lowell, she pronounces her town See-at-tow."

"Seattle," Luis said. "The seventeenth largest city in the United States in the 1970 census. It is the principal city of the state of Washington and the Pacific Northwest."

"Save your vast storehouse of trivial knowledge for somebody who cares, Luis. The place is up there in the distant north with snowstorms and Eskimos. The relevant thing is that Miss Lowell is raising hell and demanding answers."

"Answers? She is not satisfied that you have Proctor Smith in custody?"

"More or less," Hector said, rocking a hand. "She is too polite to make an elaborate, noisy fuss, but her implications are that our investigation is sloppy and that the Cancún Hotel Zone is a fleshpot of spontaneous, unbridled raucousness."

Luis could not defend Hector and his jurisdiction on those charges. He said nothing.

"Miss Lowell accepts the reality that her dead sister was no candidate to be canonized. We will never see her likeness molded in plastic and magnetized to a dashboard. Mary Ann as María sucked and fucked for generous pay. Her objections are that Gilbert rampaged for so long and that we tolerated Mary Ann/María's whoring. We have no rapport, Luis, she and I. She has been exposed to and believes the gamut of horror stories concerning Mexican police officers."

"Why did Mary Ann Lowell become a Mexican prostitute named María López? Was she schizophrenic?"

"An early question of mine to Miss Lowell, who either does not know or declines to confide in me."

"You brought Denise Lowell here to dump her on me?"

"Not initially. I suggested the North American attorney Ringner. Despite and because of his affiliation to Proctor Gilbert Smith and Tropical Language Scholars, I felt that he would be an ideal—how should I say?—dose of reality. You are welcome, Luis."

"Thank you?"

"You are welcome for me not suggesting your worthless lawyer friend Ricardo Martínez Rodríguez instead. I saved his contemptible life. The lady's delicate loveliness shrouds an unmistakable toughness. Ricky would instantly put the make on her and as a result have his scrotum pulled over his head like a stocking cap. The lady is no dyke, but neither is she in the frame of mind for the ardor of a Latin lover boy."

"Ringner refused?"

"She refused Ringner based on his profession. She hates lawyers more fervently than she hates Mexican cops. The lady harbors strong prejudices.

"I subsequently suggested a detective. She was extremely warm to the concept. I played the game of going through notebooks and whatnot to come up with the best hard-boiled private eye/dick/shamus in Yucatán. After my research, I came up with you.

"Miss Lowell is in mourning pain and she has monumental pain-in-the-ass potential. Do this for me, Luis."

"Miss Lowell harbors strong prejudices," the detective said. "You said so yourself."

"Not racial prejudices. Luis, frankly, you take your oppressed dark-skinned-native-minority bitching too far. You really do. Not that we are not oppressed. But I do not oppress you, and Miss Lowell reacted semi-excited when I said you were Maya."

"Sorry. I am guilty of that."

"Good. I can expect you to moderate in that area? Quit boring the hell out of me continually portraying yourself as the native martyr?"

"No," Luis said with his first smile of the night.

"Okay. Just thought I would ask. It may be a situation of Denise Lowell having seen Chichén Itzá or Tikal or Copán in *National Geographic,* or it may be the influence of North American western movies. I watch them frequently. John Wayne and Tom Mix and Audie Murphy. When they let

Indians be the good guys, they are the scouts. They study footprints. They read animal turds as if they are tea leaves. They look at scuffed tree bark and find clothing fibers on limbs and lead the Duke to the bad guys."

"I am expected to interpret jaguarundi droppings?"

"No. The lady is no moron. Be her guide and confidant for the next three, four, ten days. That is all I am asking, Luis, and I am in actuality begging. Keep her out of my hair. Her sister's body will be released soon and then they can both go home to Seh-awt-leh. The sensationalism of Gilbert is stressing me. You are removing from my system a stress object. You are postponing my fatal heart attack for a couple years. Spy on her too. We do not even know the location of López's permanent residence. Find out for me. Okay?"

"Okay." Luis was aware that he could never, ever refuse Hector a request that was not suicidal or too illegal. "But why do we have to do this in the middle of the night?"

Hector grinned victoriously, clamped a plump paw around Luis's wrist, and led him toward the Dodge Dart. "It is not the middle of the night. It is nearly dawn. Look eastward. Do you not see a faint orange glow at the treetops?"

"No."

"Trust me," Hector said, tugging. "It is there."

CHAPTER THIRTEEN

We insure drivers like you," Denise Lowell said.

Luis wondered what she meant by that. Hector had introduced them, Luis the extremely adroit independent detective, Denise the grieving vengeance-entitled sister, then had installed his round, embarrassed, and unburdened person behind the wheel of his car and escaped. The Dodge Dart shuddered down the pocked road, sounding like a pocketful of change.

Luis and Denise had gone inside his house. Esther had not returned to sleep as instructed, but instead was awake and dressed. Rosa was up too, roused by Esther. The girls and Denise exchanged small talk and drank boiled coffee, ill at ease like different species encountering one another in the jungle. Not unfriendly, not hostile, Luis thought, but with the mutual shyness of dissimilar beings.

Hector had lied about the emerging sun; according to Luis's wall clock, it was not due for an hour. He invited Denise to see the Tulum ruins at sunrise. She eagerly accepted. A stranger, a tourist by default, somebody you did not know what to say to, you took them to a sight, an attraction.

"What do you mean, you insure drivers like me?"

"I wasn't insulting you," she said. "I don't know your traffic laws or whether you have any. I shouldn't pass judgment. You didn't stop before you pulled onto the main highway, you have a lead foot, and when you passed that truck, well, you cut it awfully thin. And there was the blinking."

Luis had accelerated around a laboring flatbed splayed with concrete pipe, but acceleration in an exhausted VW Beetle was a relative term. Parallel to the truck in the left lane, an oncoming automobile hundreds of meters ahead blinked its headlights, flashing high beams in Luis's eyes. Luis blinked, the oncomer blinked, et cetera.

He said, "Headlight dueling is customary in Yucatán night driving. You flick your beams to ask someone to please flick theirs to low beam. They already have, but the aim is usually wall-eyed. They're offended, so they flick their brights and it proceeds in earnest. Same with passing. You're encroaching and they tell you so, despite having ample room to get around the car you're passing."

"I saw the driver's mustache. He was overdue for a trim."

Luis smiled, pleased at her sense of humor, pleased that they were talking, conversing, not just parrying with monosyllables. "You should drive in Mexico City. Everybody packs a gun in the glove box. You don't dare honk your horn. We're civilized. What do you mean by 'insure'?"

"I'm an insurance claims adjuster for Unity Property and Casualty Insurance Company in Seattle. Auto, personal lines, and commercial. My biggest headaches come when a policyholder gets into a car and takes a goofy chance."

"Claims?"

"Yes. Our policyholder hits somebody and it's their fault, we pay. Unity writes some horrible risks. There's a running joke in the office that Unity writes anybody. Unity Writes Anybody. Our slogan. We had group life on the Seventh Cavalry, hull coverage on the *Titanic.*"

"The White Star liner *Titanic.* Unsinkable. Fifteen hundred people sank with it on its maiden voyage on April 14–15, 1912. What's the Seventh Cavalry?"

"Custer."

"I remember. June 25, 1876, the Battle of the Little Big Horn. Zero survivors."

"You're amazing. How did you do that?"

Eyes on the road, a casual arm draped over the wheel. Luis felt Denise Lowell's eyes on him. She *was* amazed and he liked it.

"Reference material I read a long, long time ago," he said. "It was how I learned English and it won't disappear. It refuses to fall out of my head."

"My profession is why I declined Inspector Salgado's offer to connect me with lawyers for assistance. It was a knee-jerk reaction, I know, but adjusters and attorneys are natural enemies, like cobras and mongooses. Or is it mongeese?"

"Mongooses," Luis said.

"Tulum," Denise said. "That's a famous ruin, isn't it, a big fort on the coast? I read something on Tulum on the airplane, in an in-flight magazine. I wasn't prepared to fly off and be a Yucatán tourist. I was having coffee in the office lunchroom, morning break, and flipped a page of the newspaper. This Gilbert, how they caught him, and María López. Mary Ann. I *knew* it was her. It was like being hit in the face with a club, reading what happened, what he did to her, finding out that way. . . ."

Her voice trailed off. She turned and stared out her window. Luis did not speak. He came to the Tulum entrance road and pulled in. Denise Lowell blew her nose and said, "This is good of you, bringing me here, but I don't think we're allowed. That sign said they open at ten."

The bazaar's shops were shuttered, gated, zippered, and dismantled, whatever the individual merchant thought was required to protect his inventory. The lot was empty, yesterday's tire treads imprinting the grayish limestone soil like ghost tracks. In six hours, Luis visualized, diesel bus engines would be baying at the vertical sun and an unprecedented bargain in hand-tooled leather would inevitably become available to the discriminating buyer.

"Take my word for it, Tulum looks better at this hour," Luis said, parking and getting out of the car.

"Yes, but the sign says ten A.M. and I don't see any turnstyles spinning."

A guard approached from the wall, saw it was Luis, and nodded.

Luis waved to him. They walked into the ruins. Luis ignored the guard's smirking leer, although he did read his mind.

Gringo lady wants it on a stone slab. Kinky travelogue fantasy in her head. Goes home, tells her girlfriends how she got it like the virgins did in ancient Maya times. Spread out like an X and bound to the hot stone, ravaged by a purebred Maya.

"He's obviously a friend of yours, but won't he get in trouble for letting us in?"

"No. And he thinks he's doing it for a good cause."

"What cause?"

"Perfect timing," Luis said, evading her question, pointing eastward. "Sunrise."

Hector's orange glow outlined the hard, rectilinear edges of the structures. Denise said, "Absolutely gorgeous, but I'm curious why you brought me here. That's a rude thing to say, I know. I'll blame it on lack of sleep and being punchy from the travel."

"You need to talk. Tulum, now, the solitude, you can cry, scream, get it out of your system. I'll take a walk."

"Thanks for the thought. It's considerate of you. But, no, that's done. I cleared out the lunchroom in a hurry. Nobody had the nerve to reenter until I went hoarse and my tear ducts ran dry." She was crying and laughing. "God, I'm sweating. Is it ever cold around here?"

"No."

"Were your daughters afraid of me? They were looking at me funny. Is that the real reason we came to Tulum?"

Luis finally had sufficient light to see Denise Lowell well. She matched Hector's description of her sister: slight, dark, pretty. Luis did not regard her as beautiful. Her eyes were too widely spaced, her nose too small, an upswept Caucasian nose that hardly qualified as a nose. Denise Lowell was no representation of a 1940s actress either. Her hair was short and straight, and instead of elaborate, flowing finery she wore sensible cotton—a loose-fitting blouse and slacks. She was desirable, yes, although Luis did not see in her the ability or willingness to charm and manipulate male libidos out of their last dollar.

"They weren't afraid of you," he said. "They liked you. Rosa was analyzing you, your coloration and your taste in jewelry, preparing her pitch. Esther was probing deeper, storing impressions."

"Inspector Salgado said you wear several hats."

"Too many hats for the hours in the day, too few for the money that comes in."

"Are Esther and Rosa in school?"

"They attended the Akumal school. What are you asking?"

"I'm sorry. I struck a nerve."

"No you didn't," Luis lied. "What is that North American term? Options. My babies are bright and they went as far as they could in school and they have no options. There isn't a college or university in Quintana Roo State, as if they would be admitted."

"Ethnic discrimination?"

"And sex discrimination too. A long story. How did you like Hector?"

"He has a flying start on the Mexican cop stereotype," Denise said. "Add a sombrero and bandoliers and you'd have it. I liked Inspector Salgado. I can't say the same for his cronies. In spite of his blatant unloading of me on your porch, he's a warm, decent man. He thinks the world of you."

"He told you why?"

"You're the top private detective in Yucatán, he said."

Luis smiled. "Hector exaggerates. I haven't a license or a gun. I just poke into things for people once in a while."

"He said you were a policeman who wouldn't knuckle under to corruption. A rich kid killed a Maya family with his sports car. They defeated you, the kid's money and the criminal justice system, but you put up a good fight."

"Also a long story. Hector asked me to spy on you too, by the way."

"Because I was complaining so much?"

"Yes. Your vagueness about your sister too."

"Are you going to report what I say to him?"

"Could be."

"Isn't there a code of confidentiality or something for private eyes?"

"In the movies there is," Luis said.

"The inspector's going to be disappointed. I haven't an address for Mary Ann. Every time we received a card or a letter, it came from a different post office box. She sometimes signed herself as María López, sometimes not. I assumed it was a private joke between Mary Ann and herself. It wouldn't've been the first time her bizarre behavior went without explanation. This missionary person, Smith, is he the serial killer, this Gilbert creature?"

"The evidence says yes."

"You're not sold."

"An investigation should be thorough," Luis said ambiguously. He did not define his doubts, the inconsistencies in the case. Rape of the first victim, absence of sexual assault on the next two, or indication of such an attempt on María López/Mary Ann Lowell. The significance of the sacrificial knife. Assistant Curator Figueroa's rabbity behavior. Ellen Smith's credible evaluation of her husband's innocence. Luis's own impression of Smith as an overreligious bumpkin, but not necessarily a homicidal one. His locksmithing skills, however, deflecting the brunt of the doubts.

Denise said, "That's what I said at the police station and I guess that's what made me a shrew, a mouthy broad. What is a *puta?*"

A whore, Luis did not say. Denise Lowell's sister was one, Denise Lowell was not. But if she were, so what? The Virgin of Guadalupe could stroll into a police station, assault manhood by insisting on efficiency and plausible answers, and She would be a slut bitch.

"Is that supposed to be a Spanish word?" Luis asked innocently.

"I'm positive it is. My accent is probably wrong," Denise replied. "Inspector Salgado's men were talking among themselves. That word was repeated again and again."

"Bad acoustics. Garbles you in every language. Look," Luis said. They had walked past El Castillo to the edge of the cliff. The low sun was plating the Caribbean's surface with copper.

"On our ocean, the Pacific, this would be a sunset. We couldn't compete. This is too spectacular. You have a knack for changing the subject, don't you? Proctor Smith's missionary organization, you and the lawyers are working for them?"

"I haven't seen any money yet."

"Tropical something?"

"Tropical Language Scholars, Incorporated. Headquartered in Dallas, Texas."

"We grew up Presbyterian. Mary Ann was my only sibling. She was two years older. We went to Sunday school. The church sponsored a missionary couple someplace in Africa. Cameroon, I think. There were jokes about them being eaten. We never met them. They never came home while we attended that church. We knew them by photographs. They were homely people with big smiles who always seemed to be squinting into the sun and standing in front of straw huts next to black people in loincloths. Our Sunday school teachers would show us the pictures and pitch us an offering.

"We had to attend the main services with our parents afterward. The offering plate came around again. Today they call it double-dipping. Mary Ann rebelled at an early age, against church among other things. Church didn't take for me either, but I kept my mouth shut and went. I don't know to this day if Mary Ann died a card-carrying atheist, but when she was a junior in high school and I was a freshman, she raised so much hell that our folks gave up on getting us to go. There were occasions when I benefited from her rebelliousness.

"A percentage of the money we sent to the Cameroon couple was allocated for maintenance of a school and a clinic they supported along with other Presbyterian churches in the area. I didn't resent their nicking at my allowance quite so much, knowing some of the money actually benefited the people. It wasn't as if every cent went for Bibles and prayer cloths.

119

"Tropical Language Scholars. Do they operate schools and hospitals?"

"Not in Yucatán," Luis answered. "None that I know of. They do no good works, which makes them at least partially honest. They aren't bribing you with underwear, vitamin pills, and oatmeal. Tropical Language Scholars missionaries meander through villages and aim directly for the immortal soul."

"You're sort of defending them, but that's a damned cynical endorsement. You're a puzzle, Luis Balam."

"María López was also a puzzle. She passed as Mexican. You, too, could almost be Hispanic, but not quite."

"You're seeing a recessive gene. A great-great-whatever and her Mediterranean-type gigolo. That's my favorite fantasy on the subject. Our ancestors were English and our family has been in America since the *Mayflower.* We have a heritage of being straitlaced. We graduate from college and pursue secure, conservative careers. Dad is a certified public accountant and Mom teaches special ed at an elementary school. I guess I'm continuing the tradition. Mary Ann shook the family bedrock, needless to say."

"Your sister's personality passed her as Mexican. I don't think, from what I've been told, that her coloration did."

"Mary Ann was an aspiring actress. Went to Hollywood right after high school, the whole bit. No career in an insurance office or anything else dull and ordinary for her. She was an okay amateur actress too. She usually won the lead in the school play."

Anger flared in Denise Lowell's voice, the cold, modulated anger of resentment. Was she resenting her sister's life or her death? Luis asked, "Did she win any Hollywood movie roles?"

"No. She wasn't that one in a million who make it. She went away eleven years ago this month, this June. We didn't see much of her after that. Occasional holidays and birthdays. She'd always just pop in. We'd never know she was coming. Phone calls and letters were sporadic too. That's how she was. Mary Ann's charm was her combination of wildness and sweetness. She was born with gobs of both. Basically good but untamed. Untamable."

Which, to Luis, confirmed María López's allure in the Hotel Zone night spots. She was pretty, adorable, volatile, mysterious, and feral. A solitary tourist whose pants strained with the twin bulges of sexual frustration and traveler's checks would be easy prey. "In those eleven years, before she came to Cancún, how did she live?"

"She was evasive. We had hunches we didn't want to dwell on. You know, the things failed Hollywood actresses fall into. Topless dancing. I don't know what else. She had a short-term drug problem, we're fairly sure. She licked it. The last time we saw her, two years next Thanksgiving, she was bright-eyed and had put back the weight she'd lost the previous time we saw her."

"Prostitution?"

"I can't frankly say we were surprised. We had no direct evidence, and if there were little signs, we conveniently blocked them out of our minds."

"When did Mary Ann move to Cancún?"

"You don't know, the police don't know, I don't know. A year to eighteen months," Denise said bitterly. "The cards and letters didn't exactly pour in. Communication was primarily between Mary Ann and me. Mom and Dad had washed their hands of her. She was pushing thirty, and if you couldn't act like a responsible adult by that stage in your life, well, you were hopeless.

"She was animated, if you can be animated on a four-square-inch space on a picture postcard. She said her acting career had revived. She was re-creating—and I quote—'electrifying Mexican actresses from the golden days of the silver screen.' She signed herself as María López on those cards. I thought she was doing gigs in supper clubs. Was I wrong!"

"Lupe Velez," Luis said, clapping his hands. "The Mexican Spitfire."

"I've seen her," Denise said. "We have a cable channel that's entirely old movies. I'm an old-movie buff. The forties flicks are my favorite. *Films noirs,* the musicals, I love them all. Mary Ann did too. That's about the only thing we had in common that stuck through the years. We'd watch them on 'The Late Show' when we were kids. Lupe Velez and Leon Errol. They made four or five Mexican Spitfire movies. Not great cinema art, but they sure were fun."

"Your sister adopted a Lupe Velez persona? She became the Mexican Spitfire?"

"She might have, yes. She was zany enough. If she was a —Jesus, I can barely say it—a hooker, leave it to Mary Ann to sell herself with flair."

"You have no luggage." Luis had just noticed.

"Inspector Salgado took me to a Cancún City hotel to check in on the way to see you. It's occurring to me, Luis Balam, that I should *not* be seeing you. You're working for people associated with the person who probably killed my sister."

Luis shrugged.

"On the other hand, I've been in Mexico for less than twelve hours and I have nobody else to confide in."

"Did your sister like men?"

"Mary Ann liked Mary Ann," Denise said. "She used people. She especially used men. What are you driving at?"

"Could she be easily romanced? How should I say it? Swept off her feet?"

"No. She's always been the sweep-or, not the sweep-ee."

Luis looked at her. "Those words aren't in my English vocabulary."

"Sorry. Bad slang. Men fell in love with Mary Ann, not vice versa."

"Was she a good judge of men?"

"Could she pick a psycho out of a crowd? She could. She was impulsive and promiscuous—beyond promiscuous, it appears—but she was careful. She wouldn't bring a nut to her room and it wouldn't be easy to surprise her, you know, in an attack. She'd bite and scream and yell. She could take care of herself. Wait a minute, are you saying she invited this missionary to her room?"

"No," Luis said. Not Proctor Smith the locksmith, he neglected to say. "He is a big, strong man. He could overpower her quickly."

"Who's that?" Denise said with a start, looking inland.

A gawky young man with a silly grin on his face was ambling past the Temple of the Frescoes, heading toward them.

"Nobody. Who is Tonto?"

"The Lone Ranger's Tonto?"

"Yes."

"He was his faithful Indian companion. Those shows date from the fifties."

"What else is Tonto?"

"I don't know, unless it's the negative stereotype you're referring to. The Indian as inferior and subservient to the white man. Native American rights activists mention Tonto, as in the Tonto Syndrome."

"Tonto," Luis said, speaking essentially to himself.

"Who *is* that?"

"Nobody."

CHAPTER FOURTEEN

Who's she, Mr. Balam?"

Luis was dragging Dave Shingles by an elbow, jerking when he resisted, bound for the hole in the wall, the entrance that from their direction was an exit. As skinny as he was, an uncooperative Shingles was a load. On the positive side, Luis thought, his vile breath was annihilating insects in their path. Malaria would not be contracted today.

"Nobody."

"She's super-cute for nobody," Shingles said.

"How did you get in?"

"Coupla bucks. I had to promise to stay quiet and not mess with stuff."

Coupla bucks was how much? Five, ten, twenty? Irrelevant. Bribery was bribery, an intimate contract between buyer and seller. Bribery, the universal language. "Why did you get in? The saucers are coming to Cobá, yes?"

"I look at my notes and I think, Tulum, and I look at them an hour later and I go, well, Cobá's it. The day, next Tuesday, we're on." Shingles stopping moving, dug his heels in, and Luis did not think he could dislodge him without separating limb from body, not an unpleasant notion.

"I can't be two places at once," Shingles whined. "I go to Cobá, I go to Tulum. I go in the day, I go at night. Sacking out on the Xcacel beach was bor-ing. I'm waiting for a sign and they're not giving me one, Mr. Balam."

"*Mr.* Balam?"

"You don't like 'mister,' I can go 'sir' or 'señor.' Since I'm working for you on your murder case, it's only proper that I address you like a boss."

"You aren't working for me," Luis corrected. "Call me Luis."

"Oh, you don't have to pay me. I'm killing time till Tuesday. Money's unimportant. I'll bet even money that money doesn't even exist where I'm going. Lucky we keep bumping into each other, huh?"

"Go away," Luis said. "Go away to where you're going. Venus, Mars. No, Saturn. Saturn is farther and you'll love the rings. If I had spare money, I'd give it to you to go to Saturn. They may have their own currency on Saturn. Don't say they don't unless you've been there. You don't know. I'd gladly pay you in dollars. Everybody in the galaxy takes dollars. I'm confident the exchange rate will be to your advantage."

"Hey, c'mon, Mr. Balam, don't yell. The lady's looking at us funny. You can listen to what I've developed on your Gilbert thing, can't you? I went to a bunch of trouble."

Luis sighed. Confiding in Shingles at Cobá had been a major error. "I can listen. I can't restrain my curiosity."

"Okay. I hitchhiked into Cancún and did some snooping, some asking around."

"Snooping and asking where?"

"Just around. The hotels where they were killed. The newspaper. The library. Government offices where they'd speak to me. They weren't super-cooperative. Those hotel managers were bordering on hostile. They'd freak out when I'd ask blunt questions and whip out my notebook to take notes."

"Just around," Luis muttered. "Not on my behalf? You didn't identify yourself as my representative?"

"Nah. I played it cool. Okay. The first girl, Foster, she was killed on March seventh, a Saturday. Judy Jacobson, April ninth, Thursday. Alison Hall, Sunday, May tenth. The last girl, Thursday, June fourth. Those dates, in order, are Pisces, Aries, Taurus, and Gemini."

"Astrological signs apply to birthdates, not death dates," Luis informed him.

"Death is merely a bridge between one life and the next. Most religions and philosophies buy that at some level. Your ancestors believed in dualism, you know, the struggle between opposites. Good and evil, rain and drought, life and death."

"The horoscopes in the paper go by birthdates, but you know more about astrology than I, plus your great, scholarly command of the afterlife."

"No, no I don't. I'm not into astrology."

Luis laughed. "That's incredibly difficult to believe."

"It's true, Mr. Balam. I was searching for patterns."

"Patterns," Luis said. "Patterns as in mystery clues? Why didn't I think of it? Did patterns come to you?"

"Hey, c'mon, lemme proceed, okay? I checked the

birthdates too. Foster, October seventh, Libra. Jacobson, November twenty-fourth, Sagittarius. Hall, March thirtieth, Aries."

"Patterns? Aries came up twice."

"Nope. Forget it. No patterns. I looked into the moon phases too. Man, people do some weird, gross stuff when the moon's full."

"You developed a lunar pattern?"

"Nope," Shingles said. "Moon phases didn't coincide."

"No patterns?"

"No patterns is a pattern. If you don't have a pattern, what do you have?"

"I don't know what you have," Luis replied. "You don't have anything, do you?"

"Yeah, you have something. You do have a pattern. It has to be a pattern. Loony-tunes killers, they always do things in patterns."

Luis had him moving again. They were within steps of the exit. He stopped and asked, "No patterns is a pattern?"

"Yep," Shingles said with a proud, lopsided grin. "Chaos is a pattern. Randomness is a pattern. The guy is deranged, but he has a pattern whether he's consciously making one or not."

"Proctor Smith remains your top candidate?"

"Has to. Like I said before, God talks to you, He says some goofy stuff. Smith's your Gilbert. Unless he isn't."

"Excuse me?"

"Unless there's more than one killer. My money's on Proctor Smith, but I could be wrong. Erratic patterns, chaos —it isn't erratic and chaotic if it's two or three killers doing things differently."

Luis had stored the multiple-killer possibility in a dusty corner of his mind. When he suggested it to Ricky and the junior, he had been teasing. He dreaded the contemplation of Gilbert as twins. Or triplets. There were so many factual inconsistencies, though. The knife in Mary Ann's chest could be connected to Alison Hall's murder alone, providing laboratory results weren't contrived to dovetail with expediency. The sexual molestation angle. Shingles's randomness-chaos insight, based on birthdates and zodiacs, was yet another contradiction. Bizarre as the kid's methods were, he had produced an argument of unsettling clarity.

"I appreciate your help. I'm grateful," Luis said. "Drop out of the case now. You've done what you could. People along the coast are sensitive about Gilbert and his effect on their tourism income. You received a small lesson in Cancún. Push people too hard and you'll be pushed back. Pushed harder. Take my advice and enjoy the Xcacel beach until your flying saucer comes."

"Hey," said an unhearing Dave Shingles, "I wasn't able to come up with María López's date of birth. I don't think anyone knew it. Maybe we have a pattern after all."

"January eighteenth," Denise Lowell called out from a distance.

Shingles's jaw went slack. Luis smiled. The Lowell woman had Rosa's hearing.

CHAPTER FIFTEEN

After Dave Shingles had gone, Denise Lowell asked who he was. Luis said nobody. Everybody is somebody, Denise countered. Very well, Luis said; he is waiting for a flying saucer like normal people wait for a bus. Denise said excuse me for asking.

Luis said he was serious, Denise said have it your way. They got into the Beetle and drove to Cancún City.

Ten kilometers along, Denise said, "Oh, wait, is he one of those?"

"Those who?"

"There've been books written that claim aliens from outer space were responsible for building the great monuments of the past. Those markings on the ground in Peru that go on for miles, supposedly they were laid out from the air and outer space. Easter Island statues and the Egyptian pyramids too."

"Yes," Luis said. "He is one of those."

"What on earth, pun intended, are you doing associating with the likes of him?"

"He volunteered to help me solve the crime."

"A crime that has probably been solved. Is he helping?"

"No. He is only confusing me," Luis said with a finality that ended conversation until they reached the outskirts of Cancún City.

Denise asked if Luis would take her around to do what had to be done to secure the release of her sister's body. Her parents were numb with grief and guilt, and wanted a proper funeral as soon as possible. She dreaded dealing with a bureaucracy that spoke a language she did not. She said she would pay Luis for his time. Luis said her dread was justified and to forget payment; his time was cheap.

They stopped at her hotel on Avenida Yaxchilán. Luis waited in the car while she went to her room to bathe and change. Hector had made a good choice of accommodation. The Hotel Sol y Mar was clean, inexpensive, and looked like a hotel. It was two stories of stucco and shuttered windows, not a glassed-in Maya temple.

She came out in a sun dress printed like a botanical garden. She had gone without sleep last night, but the bath and the vivid colors seemed to energize her.

Luis drove to the Quintana Roo State Judicial Police station. This time Denise waited in the car while he went inside. There would be *three* bureaucracies to encounter, Hector advised him. A body that was a homicide, that was to be shipped out of Mexico, that body provided employment for multitudes of clerks. Hector wrote notes requesting cooperation to cronies in each of the agencies.

Luis accompanied her into the various agency offices and served as interpreter. The process went remarkably smoothly; Hector's notes neutralized the instinctive Mexican resistance to expediting business for a *gringa* and an Indian. Promises could not be elicited and timetables were evaded, but Luis and Denise sensed progress.

By noon they were finished. Bureaucratic momentum gives one an appetite, Denise told him. And since you will not accept my money, I insist on buying lunch.

Luis said fine, but let's see if we can't coax two lawyers into buying our lunches instead. Inspector Salgado's attorneys? Denise asked. I don't know if they'd be good for my digestion; please brief me on them. Luis summarized Ricardo Martínez Rodríguez, skipping Ricky's lothario characteristics—she would inevitably learn for herself—and his impressions of W. W. (Lard) Ringner. Lead the way, Denise said without hesitation. Know thine enemy.

Ricky's door was locked. A note taped to it read: GONE TO LUNCH WITH MR. RINGNER. LUIS, IF IT IS YOU, YOU KNOW WHERE.

They descended the stairs, Denise humming along with "La Bamba." In the car she asked, "Is this restaurant a hangout?"

"No. The Crazy Cow. The steakhouse where I met Mr. Ringner."

"I'm trendy," Denise announced. "I worry about cholesterol and seldom eat red meat."

"I can arrange for other dishes. I am not fond of cow meat either. I know an assistant chef."

"You?"

"Me what?"

"Do you worry about cholesterol?"

"Do I worry about cholesterol clogging my arteries and heart and killing me?"

"Yes."

"Not much," Luis said, not elaborating on the actuarial fact that the Maya do not live long enough to lethally clog their arteries.

They entered the dining room just as Ricky and Ringner were being served, Ricky a steak sandwich, Ringner a pinkish slab of fatty meat, fried potatoes, and a bourbon-rocks refill. A walking cane was hooked over the back of the Dallas lawyer's chair. Denise said something under her breath that may or may not have been "drugstore cowboy."

"Luis, fabulous timing. Come join us," Ricky said, eyes locked on Denise.

Ringner forked a chunk of beef into his mouth and saluted with the utensil. Ricky sprang out of his chair and pulled the one next to him out for Denise.

Luis said, "Lard Ringner, Ricky Martínez, this is Denise Lowell. She is—"

"Famished," Denise interrupted, abbreviating the introduction.

Luis stopped talking and sat down. She had her reasons for secrecy, he figured, reasons that would later be revealed.

Ringner drank whiskey and said, "Lowell. You're not Mexican?"

"Seattleite."

"Great white north." Ringner cut his meat.

"Welcome to Cancún, Miss Lowell," Ricky said. "Whatever suits your interest, whatever glamorous sights and activities appeal to you, please be assured that I am at your disposal. My knowledge of the region is intimate."

"Thanks," she said, then to Luis, rolling her eyes, "Is this our waiter coming?"

It was. Luis discussed nonbeef choices with him and Denise, then ordered a chicken sandwich for her, tortillas and black beans for himself.

"Unfortunately, we have business to discuss and will now be unable to," said a rebuffed Ricky in Spanish.

"We can talk business," Luis said in English. "Miss Lowell is familiar with the Gilbert case. Everybody is familiar with the Gilbert case. Unless, of course, there has been a recent development that should be kept secret."

"Nothing's been secret on this thing," Ringner said. "Besides, it's just a hop, skip, and a jump from not being our thing any longer. Unless you got something new for us."

"No," Luis said.

"Luis, is that the absolute truth?" Ricky asked.

"Ricardo, Ricky, old and dear friend," Luis replied, aghast. "Have I ever lied to you?"

"Luis, Mr. Estrada personally handwrote a letter of complaint regarding you and had it delivered to me by a man who would terrify the sum total of vipers slithering in the jungles of Yucatán."

"Bandit mustache? Nasty little eyes? Neckless and fat and big as a rubbish heap?"

"That is him in the terrifying flesh," Ricky said. "Who were you harassing?"

"The junior's personally handwritten note did not specify who I harassed?"

"An unnamed guest at the Club Estrada. You were pestering him at the pool bar. You allegedly menaced him in a manner that Mr. Estrada did not divulge to me."

"Not me," Luis said. "Ricky, we Indians all look alike."

"Please, Luis, behave," Ricky admonished, sighing, and adding for Denise's benefit, "I am not a physical coward, you know, but that organism of Mr. Estrada's was potentially deadly."

"You don't have to go powder your nose, do you?" Ringner asked Denise. "The things we have to kick around, they're pretty boring for a gal."

"Thank you for your concern." Denise smiled sweetly. "You gentlemen could never bore this little gal."

"What is your sign?" Ricky asked Denise.

Luis pointed at Ringner's cane. "What happened?"

Ringner lifted a slippered foot, a mismatch for the other, which was encased in scrolled cowboy leather. "Parasailing isn't the piece of cake they sucker you into believing on those TV travel programs. Especially when you've had a couple of drinks and your coordination loses its razor edge."

A couple or twenty drinks, Luis thought, nodding sympathetically.

"Ricky's girlfriend's best girlfriend—"

"I have no steady lady friend," Ricky broke in, looking at Denise. "Hortensia is simply a very good friend. Denise, I am a Cancer. We Cancers are noted for our sensitivity and passion."

"Yeah, okay," Ringner said. "Anyway, Carla, Hortensia's bosom buddy, I call her Chiquita Banana, Chiquita talks me into parasailing. She loves it. She 'gets off on it' is how she puts it. A cute little Mexican gal saying 'I get off on it' with a Spanish accent, well, that's the cutest thing this side of my wife's Lhasa Apso, but I reckon you'd have to've been there.

"You rise up in the air, yanked up off your feet ungently, and the beach shrinks to a ribbon and the people to ants. What happened was, the bottom line of the situation, I landed funny and twisted an ankle."

"I did not hear what you said your sign was, Denise," Ricky said.

" 'No Parking in This Space,' " Denise said, eyes aimed straight ahead at Ringner.

Luis remembered Hector's prophesy on Ricky, Denise, and love. He changed the subject, asking Ringner, "Damage control? Any headway?"

W. W. (Lard) Ringner pondered a response. He lit a long black cigarette, sucked smoke to the floor of his chest, exhaled, raised the whiskey tumbler to his lips, changing the color of the ice cubes from amber to clear, and pondered further with a second long drag.

Luis was going to ask him if charging his clients by the hour was ethical when Ringner at last said, "Damage control. Damage control, at this point in space and time, boys and girls, is irrelevant, inoperative, and immaterial. And impossible.

"I visited my client, Mr. Proctor Smith, that paradigm of hard-shell, Jesus-flogging, evangelical Christianity. I kid you not, a fundamentalist preacher has got to be the dumbest critter on the face of the earth. I already sent my recommendations by fax to the TLS brain trust, a term I'm using loosely, thanks to my *mucho compadre* here, Ricky, who has amazing communications connections.

"Whoa, am I stepping on any toes? You Mexican people are predominantly Roman Catholic, aren't you?"

Ricky crossed himself.

Luis said, "I am a secular humanist."

"Okay, no harm, no foul. Smith stonewalled me. No, correction, he didn't do me the courtesy of stonewalling, bullshitting—pardon my French, little lady—no, what he did was provide name, rank, serial number, and I had to wring that out of the sumbitch. And, oh yeah, he said he was innocent. Swell.

"Smith is poor white trash of the first order. He's a bigfoot, clodhopping goat-roper from the sticks. He's sitting there on his bunk, I'm trying to talk to him, me, his attorney, and he's staring at his feet. Ricky, is there an insanity plea option in the Mexican justice system?"

Ricky stroked his waxed, pencil mustache and droned pessimistically, "Yes, but it is rarely implemented. Procedural impediments discourage its utilization. It would be a futile gesture."

"Well, hell, Smith isn't crazy anyhow, not crazier than your average serial killer. But he sure isn't firing on all cylinders. I think he got kicked in the head by his mule. I'm not qualified to say he's certifiable, but any man on the street can see that Proctor's elevator's not running all the way to the top. I have a hunch, too, that he's been getting some bad advice, especially in the area of venue change. He's been stonewalling the public prosecutor in that regard. The prosecutor is a reasonable man, and venue cooperation is Smith's best shot at copping a plea and saving his hide. The prosecutor"—Ringner smiled and paused to relish a memory—"him and me did a spot of pub crawling last night.

Saturnino's a good ol' boy. He's congenial as can be and he's some kind of *puta* hound."

"*Puta,*" Denise said. "That word again. I think I've translated it."

"So the bottom line, gents, is," Ringner went on, ignoring Denise's comment and rotating his head from Luis to Ricky, "cutting our losses. I've been in constant telephonic and fax contact with our benighted and holy leadership in Dallas. They're in sync with me in respect to distancing ourselves from our boy if he insists on making a public spectacle of himself and Tropical Language Scholars in a Cancún trial.

"The philosophy, theirs supported by my counsel, is anybody who'd slash four foxy little gals has extreme personal problems that shouldn't reflect on his profession or his employment. Hell, he could be working for GE or IBM or the USAF as easy as he is for TLS. A wacko is a wacko. Identification with TLS is what we have to avoid."

Luis looked at Denise. Her unblinking eyes were set on Ringner, but they revealed no emotion whatsoever. He asked, "The suspicion of embezzlement?"

"Yeah, glad you reminded me. Proctor Smith scarfing a few bucks out of the collection plate is as pertinent to girl slashing as the price of tea in China. It defines the man's basic character is maybe what it does. Funny thing, I confronted him with the allegation just for the hell of it. I was tired of listening to the sound of my own voice.

"I got a rise out of him. He denied it with a no and a head shake. Strange. Being nabbed with his hand in the cookie jar seemed to offend him worse than his homicide situation. I'll tell you, people are strange."

"How do we proceed, Lard, Luis and I?" Ricky asked. "The seriousness of the crime, I sincerely feel, warrants documentation of the case, legally and investigation-wise, to the extent of our abilities."

"Yes, come to think of it," Luis said. "When will we be paid?"

"In the immediate future," Ringner replied, frowning into his depleted drink. "In the meantime, you boys just keep plugging along, doing the stellar job you've been doing. The Dallas leadership prays hard enough for Proctor, maybe he'll be divinely inspired to come around."

"Could I interject a silly question?" Denise asked sweetly. "Us gals aren't up to speed on legal complexities, so I assume I've missed a key phrase or nuance."

Ringner took a replacement drink from the attentive waiter, tasted it, nodded in satisfaction, smiled, and said, "Fire when ready, hon. It's a stupid man who isn't wide receptive to new input."

"You spoke of Proctor Smith's unwillingness to accept a deal. Did it occur to you to presume his innocence and fight the charges?"

"That's super in the sentiment department, hon. We'll get right on it as soon as pigs can fly."

Ringner snapped his fingers, turned to Luis, and said, "You and that cop, Hector, you're tight, aren't you?"

"We are friends." Luis said warily.

"Could you do me a little favor? There'll be something in it for you if you do. After the smoke clears, give me first crack at buying that knife. I'm not what you'd call a patron of the arts and crafts, but I don't mind speculating when the piece and the price are right. This knife, in terms of historical value, is a twofer. Sacrificing virgins in the old days, sacrificing nonvirgins in the present. It'll appreciate faster than gold during Armageddon. It'll be worth mucho bucks a few years down the road."

An idea came to Luis. He was stunned by its simplicity and lustrous clarity. He said, "No. The knife is an antiquity. Ricky?"

"Transporting it out of Mexico would be illegal," Ricky confirmed.

Denise was on her feet, glaring down at Ringner. "You shithead," she said, her voice steady and cool, no louder than a whisper. "You fucking creep."

She walked out of the Crazy Cow at a normal pace, with considerable dignity. Nobody had overheard. The glances that followed her exit were standard male glances. She had created a microcosm of a scene, Luis mused admiringly.

Ricky sighed and made a face. Denise had lost her appeal to him, Luis knew. Ricky despised females who talked dirty, except in bed.

"Guys," said a dumbfounded Lard Ringner. "Was I out of line? What did I say?"

Then to Luis, "What, Kemo Sabe? Was it the wrong time of the month for her? What?"

CHAPTER SIXTEEN

t was midafternoon, too early for Black Coral to be closed, but it was. The rain, Luis thought; the rain. A downpour had commenced moments after he left the Crazy Cow and intensified between there and here. Wind and wet howled across Highway 307 from the sea, forcing Luis to hold the Beetle steering wheel forty-five degrees left of center to keep from being blown off the road into the scrub jungle. Chac, the Maya rain god, was too generous.

Luis eased the Volkswagen onto his slick slime of a parking lot. The potholes had their own surf and were overflowing. Tent ropes were as taut as guitar strings, and canvas segments were convex. But why was Black Coral *closed,* the CLOSED—CERRADO sign swinging to and fro from the front flap? A useless gesture. Why bother? Who would be out on the road in this weather? Besides himself, he'd seen only five or six other idiots, none of whom were parked in his lot.

His girls couldn't be gone; they depended on him for transportation. He split the flap and saw that they weren't gone.

"Indian, we were growing impatient with you," said Raúl Estrada Estrada's chauffeur-bodyguard-pimp. "We considerately closed your shitty little trinket shop on account of weather. In case you did not see our car, we thoughtfully parked out back so you could park wherever you liked."

Luis did not move or speak. The lights were out. He couldn't react properly until his eyes had adjusted to the dimness.

"We were bored, Indian. You showed up none too soon. These daughters of yours, I think they would like to relieve our boredom. Indian girls excite me, you know. You are all ugly as sin in the daylight, but, man, with those wide flat lips and big tongues, Indian girls can do wonderful things to you in the dark."

We? There he was, behind Estrada's goon and to his right, not touching but within grasp of his babies. They did not look injured or even disheveled, but they were in each other's embrace, fearful faces foretelling what was to come. The secondary goon was Luis's height, though as wide and ugly as the big boy. They dressed like improbable twins, identical in dark slacks, white shirts, and string ties. Thugs so confident and formal would be trouble. They were accustomed to doing their jobs without wrinkling a crease, without breaking a sweat.

The secondary goon was biting necklace strings apart, watching with fascination as the black coral beads fell, clicking, one by one onto the hardpacked floor. Primeval, Luis thought.

"I have a notion what this visit might be concerning."

"Indian, you have been told to mind your own business.

Are you hard of hearing? The words, do they lose their direction from your ears to your brain?" asked the bigger goon.

"Pardon me?" Luis said, cupping an ear. "Could you repeat yourself?"

The big guy shook his head sadly. "I try to treat you like a human being and you are acting like the fucking animal you are, insulting me by doing a nightclub comic number. Ha ha. You are not demonstrating respect."

Luis was not eliciting laughs. He was attempting to elicit a response from the secondary goon. Preferably to anger him. To encourage a slap in his Indian face for impertinence. Anything. Anything to draw him out of range of his babies. Luis did not detect a wide emotional range in the man. Fury would have to suffice. But the secondary goon's reverie with the falling beads, which he appeared to be counting, remained unbroken.

"I am really and sincerely sorry," Luis whimpered. "Please leave us. I promise I am through with the Gilbert case forever."

"I have to doubt your sincerity," said the larger goon. "I have to impress our position on you so you do not forget."

"Hey," Luis said to his partner. "I have a string that long in lapis lazuli. Lapis bounces higher off the floor than black coral."

The secondary goon still did not reply. The bead-dropping procedure had slowed. He was pinching them between curled thumb and index finger, digits like sausages, then, aiming and squinting, releasing them as if from a bomb mechanism.

The primary goon withdrew a sap from his pocket and

walked forward with the leisurely swagger of one who enjoyed a successful career as a professional bully. The sap was a lead slug wrapped in leather thongs. He swung it like a watch fob, saying, "Take it like a man. Profit from the experience. I am going to build your character. When we are done, we will not doubt your sincerity."

Luis raised his hands in front of his face, spreading his fingers to widen the pathetic shield. "Come on, boss, hurt me a little bit, but not my girls."

" 'Boss'? Last time I was 'fatso.' Exercise stiffens my cock. I cannot help it, Indian. Your girls will love us."

"Please, boss, do not let him touch me," Luis said. "Your associate."

The primary goon paused, puzzled. "Touch *you?*"

The secondary goon was looking at Luis, bombshell delayed in finger mechanism.

"He is queer," Luis said. "You do not know? Wake up, boss. I read him as a homo the instant he laid eyes on me. Beat me up and knock out my teeth, but as the normal, masculine Mexican male that I know you are, please, I beg you with all my heart and soul, guard my unconscious body from *him.*"

Luis jabbed a melodramatic finger at the secondary goon, whose attention was his at last. "Turn your back and he will yard my pants to my knees in a second," he cried. "I refuse to spell out in front of my daughters the sins he will commit against God and my body."

The secondary goon flung the remaining bead-string-bomb rack to the ground and came at Luis in a couple of long strides, fists and mouth clenched. Conversation, more than ever, was extraneous. Manhood impugned, manhood mocked, his Mexican machismo had suffered the ultimate insult.

Rosa and Esther scuttled on their hands and knees to the rear of the tent. Primary Goon shifted his attention to Secondary Goon, saying, "Hey, you dumb fuck, what are you doing? He is tricking you. The girls are getting away. The Indian is mine to teach a les—"

Luis interrupted him by driving a foot into his crotch, lifting him to his tiptoes. He groaned and staggered against a table, crashing down on top of it. Luis ducked the swing of his emasculated companion and buried a fist into a gut softer than it looked. Secondary Goon made a noise like an air lock in a science fiction movie and slumped to his knees.

Luis's head jerked sideways. Pain jolted him behind the left ear. He dodged the second swing of the lead sap. Luis marveled at the big boy, crazed and keening yet pressing the attack: he should have been paralyzed for a month.

Luis feinted left and slipped right, rotating toward his adversary, his plan to slam knuckles under his rib cage and upward. Even a caveman with steel gonads still had to breathe.

Simultaneously, Secondary Goon grabbed Luis by the ankles and began retching. Luis lost his balance and fell on the toppled table. Primary Goon wasn't far behind, lunging and swinging the sap. Luis heard and felt his cheekbone crack. Warm liquid flooded his left eye, and it wasn't tears.

Luis fended off Primary Goon with a knee. *His* head jerked.

A metallic thud. Then another. Esther was pounding the

top of his head with a griddle. His hair sizzled. The griddle was still hot from luncheon tortillas. It must have been left on the camp stove—no, they were cautious about fire, they had hurriedly reheated it for this occasion. Primary Goon merely touched his head and grunted. Science fiction movies came to mind once more, the immortal beast emerging from the ooze, aroused to anger by the pesky humans.

"Run! Run! Run!" Luis yelled until Esther and Rosa scampered out.

Luis's ankles remained locked. He grasped wrist in hand, pivoted at the waist, and snapped Secondary Goon's head back with his elbow. His front teeth sounded like fallen china. Luis's ankles were free. He lurched to his feet, but Primary Goon took him by the shirt and hoisted himself up also.

Luis was blinded by his own blood. But at such proximity, vision was irrelevant; at such proximity, Luis smelled stale garlic and chilis. They traded punches, grunts, and curses. Luis shortly realized that this was not an advantageous strategy. Primary Goon outweighed him by a factor of two. His head was made of stone, and Luis's repeated and ineffectual blows to his body were converting Luis's arms into same. He should have cut and run with his babies.

The big boy was boring in. His arms weighed a ton apiece by now too, so he was pummeling with his shoulders and his bulk, rather than boxing. He was falling in on Luis, wrapping him up, pressing him to the ground, fingers clawing like pudgy insects for his neck, locating it, squeezing, clamping.

What a senseless, pitiful, sorry, humiliating way to die,

thought Luis. Like a woodcutter crushed by the tree he had felled.

Suddenly the tent filled with bright white light and flashes of yellow. A horn and siren screamed. The tent imploded, rough canvas collapsing, smothering him.

Passage to the next world.

Not even the devout claimed it would be easy.

CHAPTER SEVENTEEN

*L*uis," said Hector Salgado Reyes, "you look like death warmed over, except they forgot to turn on the oven."

It hurt terribly to smile, but Luis Balam could not keep a straight face.

"Explain to me once more how this mayhem occurred."

"I tripped and fell down and bumped my head."

Hector threw up his hands and said to Denise Lowell, "Talk some sense into him, will you, miss? You rescued him from his fall and took him up the highway to the doctor and drove into the city to notify me. How many men were on top of him when he had his accidental fall and head bump?"

Denise looked at Luis, who shrugged. They were in front of Black Coral, such as it was. After storming out of the steakhouse, Denise had rented a car and driven to Black Coral to apologize to Luis for her outburst. Not for her profanity per se, not for the words inflicted on the Texas lawyer, not for rebuffing lover boy, but to Luis, the innocent by-stander.

She had arrived just as Rosa and Esther burst out of the

back of the tent. They ran to her and chattered their story in Spanish, English, and Yucatec Maya. Denise understood a dozen key words, which she confirmed by peeking into the tent. She waved the girls off to a safe distance, turned on the car alarm, headlights, emergency flasher, and drove into the tent, breath held, teeth gritted, thumbs pressed on horn button.

The two intruders fled on motor scooters. The larger of the two, she swore, had NFL dimensions. There was so much of him, she could hardly see the bike underneath.

Her assault rendered the tent as damaged as its owner. The front half was collapsed. The storm had ended and moisture steamed from small puddles trapped in the slumped canvas. Black Coral looked as if it had melted.

Denise took Luis's shrug as permission to speak. "Two. One of them—Inspector, are you familiar with American football?"

"Absolutely. The miracle of satellite TV. I love the New York Bears and Chicago Giants."

"Then you can picture how massively oversized a lineman is."

"The Refrigerator," Hector said, wrapping arms halfway around an invisible tree. "Various gentlemen named Reggie, Otis, and Bruce. Smash-face football. Pretty blond quarterbacks broken into bite-sized pieces. I love those huge, mean guys. I identify supremely with them."

"Oh, now I know who it is! Miss Lowell, was his companion a squat version? You know, how these modern photocopy machines reduce things. You retain the essence, although it can thereafter be depicted on a smaller sheet of paper."

"An excellent analogy. I didn't think I had a good look at him, but, yeah, a bowling ball with arms and legs. Who are they?"

"That is him, that is our boy. Luis, speak up. Do the honors," Hector demanded.

"Hector, what's the use? They belong to Estrada. They're untouchable."

"Estrada?" Denise asked. "The rich kid you call a 'junior'?"

"No longer a kid," Luis observed. "Not chronologically. He's losing his hair and putting on weight."

"A spoiled child until he dies," Denise said. "I know the type."

A red-faced Hector jabbed a finger at Luis. "I will decide who is above the law, not you. You're going to cooperate with me, Luis. I guarantee it."

"I don't know their names," Luis said. "Interrogating them will be difficult. The stumpy one's busy spitting out teeth and the big boy is a soprano."

Hector laughed.

"God, you're both incredible," Denise declared. "Does the machismo ever cease?"

"Despite our rich, ethnic Indian heritage, Luis and I are indigenous, normal, healthy Mexican males," Hector said flatly, a statement intended to suffice as sociological justification.

"Don't be too proud. You don't have a patent on it. I know men at home who put your machismo to shame, one ex-boyfriend included."

Hector grinned. "North American machismo guys? Come, come. They try, like counterfeit money tries."

"A yuppie with a membership in a health club," Denise said. "Top that."

Hector sought interpretive guidance from Luis, who helplessly shook his head.

"Their names are Romero and Hernández," Hector said. "They were *federales*, members of the federal judicial police. The federal boys have a swagger and an arrogance and they do precisely as they please. Within limits. Romero and Hernández do not know the meaning of the word 'limits,' however. Hernández, the fire hydrant, does not know the meaning of most other words either. He should be permanently confined to a tiny cage constructed of barbed wire and high voltage. In a certain respect, the Ram and Giant replica, Romero, is more hazardous. He has functioning brain cells.

"Raúl Estrada Estrada likes vicarious danger, so he surrounds himself with the disreputable of the disreputable. He pays his muscle well and they do what they are told."

"Well, can't you arrest them?" Denise asked. "How untouchable is Junior Estrada?"

"Luis, in this case, could sign a complaint. You and his daughters could file witness statements to this savage, unprovoked assault. I could toss them in jail. Estrada could then pull strings. Or he might not.

"Luis does not exaggerate. One attacker violently gelded, the other toothless. I can visualize. They look worse than Luis. The muscle did not do their jobs. They shamed their master by being held to a draw by one sawed-off runt of an Indian. The junior might cut them loose in disgust, to rot in my jail. They are replaceable, they are disposable."

"Thanks anyway," Luis said. "I'll handle it."

"No, no, no, you can't dismiss me so nonchalantly. Why,

Luis, would an elegant rich boy like Estrada slip Romero's and Hernández's leashes and sic them on you?"

"The junior and I are old pals."

Hector's face reddened again. "I of all people am cognizant of your relationship. Don't get smart-ass with me, Luis. What did you do to stir Estrada up?"

"I made some inquiries."

Hector looked sidelong at Denise, cleared his throat, and said softly, "You made some inquiries. Regarding Gilbert?"

"Yes. The favor I asked you last night at Ho-Keh, the curator, for instance. Indirectly, the junior is involved. I also had a confrontation with Enrique Bud Rojas at the Club Estrada, and with the junior in the flesh at Ricky Martínez's law office, and with Mr. Romero outside Ricky's office just prior. In my opinion, they weren't serious confrontations. But, apparently, my opinion wasn't unanimous."

Hector closed his eyes and shook his head slowly. "Luis, you are astounding."

"It's my responsibility, Hector. I'll handle it."

"Luis, how often must I lecture you on the differences between operating as a policeman and working as a freelance detective? You cross the line and you get stepped on. What did the doctor say about your injuries, by the way?"

"He said I'll be as good as new in two to three weeks."

"Can you see out of your eye? I do not see a lot of eyeball through the black-and-blue and the puffy raw meat."

"I can see out of it."

That was also a lie. The doctor on the highway could treat some infections, set bones, take a stab at a diagnosis, and make recommendations. His recommendation to Luis was to check into a Cancún clinic or hospital. The doctor had no X-ray machine, but the cheekbone felt under the swelling as though it was possibly cracked. And who could guess, with the trauma and capillary ruptures inside the eyeball, how long it would be before sight returned, if ever? Luis did not answer yes or no to the hospital recommendation, so the doctor, muttering about patients treating themselves, knowing what Luis's true answer was, gave him ointments and antibiotics, directions on their application and dosage, and a sincere wish of good luck.

"You can see out of *that?* Luis, are you sure you don't want to be driven to a hospital?"

"No, no thank you, Hector. Things will appear fuzzy for a while, but I'll be all right."

Check into a hospital, for how long, and what would happen to him? What would happen to his babies in his absence? What would happen to his babies if somebody made a medical error and he never checked out? And what could they do for him? How did you put a plaster cast on a broken cheekbone? And how were they going to fix his eye? With an ether mask and a scalpel? No.

"Will you be reopening your store?" Denise asked him.

"Not soon. We'll prop up the tent and take our merchandise home. I can't be with Esther and Rosa every minute and I can't leave them here alone. They will be staying in Ho-Keh until the matter is settled."

"The matter may never be settled unless you have Romero and Hernández arrested."

"I'm optimistic. As Hector said, they're replaceable."

Hector shifted from English to Spanish. "I have obtained

the information on Figueroa you extorted me last night into acquiring. I shall rattle it off ultra-quick. It is rude to linguistically exclude a person from a conversation. She will be pissed off."

"Look at her, Hector," Luis said in Spanish. "She *is* pissed off. Miss Lowell saved my life. She thought fast and she was brave. She came to Cancún to take her dead sister home. We owe her better treatment and higher respect."

Hector reverted to English. "My apologies, miss. Boy talk. It is rude."

"And tacky."

"I'm telling her about Figueroa," Luis said, and did.

"A museum curator on vacation may have faked identification of the knife that was used to kill my sister and the three other women? Why?" Denise asked.

"Not the knife's identification, its origin," Luis replied.

"Okay, but how come it's important whether or not the weapon is new or old?"

"It's important because somebody thinks it's important. Hector?"

Hector consulted a notebook in his hip pocket. "Mr. Figueroa moved into a plush suite in the Club Estrada the morning after the fourth Gil—after your sister was murdered, Miss Lowell.

"He had purchased for himself and his family a ten-day tour from Mexico City to Cancún to Mexico City. It was a low-budget vacation package. Transportation was provided by a terrifyingly inept domestic air charter company. You can go to the airport and tell which airplanes are theirs by the gobs of oil dripping on the tarmac under the engine

nacelles. The Cancún City hotel contracted to supply room
and board is less than sumptuous. The cockroaches are so
aggressive they have tattoos."

Denise and Luis laughed, the latter with considerable
pain.

"Mr. Figueroa is a small-time Mexico City bureaucrat
and intellectual," Hector went on. "He bought the vacation
of a lifetime for his wife and children. He, an exemplary
family man and an honest white-collar pauper, selected his
dream holiday in paradise and bought what he could afford.

"From fleabag dump to lap of luxury the Figueroas went.
Two thirty-five per night plus four-star meals for a husky
wife and two growing children, and mucho Corona that he
drinks day and night at lounge and pool-bar prices. We have
not a clue to the source of his sudden wealth. The plain-
clothesman I dispatched observed no money change hands.
Mr. Figueroa does not even sign chits for the beer he drinks
to become unhappily inebriated."

"He's been bribed," Luis said.

"Brilliant, Luis. The question is why."

"Let's find out," Denise said.

"A more germane question than why is why should we?"
Hector said. "Your assumption is that Figueroa was bribed
to falsify authenticity of the flint knife. Could be that he did.
Could be that he did not. Could be that later on in the
criminal justice process it will be reexamined by a second
expert. So what if it is bogus? Proctor Smith bought an un-
traceable weapon on the street from a black market sharpie.
People make all kinds of junk and peddle it to tourists. So
what?

"Or could be Mrs. Figueroa is Mr. Estrada Estrada's long-lost cousin. Overwhelmed by the surprise reunion, Mr. Estrada Estrada touchingly and generously lavished his facilities upon the Figueroas.

"Miss Lowell, there is an old Yucatán custom. You save a person's life and it is your responsibility to guard that person to the best of your ability. In Yucatán the God of Death is given two chances."

"Really?"

Luis examined his fingernails. The God of Death. Hector, a Zapotec, was astounding. He was inventing Maya folklore on the spot.

"Miss, these are legends derived from the writings of the ancient Maya," Hector continued resolutely. "They are, to be sure, superstitions, but how often is it that we discover superstition is in actuality based on substance? Who can truly say? This evil spirit must be thwarted. It is up to you.

"Luis at this minute is contemplating foolish vengeance, rather than steering his energy to recovery and to constructive projects. He requires supervision. Otherwise, he is going to be one of those self-activating prophecies."

Luis translated Hector's drivel: Keep tabs on him, and both of you stay out of my hair. The simple and lustrously clear idea that had come to him at the Crazy Cow was making an encore appearance.

"I accept the responsibility," Denise said.

Luis looked at her with his good eye and said, "I promise to be constructive. Tomorrow I'll take you sightseeing."

CHAPTER EIGHTEEN

wo types of passenger ferry ran between Playa del Carmen and Cozumel Island—conventional hull craft and water-jet catamarans. The catamarans' fares were higher, but they covered the nineteen kilometers faster than the conventional boats, twenty minutes as opposed to thirty. In rough water, though, the catamarans were forced to throttle back, more or less equalizing the crossing times. The boats should also have slowed in choppy seas, but as far as Luis could determine from his countless buying trips to Cozumel, they didn't. He theorized that the captains were showing contempt for their newfangled, sexier counterparts by beating them to the dock. Testosterone, he thought; we Mexicans secrete an ocean of it.

So, for this reason, it was unfortunate that Luis had picked a conventional hull instead of a cat. He wasn't just saving pesos. The sea was a jade sheet when they pulled out from the Playa del Carmen pier. On the other hand, he knew how quickly a squall could blow up and whip the water into froth. Halfway across, one did.

The boat was plowing along at cruise speed, bouncing and thudding as if through a field of bomb craters. Green-tinged passengers sat rigidly in padded plastic seats. Music videos and travel shorts played on a projection screen. Perky young hostesses in blue uniforms patrolled the aisles with cheery smiles and barf bags.

Denise had said early on, when they crested the first swell, that she shouldn't have had the *huevos rancheros.* Using his experience as a tour guide, Luis tried to take her mind off her stomach. If she could save his life, he could at least do his utmost to save her breakfast.

"Cozumel means 'Land of the Swallow,' " he said. "Fifty kilometers long at its longest and fifteen kilometers wide at its widest, Cozumel is Mexico's largest island."

"Uh-huh."

"Cozumel was a sacred Maya island. My ancestors made pilgrimages from the mainland to worship at its shrines. Women sought fertility, among other blessings."

"Uh-huh."

"Hernán Cortés cruised by in 1518 and things went downhill. He stayed long enough to desecrate temples and deposit smallpox germs, then he sailed up to Veracruz and had some more fun."

"Uh-huh."

"Later, pirates such as Jean Lafitte and Henry Morgan hung out. Cozumel was a good refuge and staging area for their activities. In World War Two your country built an airstrip and a submarine base on the island."

"Uh-huh."

"Diving got started around then. Scuba diving, snorkel-

ing, and fishing, above all else, are what Cozumel is renowned for."

"Uh."

Denise had raised her head at an unfortunate moment,
while a cola beverage commercial was being projected on
the screen. Affluent light-skinned young Mexicans, arche-
typal juniors, giddy over the sponsor's product, were drinking it with a nice restaurant meal. On the table were enchiladas, refried beans, tamales, and chilis—an oily and starchy
assortment of fiery delicacies.

Luis reacted in the nick of time, shielding her eyes with
a hand, saying, "Don't look. Never mind. Hang on. Only five
minutes to go. Breathe deeply."

"Five minutes?"

"Six at the maximum."

"Okay, Denise, keep yourself occupied. Luis, you
said you buy your black coral from this . . . what's his
name?"

"Black coral and ninety percent of my other stock. His
name is Alejandro. Alejandro quotes me the best wholesale
prices on the coast."

"Have you ever bought a replica of a Maya flint knife
from him?"

"No. I wouldn't sell anything like that."

"Don't be so defensive. Does he sell them?"

"I don't know."

"So why are we going to Cozumel to see him?"

"Because Alejandro is Alejandro. If he hasn't sold it, it
hasn't been invented."

Denise Lowell inhaled and exhaled, inhaled and exhaled. She squinted out her window. "I may survive. Is that dry land?"

Viewed with only one eye, the world was as flat as a mural. That handicap, coupled with glass streaked by salt spray, and he might as well have been looking through the porthole on a washing machine door, staring at foamy, swirling underwear.

He said, "Yes. There it is. I see it. We're almost there."

Cozumel's town of San Miguel was conveniently and not coincidentally at the ferry landing. The *malecón*—the sea-wall—paralleled the beach. Directly ahead was a dense concentration of shops and cafés, the sweet spot of tourism. The market district was an attractive compromise of picturesque and seedy. On the whole, San Miguel was eclectic and clean. Mexicans liked it. Tourists liked it. Luis Balam liked it. It had none of Cancún's electroplated glitz.

A planet beneath their feet that was not undulating did wonders for Denise's health and her outlook. Luis led them across the *malecón* toward the handicraft market. She said, "Do they take major credit cards?"

A full recovery, Luis thought. "Major credit cards, minor credit cards, obscure credit cards. They love cash and traveler's checks too. You can buy ceramics from Oaxaca, Hector's home state. Hammocks from Yucatán State. Carved wood, blown glass, weavings, fabrics, and jewelry made throughout Mexico and Central America."

"Cheap?"

"Yes and no. Relatively cheap. Spot an item you can't resist and I'll bargain for it. If you are homesick for North

American prices, we can go into gift shops with carpeting and air-conditioning."

"This Alejandro, I'm hazy on who he actually is."

"Me too," Luis said. "He owns a small factory that makes jewelry from the black coral the divers bring up. He buys and sells everything imaginable to retailers like me, plus he's silent partner to various street-corner and market peddlers."

"How do you know he'll be at the market? It seems to me with all the irons he has in the fire, he'd be in his office overseeing things."

They turned into a passageway. "I'm not dead certain that he'll be in the market. But Alejandro, to the best of my knowledge, doesn't have an office. His office is scraps of paper in his pockets and deals in his head. You think I'm weird with my retention of the 1974 World Almanac? Alejandro remembers everything that has to do with business. A merchant owes him five thousand pesos from a 1983 shipment, Alejandro will remember. He catches up to him, he'll adjust it for inflation and exchange rates in his head and tack on the prevailing interest rate."

"So why do you feel he'll be here? Oh my God."

Amid the indistinguishable sea of silver and leather and pots was an art gallery that offered plaster Aztec clocks, freshly carved Maya glyphs on small limestone slabs, and radioactive velvet paintings. The painting transfixing Denise was of a scantily dressed woman decorated in plumed head-dress and gold anklets. She was seated atop a stone pyramid holding a torch. She looked to Luis like a young Sophia Loren.

Denise said, "A Maya princess? That's what the price tag says."

"In the 1500s a Spanish friar named Diego de Landa became incensed at the depravity of the Maya religion, our human sacrifice and our worship of multiple deities. In the name of his true God, Landa destroyed our idols and burned every devilish manuscript but three, which were hidden. To this day they are in European museums. Landa set about torturing love of Christianity into our pagan souls.

"His excesses repelled even the Spanish. They shipped him home to stand trial for mismanagement and atrocities. He spent a year in jail, where he wrote a book on Yucatán entitled *Relación de las Cosas de Yucatán.* Account of the Things of Yucatán. It preserved a fraction of the knowledge he had obliterated and got him acquitted. He was allowed to return. He was promoted and lived out the rest of his days as Bishop of Yucatán. Isn't that some justice?"

"No, it isn't justice. Your story, frankly, fascinating as it is, as far as I can tell, isn't related to Maya princesses either."

"Wrong," Luis said. "A Maya princess like her would have been immortalized in a codex. Pornography. She may have inspired my people to develop photography. The manuscripts would have survived. My forebears would have fought to the death to save her likenesses."

Denise laughed and hooked a hand around his arm. "No more tour guiding, Luis, okay? Alejandro. Again, why do you kind of, sort of insist he'll be at the market?"

"He says he hangs out to take the pulse of the consumer, to stay current on what sells and what doesn't. I think he likes the dickering and the hustling. Nor can his partners steal as much from him if he makes unpredictable appearances."

"Luis, holy sheet! Who done da calypso on your face?"

Behind a glass case of silver coins, cameo brooches, and signet rings stood a tall Mexican with bushy sideburns and a face as long and homely as a hound's. On his slender body he had chinos and a University of South Carolina T-shirt and in his mouth one of the Salems he chain-smoked.

"I had an accident. I fell down. Alejandro, meet Denise."

He bowed his head, a choppy motion that dislodged his cigarette ash. "A friend of Luis's is a friend of mine. You on a buy for your shop or you taking this fine lady round to see what's to see? Buy her lonch, mon. Put some meat on those sweet skinny bones."

"Is he talking to you or me?" Denise asked Luis. "I didn't understand three words. How does he bargain with *anybody?*"

Alejandro spoke a stew of English, Spanish, and West Indies patois that tested even Luis's understanding. "With a pocket calculator. He punches in a figure, they punch in a figure. He's emotional and entertaining. He's colorful. He does very well for himself."

Then to Alejandro he said, "No buying today. Black Coral is on holiday for a while. We're seeing Cozumel, we'll have lunch, but we really came to talk to you."

Alejandro stepped backward and raised his hands. "Bad medicine, mon. You be on Cozumel not buying. Your head got run over by a cattle stampede and you got a pretty lady dat don't act like you's butt-ugly as you is, and you say you came to talk to me."

"It won't cost you a peso, Alejandro. I just need a little information."

"Yeah? What information?"

"Where somebody would go to buy or sell something."

"This something, it ain't 'gainst da law, is it? I don't know nothing 'bout no contraband, mon."

"A Maya sacrificial knife," Luis said softly.

"I ain't no fockin' grave robber, mon!"

"Shhh," Luis said, finger to lips. "I didn't accuse you. It's a hypothetical question."

Alejandro laughed, lit a Salem from the one he was smoking, and said, "Hypothetical. Know what hypothetical is? Dat's when da mon you loaned money to disappears. Your money's gone and went hypothetical."

"You hear things," Luis said.

"I hear dat preacher mon, Gilbert, he slit da girls with a Mayan flint knife. Lucky they got him, mon. Da law was ready to pin it on da first Mayan who looked crossways."

"Don't I know. They claim the murder knife is real. What do you hear lately on the antiquities market?"

"There you go again, mon," Alejandro said with a wounded look. "I'm a grave robber *and* a smuggler of national treasures."

"Prying answers out of you is like prying the meat out of a conch shell. Genuine flint knives wouldn't be readily available, would they?"

"Not too likely. What you got to do to get ahold of them, you got to dive down deep in them sacrificial *cenotes* like dat one they got up there in Chicken Itzee. You dive or you dredge in slimy green water, but you're gonna come up empty even if no cop's looking and says to stop or I'll shoot. Dat's all been done before, for a century. What's left down in them is junk. Either you buy it or you swipe it out of a museum. Them things is scarce. What did you fall down out of, mon, an airplane?"

"How about reproductions?"

"Yeah, mon, but don't you be quoting me. Your ancestors, they sacrificed who?"

"Bones of children have been taken from the *cenotes*," Luis said. "Adults too. Many were male, assumed to be captives from other cities during wars."

"Dat's how I thought it was, but Yanqui tourists who ask, they don't know dat. All they fockin' know is virgins. Yanquis are funnier about virginity 'n us, mon." Alejandro winked at Luis and grinned a yellow-toothed grin at an uncomprehending Denise. "We worship virginity. Yanquis resent da sheet out of it."

"Have any North American tourists inquired recently about sacrificial knives?"

Alejandro lifted a shoulder. "Not to me, never, mon, but, yeah, sure, they do."

"Authentic knives?"

"Dat's what they inquire on, yeah. Yanquis who come to smuggle out national treasures, dey go for pottery or jewelry. You can wear jade, you can show off a vase on a shelf. What you gone do with a dagger, mon? Maybe they show them to girlfriends."

"There is a trade in knives?"

Alejandro held a thumb and forefinger a centimeter apart. "Teeny itty-bitty. They say they pay top dollar for da real thing, whispering like you is to me, Luis, sneaky-like, and you get whispery and sneaky-like and say, sure, mon, it's fockin' tough but come see me again in two days, like you really got to scour the continent for da fockin' thing, go to da Casbah or somewhere."

"They come back?"

"Some do, yeah. He come back, you know you got your Yanqui on da hook. You know why else they like to smuggle out a little thing like a knife?"

Luis shook his head.

" 'Cuz they're play-it-safe crooks. It's vacation sport, like tennis. They want to make a little, risk a little. Dope, da police grab you, lock you up till da Second Coming. Gold and silver, they ain't got da imagination to get it bypassed around da metal detectors at da airport. Big things, pots and stone statues, their suitcases is too small."

"How much?"

"How much they'll pay for a nice fake? Five hundred. A thousand. You talk friendly, have a drink or five, reach a friendly, agreeable price. You branching out into knives, Luis? You really ought to branch out of black coral. It's endangered. They're clamping down on big pieces being took out of the country. I'll give you a free, priceless tip. Hand a knife to your Yanqui fish in a dark alley out of a raincoat and you can clip an extra ten percent for da adventure and intrigue."

"I'm not branching out into knives," Luis said. "Thanks anyhow for the tip. Who is?"

"Nobody on Cozumel and dat's God's truth, mon."

Luis smiled. He was patient. Alejandro was ready to give, but at his speed. In passable English, he asked Denise, "You in da market for a knife?"

"No."

Alejandro offered her a cigarette. She declined. Alejandro lit up and said, "You touristing with Luis?"

"Kind of."

"You not wanting to buy a knife?"

"No."

Alejandro glanced from Denise to Luis to Denise. "No buy, no sell, no money to no mon for no knife. You writin' a book on Mayan knives? You look like a writer lady."

"Mr. Alejandro, is 'fockin' ' what I think it is?"

Alejandro did a Groucho Marx with his eyebrows. "Makes da world go 'round, mama."

"My sister was murdered with a Maya flint knife, Mr. Alejandro. I would like to fockin' know where the killer got his hands on the dreadful fockin' thing."

Alejandro looked at Luis, who said, "It's the truth."

Alejandro's hound face lengthened and his eyes seemed to bulge. "A mon on da mainland, down the coast not far from you, he makes them. Small quantities, made to order. Dat's all I know."

"Thanks, Alejandro."

Alejandro lit a Salem with a trembling hand and said, "Luis, mon, next time you come, just come with a buy order. We'll eat lonch and talk business. Murder and knives, mon, they fockin' scary."

■ ■ ■

Luis and Denise had met at Playa del Carmen. His Beetle and her rental, a later-generation Volkswagen, a four-speed Golf sedan, were in a parking lot. The only damage sustained in her assault on Black Coral was a cracked grille. Luis knew a clerk at the rental agency. He made a mental note to grease the turn-in process for her. Ten thousand pesos clipped to his check-in inspection form would render him as blind as a cave full of bats.

At their cars, Luis invited Denise to Ho-Keh for dinner. It was a spontaneous invitation that took Denise by happy surprise. At least Luis thought she was happily surprised; he thought he saw it in her skin tone, an infinitesimal flick of a blush. She accepted with a smile, yes, but Luis was less fluent in North American smiles than in words. Everybody dissembled with smiles and you had to be a native to decipher them.

Luis asked her to wait at the lot, then follow him when he returned. He needed to buy some ingredients, including pork. She had been in Mexico for less than a week. She had come from a world of refrigerated, shrink-wrapped antisepsis. Haggling for baskets and bracelets was one thing, shopping for meat in a small-town Mexican butcher shop quite another.

South they went on Highway 307, a two-car caravan. He saw the drifting streak of black smoke two kilometers before he came to the fire. Luis pulled into Black Coral's parking lot, downshifting rather than braking. Denise was in his mirror, hand over mouth. His tent was char and airborne soot.

Luis asked himself what he could accomplish by leaping

out, pacing, kicking at the piles of ash, and cursing? What? Besides giving the pork time to spoil.

He waved out the window to her, a swimming motion that said come on, come on, and accelerated onto the highway.

CHAPTER NINETEEN

*T*his is delicious, Luis. Pronounce it again."

They had finished dinner and were sitting behind the Balam home on aluminum and plastic lawnchairs, drinking warm León Negro. Years ago, Luis had scavenged the chairs from the side of the highway, bent and twisted as abstract sculpture. He had resurrected them with henequen fiber and scrounged nuts and bolts.

He said, *"Poc chuc.* Sorry for the toughness. It should marinate longer."

"Which is pork marinated in what? I'm going to steal your recipe."

"Esther's recipe. She did most of the cooking. All I did was start the charcoal in the barrel and grill the meat. Sour orange, onions, cilantro, whatever is handy, that's the marinade. Rosa boiled the rice and black beans."

"You're pampered."

Luis nodded serenely. "I am."

"Poc chuc is Maya for what? Is *poc* pork?"

Luis had to think for a moment. *"Poc chuc* is *poc chuc* like lasagna is lasagna."

"If you get tired of my questions, just say stop."

"Stop," Luis said, happy that he could now smile without sending a million volts of pain through the ruined side of his face. He diagnosed his cheekbone as unbroken; he could not have chewed the pork otherwise.

"You'll have to say it with more conviction than that." She pointed beyond a low stone fence. The scrub jungle backdropped a disorderly field. Green shoots were poking through dead, brown vegetation. "Is that corn coming up?"

"It is."

"Well, I guess I'm conditioned to pictures of Iowa corn, acres and acres of straight, weeded rows. Tasseled stalks high as an elephant's eye."

"The mess is the slash that didn't burn. We chop down the growth with machetes. In April, just before the rainy season, we burn. We plant by poking holes with a sharp stick and dropping in seeds. No John Deere machines in Yucatán. The rains come. The corn grows. We harvest in October and November.

"Our cornfields are called *milpas*. We've always farmed slash and burn. Now we're being told we're wrong."

"How so?"

"They say we're burning down the tropical rain forest."

"Aren't you?"

"It's all in your point of view. Yucatán topsoil is nil. Dig a few inches and you hit solid limestone. The burned ash makes the soil sweat, makes it fertile. We get two good years of crops out of an area and a miserable third. Then the fertility is gone. It lies fallow. We hack down vegetation next to it and burn. Two or three years later, the area next to it.

By then the first area has renewed itself and the cycle repeats.

"They compare us to Brazil and the Amazon, where once it's gone it's gone. That's a bad comparison. They want us to quit slash-and-burn farming, but what should we do instead?"

"Do you farm?" Denise asked.

"I grew up farming. It's very hard. We haven't enough land, and crops aren't good every year."

"So you went to Cancún to improve your life."

"I changed my life."

"You've done well. Don't say you haven't. And you're raising two wonderful daughters."

Luis shrugged. "I'm a schizophrenic Maya. I'm in the past right here. I drive my car to Highway 307 and I'm a Maya of the future."

"What happened to the present?"

"There is no present. Change in Yucatán is too fast. We jump directly from the past to the future, back and forth, back and forth. You get dizzy."

"You paint a bleak picture of your girls' future. Too bleak, hopefully. As you said, times are changing."

"I realize you don't know Spanish, but can you guess what *buena presentación* means?"

"*Buena,* good. Pre-sen-tah-cee-own, presentation. Appearance. Good appearance?"

"Yes. In newspaper classified advertising, employers hiring for good jobs, not hotel servant jobs, but good jobs, they specify *buena presentación.* Literal translation: no Indians."

Denise shook her head. "In the States we're not perfect

in that regard. We're just subtler. Do they know about the fire?"

"No. I'll tell them tonight."

"Will you set up another tent?"

"Not right away."

"I don't suppose you have fire insurance."

Luis looked at her.

"One final stupid question. People in the village were friendly toward me. Your parents too, when you introduced us. But nobody's outside. They smiled, said hello, and ducked indoors. Rosa and Esther are indoors. Is it me?"

"With my parents it's you," Luis said. "It isn't personal. For me to bring a woman to Ho-Keh is interpreted by Father and Mother in past terms, by me in future terms. In future thinking, we merely had dinner. In past thinking, you are a prospective bride. They don't dislike you. They're puzzled twice over because you are a non-Maya *and* a North American.

"With my neighbors, it's me. The men are *milpa* farmers. Some of the wives bicycle to part-time jobs along the highway. Resorts are sprouting on the beach side quicker than you can count them. That's the extent of their exposure to the outside world. They're locked in the past. I'm regarded as the future. We're friends, but we have little in common.

"With my babies, I didn't have to ask them to stay indoors. They're typical romantic adolescents. A question for you."

"Fire away."

"What is Kemo Sabe?"

"Kemo Sabe is what Tonto called the Lone Ranger. I don't understand your Lone Ranger questions."

"I don't understand the answers."

"Oh, wait, one final *final* question. Was Inspector Salgado's God of Death a lie?"

"Yes and no. My forebears worshipped multiple gods. They were aspects of the cosmos, so from that standpoint they were one god. Our death deity was known as Yum Cimil. He should not be confused with separate gods of human sacrifice and suicide."

Denise laughed, placed a hand on his forearm, and said, "Luis, you evade in English better than I do. I'm referring to the inspector's statement that the God of Death has two chances and that I'm responsible for thwarting his second attempt, and you know it."

Luis's arm tingled. Her hand was as warm as blood, soft and moist as a womb. "In this day and age, today, now, there are Yucatec Maya who believe that Yum Cimil breaks into the homes of the sick, on the lookout for customers."

"Okay, I also believe," she said playfully. "As I told Inspector Salgado, I accept the responsibility. Providing you can tolerate my protection, you got it. I'll carry a mirror and a wooden stake. Yum Cimil makes a move, he's dead meat."

"Now I'd like to ask a final final *final* question. This is a very serious and very stupid two-part question."

"Fire away."

Denise drank the last of her León. "Did Romero and Hernández burn your tent? Why did Romero and Hernández burn your tent?"

Luis took two bottles of beer from the bucket of tepid

water where they had been psychologically cooling, opened them, and said, "They probably burned my tent. They probably burned my tent because I hurt them while they were hurting me. They're hired goons. Raúl Estrada Estrada says to burn a tent, they burn a tent."

"You were cramping his style, but it goes further than that. You haven't been totally up-front with me on Gilbert, Luis, I know you haven't, and I have to say, unladylike as my language sounds, that it's kind of pissing me off. Warding off the God of Death deserves some quid pro quo."

Luis was tempted to tease and say that the beer was responsible for her feisty talk. Wisdom prevailed. A conking on the head by the shank of a León bottle would compound existing injuries far beyond any reasonable threshold of pain.

"Aside from Figueroa and the knife, I'm not onto anything that would jeopardize the junior."

"He doesn't know that."

Luis shrugged. "That is his problem."

"This dark beer is delicious, but maybe you should slow down. It's maybe making you sound cockier than you are. Is that the truth?"

"As far as implicating Estrada is concerned, I'm sad to report, yes."

"Aha. As far as *Estrada* is concerned. The tone in your voice. You're holding out."

Luis related his conversation with Ellen Smith.

Denise was silent for a minute. "Proctor Smith is a locksmith?"

"A highly skilled locksmith according to his wife."

"Have you told anybody?"

"No."

"Why not?"

"It's exclusive information. It's worth setting aside."

"Well, maybe it's the clincher. Proctor Smith is Gilbert. God! This creepy-crawly preacher prowling hotel corridors, able to enter any room in Cancún."

"That's what the authorities would conclude. Minds would snap shut. End of the investigation."

"Luis, honestly, is there an investigation aside from what you and those Tropical Language Scholars lawyers are conducting? I mean, are the police seriously making an effort to be positively certain they have the right person?"

"I don't think so."

"Me neither, but everything points at him. Maybe Smith is Gilbert and we're wasting our time and you're causing yourself a lot of pain and suffering for no valid purpose."

"Yes," Luis agreed. "Maybe he is. Maybe I am."

"But does the knife bug you as much as it does me?"

"At least."

"So we should follow up on Alejandro's lead."

"We should."

"Have you a clue who the 'mon' who makes phony knives is?"

"No. Cancún to Chetumal is four hundred kilometers and a quarter million people."

Denise swigged her León and said, "The proverbial needle in the haystack."

"His name is Hugo, Father," Rosa called out from inside, Rosa with the hearing of sonar. "Two or three months ago, a tourist in the shop was whispering to his girlfriend that he had a deal to buy a knife that was used to cut the hearts out of human-sacrifice victims a thousand years ago. You know Hugo, don't you?"

"Hugo in Tulum City?" Luis asked.

"Yes, him."

"Rosa, honey, how did you know it was the tourist's girlfriend he was whispering to?" asked a grinning, delighted Denise Lowell.

"Because he was trying to impress her. She couldn't have been his wife."

CHAPTER TWENTY

*L*uis knew it was going to be the hottest day of the year because it was the hottest morning of the year. The sky was cloudless and the moisture from the absent clouds coated the skin of human beings. The clouds were taking a holiday to torment the humans who complained about them. This was Luis Balam's theory on blue-sky humidity.

Denise thought his theory would be more charming if he had told it to her in an air-conditioned cocktail lounge. Rosa and Esther groaned in unison, having heard it more times than they could remember.

Hector paid a surprise visit too late to hear the blue-sky humidity theory. But he, too, had been treated to the theory before and would feel no sense of loss at being deprived of a repetition. Especially today. He glistened with perspiration, as if he had been waxed and polished. Hector, thought Luis, qualified as the theory's living laboratory, its irrefutable proof.

"My apologies for this intrusion so close on the heels of my prior intrusion, Luis. May I come in?"

"My house is your house." Luis stood aside.

"A disingenuous Mexican expression employed on the magnitude of the North American 'Have a nice day,' " Hector said. "I know you speak it sincerely, however, and I reciprocate when you appear at my door."

Something was wrong. "Then come in. Have you eaten breakfast? We had tortillas and fruit. There is plenty of left-over food."

"No thank you," Hector said, smiling at the girls, nodding to Denise, then, eyes darting, counting hammocks: one, two, three, four.

"I came to dinner last night, Inspector," Denise said. "The sun set before I realized it was so late. Luis hung up a spare hammock. I haven't slept in one since I was a child at summer camp."

"Implications of impropriety were not implied, miss. Forgive my unintended impression to the otherwise. Luis, you and I must go for a drive."

"Where? Why?"

"We can discuss the destination en route. There has been a situation."

"Miss Lowell and I have an errand, Hector. May we come in a separate car?"

"As you wish."

Hector's reply lowered the ambient temperature twenty degrees. Luis and Denise went in the Beetle. They followed Hector's menacing Dodge Dart and its trail of blue exhaust smoke.

"Doomsday device. Batmobile," Denise said to herself, then to Luis, "The inspector is in a serious mood, isn't he?"

"Yes. Too serious."

"He didn't mention your tent. He must have noticed on the way to your village."

"He must have," Luis agreed.

"Well, we'll soon find out what's bugging him. You haven't told me anything about Hugo. Is there something you didn't want the girls to hear?"

"No. Hugo is just Hugo."

"That explains everything. Like Alejandro, he has no last name?"

"Like Alejandro, everybody knows him. He has a business on the highway at Tulum City. He serves food and drink. He makes things. He sells a combination of things. In your country—I forget what a store like Hugo's is called."

"Supermarket? Discount department store?"

"No. Hugo's is too small and ramshackle."

"General store?"

They turned north onto the highway. "General store. That's it."

"After you began snoring last night, Esther, Rosa, and I had a nice talk. I'm sorry about their mothers."

Luis felt his ears and neck burn. "Thank you."

"I've had a couple of near misses, but I've never been married, much to the dismay of my parents. I'm—I was the stable daughter, you know."

"It's been many years; I don't remember what marriage was like."

Denise fanned herself. "I'd give a thousand dollars for a change of clothes. Look, the inspector's turn signal is on. That's a novelty."

Oh no, Luis thought.

"What's the matter? You're tensing up. He's going in on that dirt road to—that sign says 'Xcacel—The Wildest Beach Around.' Is it?"

"No. The waves are tame and tour buses come only twice or three times a week. There's a restaurant and a camping area. Xcacel is a nice beach to visit, a nice place to stay if you have little money."

"Then why are you so upset and driving so fast? The potholes are knocking my fillings out."

"Dave Shingles. He camps here."

"Shingles? The flying saucer kid?"

"Yes."

"And you think he's in trouble?"

Hector stopped at a campsite. Two other police cars and four khaki-uniformed officers were already there. Luis said, "Somebody's in trouble."

They got out. Hector stood between them and the activity. He raised a hand and said to Denise, "Miss, please proceed no farther. Luis, come here."

The campground was set on a rise a hundred meters from the beach. Tents and recreational vehicles occupied one site in three. Coconut and palm trees provided some shade, marginal relief from the damp heat. Campers were watching intently, but from a distance.

Hector led Luis past his officers to a sleeping bag. The upper half was covered with a blanket. The stench of putrifying flesh was unmistakable. "We threw it upon what remains above the deceased gentleman's neck. A party or parties unknown crept in—presumably during the middle of the night before last—bashed his head in as he slept, and crept out unseen and unheard. With the crash of the surf, I presume the death blows would have sounded like coconuts falling to anyone who may have been awakened. One camper recalled a noise of motor scooters at or near the highway. Would you care to have a look, Luis?"

"No thank you, Hector."

"Would you care to hypothesize regarding the identity of the deceased?"

"A North American named Dave Shingles?"

"An outstanding hypothesis, Luis." Hector pointed at a knapsack, a cloth suitcase wrapped in transparent plastic sheeting, and a portable radio. "His neighbors noticed nothing untoward until they smelled untoward smells. His face was covered by the sleeping bag cover. This radio, a shortwave portable, was on, tuned to static. The North American hippies who kindly grace Yucatán with their presence, they sleep unusual hours and long hours. Your Mr. Shingles, fellow campers believed he matched that profile, although they had never witnessed him ingest narcotics."

"*My* Mr. Shingles?"

Hector sighed, reached under the clear plastic, and produced a spiral-bound notebook. The cardboard covers were wrinkled and blood-stained. Some of the pages were missing. "He slept with it under his pillow. I further speculate that pages pertinent to the activities of the killers were removed. Perhaps discovery of the book was accidental, knocked out from under the pillow by the ferociousness of the attack.

"Your name is barely legible on a page, Luis. The remaining pages, my knowledge of written English is not proficient. But this stuff—these calculations and references to midget space aliens—it is crazy. You knew him, did you not?"

"I did."

"Mr. Shingles was a flying saucer cultist?"

"He was, though he did not belong to a cult group. He had his own ideas."

This sigh of Hector's was theatrical. "Luis, do I give a damn whether he has a membership card in an association of escaped asylum inmates? You of all people, Maya blood surging through your veins as Zapotec surges through mine, what in the fucking hell are you doing consorting with a lunatic who asserts that your ancestors were short and good at mathematics and civil engineering because *their* ancestors came from Jupiter?"

"Consorting," Luis said, shaking his head, numbing with grief and guilt. "No. Listen to me, Hector."

Luis related his encounters with Shingles at Tulum and Cobá and Tulum again. He spoke slowly and deliberately, careful to be factual and complete.

"That is the whole truth, Luis?"

"It is."

"You are prone to withhold crucial facts from me, Luis."

"Not now, Hector. Not now."

"Are you yet obsessed with the Gilbert murder knife?"

"I am still trying to trace it."

"I suppose I have to trust your word. You look like you are going to cry, so I further suppose that my trust is grounded on solid ground. I wish we could dissuade the flying saucer lunatics from their fascination with Tulum. They are not your free-spending Cancún sensualists. They mooch and hitchhike and sleep on the beach and subsist on foraged food. They do not rent cars or hotel rooms or eat in absurdly priced restaurants. They do not carry credit cards, they carry New Age crystals. They contribute scantily to the economy.

"They should make their harebrained pilgrimages to Palenque, down there in Chiapas State, with their spiritual colleagues. Palenque is remote. They have hills. They have thicker jungle than we do. Palenque has improved scenic qualities and increased eeriness. If I were an antenna-ed green man, I would choose Palenque over Tulum. But that is merely my earthly, mortal preference.

"Luis, what is sincerely and truly my preference is not the decisions of spaceship navigators. I want to know why this young man was killed."

"Not by whom?"

"We know by whom, Luis. The people who beat you and burned your tent killed Shingles. They licked their wounds after their altercation with you and came up here. Why?"

"Shingles did not know anything when I talked to him," Luis said. "He babbled about patterns that were not patterns. The people in Cancún he interviewed were uncooperative and hostile."

"So either he rubbed the wrong person the wrong way or he learned an incriminating tidbit and recorded it in the detective portion of this extraordinarily strange journal. But why did they merely remove the notebook pages? Why did they not abscond with it in its entirety?"

"As a message to whom it may concern. Lay off the Gilbert case."

Hector wiped his face with a handkerchief already soggy and took Luis aside. "This is a nightmare, Luis. Proctor Smith is arrested and we embark on the road to normalcy. But, no, it is not to be. Another gringo tourist, albeit a marginal tourist, is killed, murdered in his sleep on a lovely, idyllic Quintana Roo beach. The bureaucrats will go insane with anger. Do you realize how much trouble and paperwork there are when a foreign national meets a homicidal end? Then there are the tabloids. They will have a field day writing of blood lust and lawlessness on our beloved coast. But, Luis, do you want me to tell you what the worst of it is, or would you prefer to speculate and tell me?"

Luis nodded. "Proctor Smith may not be Gilbert."

"Yes. We have wrapped up the evangelical with the classic smoking gun syndrome, neat as the prettiest bow. Yet, incomprehensibly, you and your deceased assistant detective are frightening none other than our favorite junior, Raúl Estrada Estrada, who has a hundred alibis for each of the four killings. Your investigation in behalf of the missionary organization has been perfunctory and predicated on—what is that mercenary expression favored by lawyers?"

"Billable hours. Hector, Shingles was not my—"

"Yes, billable hours. In this instance, however, the Bible wallopers may be obtaining their money's worth. Proctor Smith cannot possibly be innocent, but maybe he is. The illogic is maddening."

"Hector, Shingles was not my assistant," Luis said loudly and angrily. "I made two mistakes that cost him his life. I agitated the junior in Ricky Martínez's office and I confided in Shingles about the case while we sat on top of Nohoch Mul at Cobá. I feel bad enough without you—"

"Luis, Luis, sorry. Please keep your voice down. My semantic clumsiness was quite unintentional."

Denise was out of the car, drawn by Luis's shouting. She stopped suddenly and threw a hand over her mouth and nose. Speaking through spread fingers, she said, "Oh God, Luis, is it him?"

Luis nodded.

A state judicial police vehicle rumbled toward them. A blue Nissan sedan, it spewed a rooster tail of dust, weaving through the slalom course of potholes. The driver's controlled wildness impressed Luis.

Hector said, "I took the liberty of dispatching a man to retrieve your lawyer and his Texas cowboy collaborator. Before you clarified to me your relationship to the late Mr. Shingles, I thought you might require legal representation. I did not for a split second believe you had butchered him, but, Luis, you are at the core of so many recent troubles."

"Ricky? I appreciate the thought, Hector," Luis said, thinking that Ricardo Martínez Rodríguez was *not* his lawyer. He did independent detective work for Ricky, yes, but would he hire him if he were in desperate legal trouble? A man who nonchalantly spoke of striking a "satisfactory arrangement" with Estrada Estrada. Probably not.

Ricky was the lone passenger. He stepped out, stretched, yawned, patted the creases in his white shirt. His eyes came to rest on Denise. His gaze passed through her. She was invisible, this toilet-mouthed shrew.

Ricky saw Luis and crossed himself. "Mary, Mother of God! Your face!"

"I tripped and fell. I will eventually explain."

"Luis, predawn police raids on my home are evidently becoming a regular occurrence. Illegal residential entry and harassment of educated professionals, those are two early warning signs of fascism. Please tell me what we are doing here?"

Luis told him about Dave Shingles, about the goons, about the demise of Black Coral.

"The Buck Rogers boy from Tulum?" Ricky said.

Luis nodded.

"Madness," Ricky told the blue sky. "The world has gone mad. Flying saucers, killings, beatings. When will you stop antagonizing Mr. Estrada? You're playing Russian roulette, you know. With a revolver that has bullets in all the chambers."

"Where is W. W. Lard Ringner?" Luis asked.

"Recuperating in bed at his hotel. He was gored at a bullfight last night."

Hector and Luis looked at each other. Hector said, "Lawyer, talk lucidly. The Cancún bullring has fights on Wednesday afternoons only and they do not permit amateurs in the ring."

"Not the bullring," Ricky said. "In order to improve business, a Hotel Zone hotel has instituted an evening bull-fighting spectacle of sorts on their beach. This and night parasailing are all the rage, the in things to do. Within a makeshift enclosure is a baby bull with either tiny horns or glued-on plastic horns. Hotel employees in string bikinis hop into the ring with red towels and demonstrate how easy it is to enjoy a harmless, mock bullfight with an animal that has been raised to be gentle. Patrons, for a price, are then invited to take a turn.

"Well, Lard, while having discarded his cane, was apparently not recovered from his parasailing mishap. Compounding the situation were bourbon and the fact that despite instructions to the contrary, Ring was snapping his red towel at little toro rather than displaying it limply.

"Lard's heel caught in the sand and the docile animal showed a burst of temper. Lard took a horn to the midsection and fell hard on his backside. Fortunately, his skin wasn't broken, but he suffered a deep, painful bruise in the vicinity of the navel."

Hector shook his head and said, "I should assign a bodyguard to the Dallas lawyer. For his own protection. I would not like him to die before he takes us out to lunch again."

"The bad news is just beginning," Ricky went on. "We were a foursome, Lard, Hortensia, Carla, and I. Hortensia and I had reconciled and the night was promising. When Lard fell, she felt a greater obligation to her best friend, Carla, than to me. Lard refused hospital treatment. It was his pride that was in the greatest agony, if you ask me.

"Hortensia went to Lard's room to assist Carla with nursing duties. Where did that leave me? Watching television as they warmed washcloths and applied them to his gringo belly. No, that is not for me. I am no nursemaid."

"Has Ringner paid you a fee?"

"Imminently, Lard assured me," Ricky said without conviction.

"Progress on the case?" Luis asked.

"None. You?"

"I am not through, but no. If I had made progress, you would know."

"Lard and I interviewed Mrs. Ellen Smith, Gilbert's wife. She is a plain, obstinate woman. The Proctor Smith situation is static. The public prosecutor has worried off ten pounds."

An ambulance had meanwhile arrived. It was an ancient Pontiac station wagon with tail fins and gaping rust holes in the rocker panels and doors. The driver sat behind the wheel, a bored statue.

Hector said, "They send a second man and a stretcher only if the subject is alive."

He motioned to two uniformed officers. They went to the end of the sleeping bag and lifted it. Luis had anticipated rigor mortis, but it had come and gone, the body and the bag bent in a U. What do I know of pathology? he mused, averting his gaze as the blanket concealing the gore slipped from Shingles's head.

Ricky did not look away quickly enough. His mouth sagged. He covered it and staggered toward the sea.

Hector smiled. "The lawyer has a sensitive stomach."

"Cancers are noted for their sensitivity," Denise said.

That would have been a cruel remark, Luis thought, except that she was with him, supporting Ricky by the other armpit as he retched.

CHAPTER TWENTY-ONE

"I'd give *two* thousand dollars for a change of clothes," Denise said.

"Sorry. Later."

"You're gripping the steering wheel like you're extracting the juice out of it."

Luis did not reply.

"I didn't mean that we had to go back to my hotel so I could change before going to see this Hugo. That's ridiculously out of our way. It's horrible what happened to Shingles. Is that what's bothering you? You look like you've turned to stone."

Luis flexed his fingers and breathed deeply. He was in the pit of an abysmal mood and it was time to climb out. He was glad he could not see his own face. The undamaged side must be even uglier than the other, he thought, a profile dark and clammy with self-pity and anger. He felt volatile, eruptive, not in charge of his emotions. Like a defective explosive. It was an extremely uncomfortable feeling.

"I don't know if I liked him or not," Luis said. "I was undecided. I killed him anyway."

"You did *not* kill him. Dave Shingles took it upon himself to get involved. You told him some things in confidence and he stepped on somebody's toes. In my line of work, insurance claims, I have to question people who don't want to be questioned and ask them questions they don't want to answer."

"Are they life and death questions?"

"No, they aren't. They usually pertain to negligence and extent of injury. People lie about what happened in the accident, who's at fault. People lie about how badly they're hurt, if they're hurt at all. Pain in a soft-tissue injury doesn't show up on an X ray. They lie for money. You prove they're lying or you coax the truth out of them, you're costing them money. They hate you for doing your job."

"Your job sounds dangerous."

"No. I'd be deceiving you if I said it was. The biggest hazard is stress. But I have been in homes interviewing people and everything's going sour. If you have a whit of common sense, you know when to say your good-byes and bail out. What I guess I'm telling you is that you can't always control what somebody else does. Dave Shingles was somewhere he shouldn't have been and he didn't know when to bail out."

Luis smiled. "You battled the God of Death for me. Now you are battling the God of Guilt to a standstill. You have to stay. I can't let you go home to Seh-awt-leh."

"Seattle," she said, turning to her window so he couldn't see her smile. "Come on, you don't have a guilt god. Do you?"

"We had a suicide deity named Ixtab. She is depicted hanging from the sky by a rope around her neck. Ixtab is

there for you when you're too buried in guilt to go onward."

"Don't you be, okay?"

"Okay. Tulum City."

"Where?"

"Here," Luis said, downshifting.

Tulum City was a village, a commercial patch on the
highway and a handful of poor homes directly off it. Two
kilometers south of the ruins, Tulum was simple markets and
cantinas, and stray dogs that displayed their ribs. Repair
garages were identified solely by the unusually large numbers of cars parked on the various properties. Tulum City
was dusty and brief, too unattractive to tourists to be threatened by prosperity. The people who did not work at the ruins
eked marginal livings from travelers.

Luis swerved in front of a bus and skidded to a dusty
halt in front of a boxy stucco building twice the size of an
average house. Denise's terrified moan and the bus driver's
horn made a strange harmony.

"Hugo's," Luis said, shutting off the ignition.

Denise looked up at a crude, hand-lettered sign tacked
on the eaves announcing CANTINA. "General store. That's an
overstatement."

"There's more to it than you can see from outside," Luis
said, getting out. "We will have to deceive Hugo. Do you
speak a foreign language?"

"I took two years of French in high school. Why?"

"You're visiting from France, then. Will you play along
with me?"

"Okay. Yes. *Oui.*"

They went into the cantina. To the left were a bar, refrigerator, and grill. The cook's back was between them and the grill. Whatever he was preparing smelled wonderful to Luis and Denise, a mingling aroma of frying meat and pungent chilis. They walked a maze through tables filled with eaters and drinkers. The patrons were locals, predominantly male. Not a man glanced from his plate at Luis; every man stared at Denise. An ancient Wurlitzer against the back wall blared with horns, accordions, and a lament about unfaithful love. On the far right were shelving and an eclectic miscellany of merchandise: Suntory whiskey, Hunt's catsup, Brut, Esso Aqui-Glide motorboat oil, Corona beer, diet Coke, Marlboros, Embasa red Mexican sauce, Friskies Buffet, Low Salt Wheat Thins, Sprite, Charmin, Tide.

"How come my first impression is that this stuff fell off a truck?" Denise asked.

"Hugo sells whatever Hugo has to sell," Luis replied, leading her through a door adjacent the jukebox.

They entered a short walkway of planks, walled waist-high with scrap lumber, then mosquito netting to a roof of corrugated iron. It led to a similarly decorated room heaped with cannibalized auto parts that reeked of solvents and sludge. A grease-encrusted V-8 dangled on a chain-and-hoist over the hoodless engine compartment of a 1960s-vintage Impala. A mechanic was listlessly removing a valve cover.

"What doesn't Hugo sell or do?" she asked.

"Hugo is a strong family man. A second cousin wants to work, he'll establish a business so the man has a job. He owns some cabins along the coast, a pharmacy in

Playa del Carmen, and a lobster restaurant up by Puerto Morelos."

"Luis, what makes you think you'll find him at this place, spread as thin as he is?"

"Hugo is a frustrated craftsman. His greatest love is inside." Luis pointed to the rear wall, which was scrap wood from floor to ceiling, and a door clad with galvanized sheet metal. "Play along, remember."

He rapped on the door.

"Who?"

"Luis Balam."

Two barrel bolts moved, grittily sliding. A man an inch taller than Luis and ten years older pulled the door open. He had flat Asiatic features and short gray hair combed forward like Caesar's. "Luis—"

At the sight of Denise he stopped talking and blocked the doorway.

"Hugo," Luis said, cocking a thumb at her, "a wealthy tourist lady who fancies herself a collector. We can make money, you and I."

"Why you speak English?" Hugo asked in Spanish. "Should we not be settling fine business details in Spanish or Yucatec as not to bore nice rich lady? And what did you do to your face?"

"I tripped and fell. We can always use practice on our English, Hugo. Do you take me for an idiot? The lady is French, not a North American. She is vacationing from Paris. She speaks a little Spanish, but not five words of English."

Luis demonstrated, saying to Denise in English, "Hugo

is half Maya and the only native Mexican I know who is richer than you are."

"*Pardonnez-moi, monsieur?*"

Hugo laughed and clapped Luis on the shoulder. "I need practice English. You speak English like gringo."

"His daughter and my Esther went to Akumal school together," Luis continued.

Denise lifted her shoulders and her eyebrows. "*Non comprendre,* bucko."

Like a gracious gatekeeper, Hugo bowed and swept an arm. They walked into a *palapa,* a circular room with a domed roof constructed of wood framing and thatch. People were at work on benches, slapping and shaping clay as if kneading dough. Others were using foot-treadle potter's wheels, forming the clay into cups and bowls. Still others were at a table doing something noisy and undetermined to fired pottery. The air smelled of stale tobacco, perspiration, and the never-ending humidity. The floor was coated with ceramic dust and cigarette butts. It was a picturesque sweatshop.

"Kiln outside in shed," Hugo said. "I used to have in here for security. I no like prying eyes. But it too hot. Die and go to Christian Hell and you would cool off. You would have to wear sweater."

Luis laughed. He recognized most of the fifteen or twenty workers. They were Hugo's nieces, sons-in-law, and maternal aunts. "Hugo, you've always done well in pottery, but you've expanded since I was last in your shop."

"Tourism expands, I expand," Hugo explained. "It is bad businessman who does not rise to demand."

"How much of this stuff is going to be sold as new on the legitimate market?"

Hugo smiled. That was his answer. Luis was being invited to believe whatever percentage he liked. "Luis, she is pretty lady. She dark, Mediterranean, delicate. French girls know tricks in bed, they say. She do?"

Luis's face warmed. "I wouldn't know."

"She only a business friend? Too bad," Hugo said, genuinely sad. "How rich?"

"She recently divorced a vineyard owner."

"Ah ah ah, Don Peridot and pink champagne." Hugo grinned. "What is nice rich lady interested in to buy?"

"What do you have that is interesting?"

"Luis, let me show you new project. You're smart guy. You can give me advice on technical problem." Hugo escorted them to the noisy table and shooed away the three young men working at it. On the table was a bucket of sand, picks, small chisels, pick hammers, and a dozen weather-beaten drinking cups.

"Boy I chase off with Pepsi T-shirt and thongs?" Hugo said.

"Your son-in-law, isn't he?"

"Not son-in-law no more. His prick never hard inside marital home, never soft outside home. I going to chop it off when my daughter come to me in tears, but he too valuable to lose over little thing like as love. Luis, I am happy this Frenchy girl of yours no understands what I am talking."

"Me too." Luis picked up a cup, an excuse not to look at Denise.

"Ratty piece, yes?" Hugo said. "Boy can age eight hundred years in thirty minutes. Rub glaze off in sand, chip here, crack there. Rare, rare talent the boy got. Fool anybody but expert."

"Archaeological rubble."

"Yes. Is junk. Historical junk," agreed a beaming Hugo. "Everyday utility pottery, of common peoples. Peasants. Fancy, elaborated junk, they belong to royalty, ruling class, bosses. Dumbest gringo knows he can't buy drinking urn of Maya king for surplus on American Express card. He know that stuff in museum or is too expensive to be had on black market. These pieces, my pieces, you can believe in, that plain folks back then drunk out of. You can pay for them. They are—how you say?—affordable."

Denise picked up a cup, looked at the side of it, looked at Luis with widened eyes, looked again at the drawing of the Descending God, pointed at Luis, and pointed at the cup. *"Le même. Sacrebleu!"*

"The upside-down guy," Luis said, sighing.

"Him popular stuff," Hugo said. "They see at Tulum ruins, they remember him. They buy. They buy more stuff at higher prices if I can beat technical problem."

The table had drawers. Hugo opened one, removed a cup, and gave it to Luis. The inside bottom was black and crusty. He sniffed. The odor was sharp and scorched, like food that had been forgotten in an oven.

"Cacao," Hugo said. "Cacao important to ancients. Whole beans were money, principal currency in trade. They also ground up the beans and drank it. In *National Geographic* they analyze, find residue in cups. I give gringos cups with residue."

"What else am I smelling besides chocolate?" Luis asked, sniffing again.

"That my problem, Luis." Hugo brought a can of Nestlé's Quik out of the drawer. "Cacao. Stuff go black when I bake it."

Luis examined the ingredients in the can. For someone who manufactured such a volume of fakes, Hugo was ridiculously ignorant of Maya history. "Hugo, the major ingredient is sugar. Sugar burns and turns into carbon."

"I should heat maybe less?"

"Our ancients didn't have sugar, Hugo. They had honey, but those who drank chocolate drank ground cacao beans without sweetening. And since cacao beans were used as money, only the elite drank chocolate."

"Peasant drinking *stolen* chocolate is what I say to gringo. Where I find cacao beans to grind up?"

Luis shook his head. "Sorry, I don't know. Actually, the lady isn't interested in pottery."

"Luis, I do pottery," Hugo said warily.

"Mainly pottery. You experiment with other things. Like knives. Flint sacrificial knives." Luis made a jabbing motion to his own chest. "That's what she has her heart set on."

Denise repeated the gesture. *"La knife. Oui."*

"I try making knifes. Very hard work. Flint very hard to chip. You wear out tempered steel chisels. Knifes is, how do I say—labor intensified."

"When did you try them? Recently?"

Hugo's eyes darted to Denise. He shifted to Maya. "Luis, you have never handled my reproductions or anybody else's at your shop. Everybody knows you were beaten up and burned out. What is the truth?"

Despite their long-standing friendship, Luis knew that in

matters of money Hugo would lie to him as casually as he would draw breath. His lying wasn't malicious, it was simply a component of doing business. Luis reciprocated.

"I'm desperate, Hugo," he said sincerely. "Black Coral is finished permanently. I need money. Swindling a gringo is fast money. Help me out, Hugo, I beg you."

"I am sorry, my good friend," Hugo continued in Maya. "I wish I could help you. I made three knives special order. A guy from Cancún was going to sell them up there. When he came for them, he changed the price we agreed on before. We argued. He said the workmanship was inferior. It wasn't. I made them with my own hands. They were perfectly faithful to photos and drawings of the originals. He took the knives. I was glad to be rid of him. He scared me. Five hundred American dollars apiece.

"Good money, but no more knives for me, Luis. They scare me too. Everybody's talking about Gilbert, how he killed with a genuine sacrificial knife. I do not need the trouble knives bring."

"Why did the Cancún buyer scare you?"

"He was not the sort you said no to. I was fortunate to be rid of him."

"Can you describe him?"

Hugo raised an arm over his head. "Huge. Fat. Bandit mustache. No neck and tiny black eyes that should belong to something that jumps you at night in the jungle."

A stunned Luis Balam could not respond.

Hugo picked up the Nestlé's Quik can and asked, "Do they make this Quik without sugar?"

CHAPTER TWENTY-TWO

"I'd give *three* thousand dollars for a change of clothes," Denise said.

Luis laughed. They were northbound on the highway en route to Denise's hotel, windows rolled down, Luis's foot to the firewall, his decrepit Volkswagen red-lining at ninety kilometers per hour. "Not long. Not long."

"You're too elated for your own good, you know. Just because Godzilla bought counterfeit knives doesn't mean he gave one to his boss so he could kill women and star in the tabloids as Gilbert."

"Doesn't mean he didn't."

"Luis, look, Estrada can buy alibis that will last him into the next decade. He probably already has."

"We'll get to Figueroa, the curator. Somehow. We'll make him recant. Somehow. We'll prove Hugo's knife was the murder weapon. Somehow."

"Wishful thinking."

"Positive thinking."

"Coincidences usually are. Wishful thinking, that is."

"Except when they aren't."

"Raúl Estrada Estrada is well known. From what I gather, he's the biggest tycoon in the Yucatán. If he were committing the murders, which occurred in luxury hotels, wouldn't he have been seen? The killer was wreaking havoc on tourism, but those places are semi-busy. Also, don't forget, his family owns three out of four of the hotels. He'd be butchering the golden goose.

"And don't go and tell me that everybody was bribed to button their lips. He couldn't have bribed hundreds and thousands of tourists and Mexicans to forget they saw him. And don't say, either, that Romero, a Hispanic Freddy Krueger if there ever was one, is the killer. God, who could forget him?"

Damn her logic. It was turning his euphoria rancid. "Money can buy anything in Mexico, Denise. You just don't know. It can."

"Okay, relax. I'm as uncertain and confused as you are. I'm playing devil's advocate. Providing that Estrada is Gilbert, how come Estrada is Gilbert?"

"Pleasure. Thrills. I said money can buy anything in Mexico. I was wrong. There are exceptions."

"Money can't buy murder in Mexico? Come on."

"Money can buy murder anywhere," Luis said. "You can buy a murder in Mexico pretty cheap. You're twice as likely to be murdered in Mexico City as New York. I read that somewhere, although it wasn't in our tame press. You don't have to dodge bullets in Yucatán, but people do kill people. Politicians and labor bosses and businessmen hire murderers to hang on to what they have and to grab what they don't.

"We kill for love too, like North Americans do. You kill the guy sleeping with your wife. Or he kills you. Or one or the other hires it out."

"You ought to hire on at the tourism board, Luis. You've just made my day."

"My point is this. You do buy those kinds of killings, killings for love and money," Luis said in exasperation. "These Gilbert killings were done for fun. You don't buy them. You're crazy. You kill the girls yourself. You don't care what the murders do to your hotel business. You can't stop yourself."

"Look, Luis, I really think your obsession with the knife is affecting your judgment on the case. What we did at Hugo's was a kick, but it's super-long odds that the knife Hugo sold Romero is the murder weapon. How many of these knives are there? For all we know, they're giving them away in cereal boxes."

Cereal boxes? Flint knives packaged inside cartons of breakfast cereal such as cornflakes? It was the stupidest thing he had heard in his life. Who was she to insult his investigative judgment?

"You look," he said flatly. "Before I'm going to be convinced Proctor Smith is Gilbert, I'm going to get to the origin of that knife. I don't know why you're fighting me. Gilbert killed your sister."

Denise looked out her window. To cry, Luis knew. Luis the lowlife verbal bully. He felt tiny, tinier than tiny, microscopically tinier than when he had bullied Enrique (Bud) Rojas, when he compressed the fingers of the Polyester Asshole, squeezing a silent scream out of him.

He didn't know how to apologize properly, so he substituted an effort at compassion. "I believe he should burn forever, this Gilbert."

"Thanks. That makes two of us."

"Denise, if I can help again in the process of you bringing her, Mary Ann, to your home city, I will do whatever I can."

"Okay, thanks."

"You don't know where she lived, do you?"

"No. I'd kind of shoved the issue of personal effects out of my mind. But I'd like to retrieve what she had, especially photos. Inspector Salgado said the police didn't know where she lived."

"When he asked me to spy on you, he asked that I obtain your sister's permanent address from you."

Denise turned to him, touching red eyes with fingertips, saying, "Sorry, uh-uh. I haven't the foggiest. As I said before, she rented post office boxes. I suppose if she was that concerned about privacy, she could pay the rent in cash and not give a physical address."

Luis nodded. "She could. No doubt she did. Your sister was evasive with regard to her whereabouts and activities in these cards and letters?"

"Yeah. She was frustrating as hell. But what else is new? Mary Ann was Mary Ann."

"Tell me what you remember from the cards and letters."

"Everything?"

"Every word."

Denise smiled and whacked Luis on the arm. "Luis Balam the private detective?"

Luis laughed. "Mystery clues, Denise. Give me mystery clues."

"Well, I did hold out on the inspector a little."

"How little?"

"Nothing major. Mary Ann had been violated to the extent that any human being could be violated and these cops were asking nosy questions that didn't seem to me to have any bearing on the case. They had their Gilbert, after all, and the victims were random strangers. To tell you the truth, they were acting like voyeurs. Mary Ann was a whore. Can we search her underwear drawer, please?"

"Hector isn't that sort of man," Luis said defensively.

"I know that now. His *puta*-talking buddies, they're a different story."

"The little holdouts, Denise?"

"She loved the Yucatán. She was planning to stay indefinitely. I'm fairly sure she bought a condo."

"Old Maya saying: Beware of bilingual realtors," Luis said solemnly. "Where was the condo she was considering?"

"Along the coast, off the beaten path. I remember her writing 'off the beaten path.' No names of towns or addresses. This was two or three months ago. In my very last letter to her, I asked whether she did buy. She never answered, but I'm sure she bought. If she wanted the place and could afford it, she wouldn't deny herself."

"Did she describe the condo?"

"No, not directly. Mary Ann, coy and cute as usual, said it reminded her of the settings for those 1950s movies starring Fernando Lamas and Ava Gardner."

"How? Which movies?"

"She didn't specify which movies. Latin American settings, I assume. They starred in that sort of movie. Villa on the beach, Spanish architecture, romance, Latin intrigue. Et cetera."

"Then what?"

"Then what what?"

"She buys and lives in this condo and then what? What *what?* Denise, have pity. I studied English like a madman, to learn the right forms, and you're feeding me grammar I never came across."

"Sorry. I forget, whose question is it to answer?"

"Yours. Aside from the off-the-beaten-track condo, what else?"

"Nothing much. Wait, one thing. She raved about the fantastic water and the tropical fish. She was taking diving and snorkeling lessons. She said the water was like crystal and you could see a hundred feet down."

"Were the condo and the diving linked?"

"Well, she didn't say so, but she wrote of them around the same time. I had the impression the condo location, the off-the-beaten-track spot, it was by or at her diving and snorkeling lessons."

"At!" Luis yelled, pumping brakes that squealed and bucked. The skidding right turn slid Denise's hip against his. Only her frantic grip on the dashboard kept her off his lap.

"Jesus," she said. "What are you doing? The sign at the intersection said—lemme look again—'Hotel Club Akumal and Villas Maya.' What's going on?"

"Coincidences," Luis replied. "This is our day for coincidences."

"Akumal. Isn't that where Esther and Rosa went to school?"

"Yes. Akumal is a village and it is a resort; village on one side, resort on the other. The village side is the side with the sewage smell. Out past them both on Half Moon Bay are private homes, condos and villas."

"Okay, why the death-defying side trip to Akumal?"

"Diving and snorkeling. Akumal is Maya for 'Place of the Turtle,' did you know? In the old days, giant sea turtles laid their eggs on the beach in May and June. They do so still, but many fewer, thanks to egg poachers and tourists."

Denise said, "Turtles and scuba gear and non sequiturs. And you damn near killed us."

"Akumal was originally a coconut plantation."

Denise sighed.

"By the 1950s, coconuts were out, diving was in. You could only get here by boat then. Akumal became headquarters of the Mexican diving club. After the highway was built, Akumal expanded into a general tourist spot with restaurants and rooms and shops. And condos. Diving is no less important here than it was. You're a dedicated diver and snorkeler on the Mexican Caribbean, you come to Akumal."

"And if you're a serious wannabe, you also come to Akumal?" Denise said.

Wannabe? "Uh, yes."

Luis parked at the side of a stuccoed arch that separated the offices of Hotel Villas Maya and Club Akumal. The former was locked and the latter handled business for both, an ambiguity Luis regarded as perfectly Mexican. The desk clerk responded numbly to Luis's inquiry until he gave him the contents of his wallet, a ten-thousand-peso note. A few coins jingled in his pocket, coins not worth the base metals from which they were stamped. When they were gone, he would be broke. Ringner and Ricky, he thought. Fees. Soon!

Mary A. Lowell, the clerk said, asking no questions. An odd, congenial dark-eyed Anglo lady, who claimed she was taking a year off from teaching school. No car. She traveled by bus and taxi, often in the evenings. No husband, no visiting friends. A loner, a spinster schoolteacher from North America who dressed too sexy on her nights out to be one. Took lessons at the dive shop. Haven't seen her in a week, probably not home.

The clerk glanced at Luis's Beetle and the woman passenger, evidently deciding that they weren't thieves, and if they were, how much could you haul away in that tin can? A kilometer north on Half Moon Bay, he said, initialing a pass that would get them by the guard station. Four units, two up, two down, hers the bottom right. Pink flamingo, white trim, red-tile roof; you cannot miss it.

Luis drove slowly. The road was paved, but narrow and pocked, segmented with speed bumps. Maya domestics— maids, gardeners, cooks—walked and bicycled, oblivious to automobiles and trucks, and vice versa. Until Estrada Estrada fired his Mercedes-Benz like a cannonball, Luis had regarded a road as the natural habitat of the bicycling Maya. Not now, not ever again. The people, his people, bent over their handlebars, they were vulnerable, as fragile as glass.

"Those houses, some of them are beautiful," Denise

said, looking at the villas on the beach side. "Wrought-iron gates. Circular drives. Manicured gardens. Fountains. Gingerbread haciendas. Who lives along here?"

"The license numbers on the cars tell you. Every Mexican license plate has an abbreviation of the state where the car is registered. Quintana Roo is QR."

"I've noticed a bunch of YUCs and DFs."

"On the fancier cars," Luis explained. "Yucatán State. Rich people from Mérida. DF is the Federal District. Richer people from Mexico City."

"A coconut plantation I can imagine, all the trees. One out of around ten is decapitated. Disease?"

"No. Gilbert, the hurricane, blew the tops off," Luis said, turning onto a cobblestoned driveway.

Denise didn't move. "It occurs to me that we don't have a key."

She was stalling. Luis sympathized. Inside were belongings and traces and memories of the human being who was her closest genetic equivalent. Denise Lowell was paying an unannounced call on a ghost.

"Security is tight. People leave their doors unlocked. I can go in alone," he said.

"No, I'm okay."

They went in together to an open living and dining area, with an adjoining kitchen beyond a barlike counter. Doors led to a bathroom and two bedrooms. No palace, Luis observed. Nor a squatter's shack. The going price would be in the neighborhood of one hundred thousand U.S. dollars.

The condo, closed up for days, was a sauna. Luis walked around pulling ceiling-fan chains. Sliders led to a covered veranda. He parted them as wide as he could and walked out onto cool tile. A small strip of lawn separated the veranda from a narrow beach and the Caribbean.

Mary Ann Lowell/María López's Hollywood-Latin fantasy, Luis mused. He visualized steamy romantic evenings on the veranda, interludes of margaritas, witty dialogue, and foreplay.

Luis returned inside, wondering if that script had ever been played. Mary Ann was an enigma and María was commercially romantic. The prostitutes he had known were as enthusiastic about sex on their own time as laborers were excited about ditches and shovels when they were off the clock. Their loins were blocks of ice.

And on second perusal, the condo didn't look like a home. It didn't look lived in. A wood-and-glass coffee table. Beat-up lawn furniture for chairs. Bare walls. In comparison, Ellen Smith's shabby apartment was an interior decorator's showroom.

The bedroom doors were open. Denise was in one. Luis ducked into the other. It was devoid of furnishings. Watersports apparatus was spread on the floor. Flippers, mask, swimsuits on towels; underwater camera.

He joined Denise quietly, maintaining his distance. She was going through dresser drawers, sniffling. The bed was neatly made, covered by a crocheted bedspread, tropical flowers standing out in relief. The closets were crammed with clothing—flimsy cotton sportswear favored by North American tourists and bright, flowing embroidered Mexican dresses. Lupe Velez costumes, Luis thought. On the walls were framed photographs. He saw Denise in cap and gown.

He saw an older couple, reserved and not quite smiling, the disapproving accountant and teacher. The room smelled of powders and lotions. It was a prim, feminine sanctuary. Luis half expected a cat curled up on a pillow.

"Luis, the top drawer of the corner dresser is bills and receipts and documents. Would you go through them? I'm not quite up to dealing with her papers yet."

Luis said that he would, thinking: mystery clues. He took the drawer into the living room, dumped the contents onto the bar-counter, and began sorting. Bank statements. Three different Seattle banks; twelve thousand dollars total. Money order receipts. Four post office box keys. Real estate trust agreements and contracts; she had paid ninety-seven-five with twenty percent down.

There was no ledger. Characters in movies and television who derived their income disreputably, whether they were gangsters or gamblers or bootleggers or hookers, always recorded their coded transactions in ledgers, and the ledgers were frequently their downfall. He should have known. María López was too smart for ledgers, too smart to bare her financial soul to the tax man.

There was a high school yearbook. He found Lowell, Mary Ann. Goosebumps raised on his arms, Mary Ann so much resembled Denise. Lowell, Mary Ann, had in this, her senior year, participated in Drill Team, Drama Club, and Student Council. Out of curiosity, Luis thumbed through the senior portraits. Less than one photograph per page was of a non-Caucasian. The exceptions were Negro, Asiatic, mestizo, mulatto. He wondered what native North Americans looked like. He didn't see anybody who remotely looked Maya.

The final item in the drawer was the strangest. It was the only other book he had seen in the condominium, a Holy Bible. The page edges were gilded, but it was cheaply made, with a mock leather binding no thicker than cardboard. Evangelical organizations deposited Bibles of similar quality in Cancún hotel rooms.

The pages and cover of this copy were flat, unrippled. Mary Ann's Christian holy book had not been extensively studied.

Luis opened it. Stamped on the inside flap in English and Spanish was:

A GIFT IN THE NAME OF THE LORD JESUS CHRIST.

TROPICAL LANGUAGE SCHOLARS. DALLAS, TEXAS, USA.

Inscribed below the stamp was:

Jesus loves you.
—*Proctor Smith*

CHAPTER TWENTY-THREE

enise packed a box of her sister's belongings: the documents, yearbook, Bible, jewelry. Also, a few clothing articles that seemed to Luis to hold certain memories. He couldn't guess whether the remembrances were happy or sad, or from what era, nor did he ask. At the Club Akumal office Denise introduced herself to the manager, told her story, and asked him to divide the remaining clothing and toiletries among the housekeepers. The horrified manager couldn't believe it, Ms. Lowell had led such a sedate, solitary life.

In the car, Denise asked Luis's advice on selling Mary Ann's condo. Luis said it probably would be complicated. An estate was involved and the deceased owner was a foreigner. Denise groaned, said please don't tell me I need a lawyer, but if I do, please don't recommend your buddy. Luis said the answer was yes and added, think about it, Ricky comes from the same gene pool as our realtors. Denise laughed and said she'd consider him, providing he ever spoke to her again.

On the highway, Denise said, "We've never addressed this, but it'd been in the back of my mind before the Bible bombshell."

"Mine too," Luis admitted, aware of what was coming.

"Tell me the truth, Luis, do you think Proctor Smith was buying my sister?"

"With money embezzled from his evangelical bosses? Yes, it's likely he was."

"I did too when you asked Ringner if he'd confronted Smith on the embezzlement and he said, and I quote, 'I got a rise out of him.' Smith was more worried that his lawyer regarded him as a thief rather than a serial killer. Fundamentalist preachers are on a different wavelength, but that's still a pretty strange set of priorities. Now, if Smith was afraid he'd be uncovered as a frequenter of prostitutes, well, that changes things. The allegedly embezzled money is secondary, the means to an end."

"He's obeying urges and the urges shame him more than murder," Luis said, shaking his head. "That's bothered me from the start."

"Number one," Denise said, index fingertip to index fingertip. "You and the two lawyers are working for fees until you're ordered to stop. Tropical Language Scholars is extremely embarrassed. They'd *love* to sweep Proctor Smith under the rug. His only faithful ally is his wife. If she knew he was stealing money to do the dirty deed with prostitutes, she might leave him dangling."

Luis nodded. "Logical."

"Number two," she said, index fingertip to tip of middle finger. "These hard-core puritanical reverends are a national joke. Several of the big-time television boys have been caught with their pants down. Literally. The tabloid press and the straight press too, if this isn't their favorite sort of story, it's in the top three.

"They have short attention spans. They'll forget Smith in a hurry if he's just Gilbert, killer of women somewhere down in Mexico."

"The North American press will forget an evangelical Gilbert fast?"

"They will. There's always another serial killer coming along to replace him. But the illicit sex angle, preachers and hookers. A magical combination. That would increase the shelf life of the story indefinitely. Smith wouldn't be able to stand it. Hard as he'd pray and hope, he wouldn't be able to make the guilt go away, not as long as he was plastered on newspaper covers at every supermarket check-out counter."

"If you say so," Luis said uncertainly.

"I say so. Will you visit him again?"

"Soon."

"Luis, you didn't happen to run across a little black book and stick it in your pocket to spare my feelings, did you?"

"Little black book?"

"Yeah. You know. Phone numbers. Dates of, uh, transactions. Amounts."

A ledger, a mystery clue. "No, honestly I did not."

"That's too bad. Wouldn't the combination of Smith's professional relationship with Mary Ann and his locksmithing expertise clear him? All you'd have to do is persuade him to confess that he walked into her room for a tryst and she was already dead. His wife could probably dig up a diploma from that mail-order locksmith school. A little black book would be the icing on the cake."

Luis looked at her. "You are satisfied that Smith is innocent?"

"No. I'm satisfied that there is one hell of a reasonable doubt, reasonable with a capital *R*. Don't get any ideas, though, that I'm signing on with your knife fixation. Even without a little black book, the Bible proves they knew each other beforehand."

"It does," Luis agreed.

"I want her killer, Luis. I want him hanged, shot, gassed, or whatever it is they do to them, but I want *the* killer, not a pigeon."

"Either Smith is the genuine Gilbert, or for Smith to be exonerated and released, they will have to find the genuine Gilbert."

"Huh?"

"There is ample evidence to convict Proctor Smith, I think, whether we prove their relationship by presenting this autographed Bible or not. Smith won't be freed until they have a replacement Gilbert. They won't just release him and start over."

"The cops will lose too much face by doing the right thing?"

"Nobody likes to look stupid," Luis said. "Nobody in Yucatán likes evangelicals. As you said, convenient."

"Mexico," she muttered.

"This never happens in the United States?" Luis snapped.

"It happens. It happens," she said irritably, and after a

pause, "Okay, let's assume Smith isn't Gilbert. What if Gilbert strikes again, what then?"

"I think he'll strike again, but not soon. Gilbert is either Proctor Smith, who is not smart and clever, or he is another person, who is smart and clever. If he can't stop killing ladies, he will move to a different city and kill them with a different weapon. He will if he is smart and clever and not too crazy to restrain himself."

"A cheerful prospect."

The Beetle coughed, wheezed, shuddered, and died. Luis coasted to a halt on a rare shoulder, one hundred meters from a rarer phenomenon—a Pemex station. They were at Puerto Morelos, twenty kilometers from Cancún. Puerto Morelos's claims to fame were a vehicle ferry to Cozumel and gasoline. There were not even half a dozen filling stations between Cancún and Chetumal.

"We're out of gas," Denise said. "I'll buy. It's my turn. I'm way overdue to contribute."

"No, we are not out of gas," Luis said. "Slide behind the wheel. I'll push."

Denise steered and Luis pushed until the car rolled to the edge of the Pemex lot, safely out of traffic.

"You definitely are out of gas, Luis." Denise stepped out of the car. "Look at the gauge. The needle's on empty."

"No. Engine trouble. Volkswagen gas gauges die when engines die," Luis lied, turning from her, inhaling and wiping his brow, pretending that he needed to catch his breath.

He was broke, insolvent, poor, a man devoid of funds. A man without the ability to buy the simplest goods and services was less than a man. The humiliation of insolvency was even too primal to be Mexican machismo. That tenet had driven Luis from Ho-Keh to Cancún a decade and a half ago. And here he was today, financially backpedaling through time to his status as a barefoot adolescent, an impoverished peasant.

How to earn money?

His present appearance ruled out tour guiding. Tulum and Cobá visitors would not rent an upside-down guy with extensive facial damage.

Sell his Black Coral inventory? No. It had taken years to accumulate an inventory. If he sold it off, hustling it out of a valise like a riffraff beach vendor, he would never be able to resuscitate the shop.

His private detective career? A sick joke. He was consumed by this case. It was impoverishing him, getting him beaten, getting a flying saucer cultist murdered in his sleeping bag. A joke, but Luis couldn't laugh. W. W. (Lard) Ringner, he thought. Tonto will be presenting a bill at the next opportunity.

"Luis, we've been running on fumes. What could it be besides an empty tank?"

"Engine trouble," he snapped. "Valves always blow on Beetles. It's hereditary. I have a friend with a truck. We'll tow it home when I can arrange it."

"Well, I can at least pay our bus fare," Denise said. "How often do they come by?"

"Bus schedules are fiction. The driver's mood and the mechanical condition of the bus determine the schedule. We'll hitchhike. I know people along the highway. Somebody will stop for us."

"Okay. To Cancún or to your place to pick up my car?"

Luis shrugged. "Depends on which direction our ride is going."

Their ride was southbound and unknown to Luis. The vehicle was a Ford pickup with an extended cab and a camper. It had British Columbia license plates and was occupied by an older Anglo couple. The driver, a man, asked Denise if she spoke English. She said a little and what part of B.C. are you from? The woman cackled and said Vancouver. The man apologized, saying she looked kind of Mexican. Shoehorned in the rear jump seats with Luis, Denise said she was not insulted, and the conversation settled into a comparison of the merits of Seattle and Vancouver. It was a friendly rivalry, give and take, the Vancouverites envying Seattle's sports franchises, although they wouldn't trade their restaurants and Stanley Park for them, Denise parrying with Seattle's Pike Place Market, an authentic farmers' market that *smelled* like a farmers' market as opposed to Vancouver's Granville Island, which was, well, a great big Quonset hut that had a little bit of a plastic feel to it, which was basically no criticism, since she always enjoyed herself up there a lot. The Canadians, according to the wife, were taking the dream trip of a lifetime. They were headed south till they ran out of money, were captured by guerrillas, or pulled into Tierra del Fuego, whichever came first. Denise said fabulous and wished them the best. The husband asked Denise if her friend was an Indian. She said yes, Luis was full-blooded Maya. The wife asked if Luis spoke any Spanish, as she had been told that some of the natives to this day communicated only in their own languages. Luis said: Vancouver, 1970 population figures, 426,000 in the city, 1,128,000 in the metro area, largest city in the province, third largest city in Canada.

They arrived at the Ho-Keh road. Luis and Denise expressed their thanks to the flummoxed Canadians and walked on in, Denise giggling and shoving him, saying you and your 1974 World Almanac. They patronized you, but they were sweet. I'd've done the same thing, except without a chip on my shoulder the size of a railroad tie, like you had. It wasn't their fault your car crapped out and you were pouting, you know. Were you purposefully behaving like a horse's butt, or did you give that impression unintentionally? Luis smiled and said he was sorry. Denise said yep, sure you are, right, uh-huh.

They walked into the village late in the afternoon of the hottest day of the year. Their hands came together spontaneously, neither the aggressor, neither inclined to let go. The two-kilometer hike felt to Luis refreshing, a hundred meters maximum.

Rosa and Esther came out of the house. While they visited with Denise, Luis ducked inside and stuffed pieces taken from the Black Coral stock in his pockets. A one-time withdrawal, he vowed. It had to be!

They drove to Cancún City and the Hotel Sol y Mar. Denise invited Luis up. The air conditioner in her room sounded like a plane in a World War Two movie, she added, but it might be a couple of degrees cooler than the sidewalk.

Luis said he would be up shortly but wanted to say hello to an old friend around the corner. The old friend around the

corner was an acquaintance named Durante, who sold jewelry and bric-a-brac at a small market. Durante's specialties
were Cancún coffee mugs, Cancún salt-and-pepper shakers,
Cancún keychains, and Cancún cigarette lighters. He also
PURVEYORED TASTEFUL JEWELRY UNDERNEATH TWENTY DOLLAR, so
stated his cardboard sign.

Luis had brought silver bracelets and rings. No settings,
no stones. This was silver stamped 925, indicating percentage
of purity. It was what they used to make money out of, in the
era when money had value. Silver was a liquid asset. Durante would weigh the pieces en masse and make an insulting offer, which he did. Luis would moan and curse and take
it personally, and ask a ridiculous sum, which he did. Durante would become exasperated at Luis's touchiness, apologize for slighting him, and hike his offer, which he did.
Whereupon, Luis would blame the hot sun for his being on
edge and lower his demand, which he did. There would be a
handshake and an exchange of goods for cash at some point,
which there was.

Luis wangled a better price than he had anticipated,
though by selling wholesale to Durante he had barely broken
even. To do this well he had agreed to accept a combination
of dollars and pesos. Denise's room was on the second floor.
She was standing outside her door, arms folded tightly.

"What's the matter?"

"Somebody's been in the room. I stuck my head in and
right back out. The somebody could still be in there."

Luis swung the door wide with a toe. The small bedroom
was in full view. Bathroom and closet doors were open.
Two suitcases were on the bed. A red blouse was on the

dresser, neatly folded. The bed was made and the floor was clean.

Luis walked in and said, "Looks like you had maid service five minutes ago."

"Do Cancún maids usually take things out of your luggage?"

"No."

"Well, everything I brought was in the bags. Someone snooped and forgot to replace my red blouse."

"Check in the suitcases," Luis said.

Denise examined them and said, "Somebody *has* rummaged in my stuff. The police?"

Luis sat on the bed. "They aren't that tidy. The police search your home, you'll think they went through with a harvesting machine."

Denise said she was going to shower and change, and sat on the bed. The mattress was mushy. As she sat, she bumped Luis, probably accidentally, but her hands on him and his hands on her were not accidental.

Denise kicked the suitcases off the bed and they lowered onto it, holding on tight, hands and tongues exploring. He tugged at the elastic of her shorts. She raised against him to help. He pulled her shorts and panties down and off in one motion. She fumbled at his belt and zipper.

He touched her, as gently as his impatience would permit. She proved as impatient as he.

"The secret's out, how much I want you," she whispered.

She guided him into her. He had not been with a woman for months. He had not been with a woman for whom he felt such affection for years. He tried to prolong, tried to think of anything except her. He pictured the ugly, the coarse, the frightening. He pictured hurricanes, he pictured Enrique (Bud) Rojas, he pictured Estrada Estrada's goons. He was unsuccessful.

"Sorry."

She slapped his side, slapped it hard. "Don't you ever apologize for your lovemaking again. You sound like all the jerks I've known. They aren't apologizing to me, they're apologizing to themselves for failing at techniques they've read about in *Playboy*."

Luis kissed her cheek and said, "I don't know what you're saying, but I know what you're saying."

"Oh my God!"

Luis twisted and sat up. The object of her alarm was the hallway. Luis sat up and hopped to the door, pants wadded at his ankles like leg irons, and slammed and locked it.

She giggled. "That's a picture I'd never dare send home on a postcard."

"Didn't you mention a shower?" Luis asked.

Later, in bed, after dinner at a nearby café—Luis's treat —Denise asked him why he had so little hair on his body. They were covered by a sheet. They had just finished making love for the third time. If their first was a sprint, this had been a marathon. The air conditioner, a window unit, *did* remind Luis of World War Two aviation movies, not of a plane but of planes, the Eighth Air Force saturation-bombing Europe. The machine had reduced the temperature of the room to moderately comfortable.

"The sun burned the body hair off my ancestors when they were building the temples."

"Nope. You were a god. They were out in the hot sun erecting pyramids to you. I saw you on Hugo's pottery, you know. You were that upside-down guy, sitting in the shade guzzling cocoa."

"We kings consorted with peasant girls. We're all the same hairless stock now."

Denise pinched him, got out of bed, opened two Leóns and a sack of tostados. "A picnic," she said. "Glad we had the foresight to run out for these goodies between rounds. We deserve 'em, the calories we've burned."

Luis was thirsty. He drank half his beer in one swallow. "Is my body hair important to you?"

"No. Don't go macho on me, okay? I was curious. Believe me, your manhood is not in question, not after you fought those animals to protect your daughters. You were fighting to the death."

"Curiosity," Luis said in good humor. "Anthropologists are curious. I was doing what any father would do. How does that make me attractive to you?"

"Have they studied you? The anthropologists?"

"Not like you study me," he said, returning the pinch. "How am I attractive to you?"

"You're dogged. You care about the truth, about doing the right thing."

"I think of male attractiveness, I think of Hollywood-leading-man handsome."

"Overrated. Tom Cruise you ain't, but so what," she said,

sitting up. "What are we to each other anyway? What's your position on us, you and me?"

"I don't understand the question."

"You do too."

Light from the street bled through the threadbare curtains. Shadows defined Denise Lowell's lithe body. Small, spherical breasts. Smooth, taut skin. A narrowed waist. Five kilograms more and he would be seeing a fold above her lovely and densely black pubic triangle, five less and he would be seeing ribs. When they were showering, he had thought she was the perfect feminine form. She looked twice as perfect now. "You could never live at Ho-Keh, going to a well for water and squatting in the bushes. I could never live where there is winter. I won't let you out of my sight again as long as you're here. I'll hate it when you're ready to go home, but I won't try to stop you."

"Honest answer," she said. "That's where I'm coming from too. I think. To be honest with you, I asked that question—and it's a loaded question—because I was afraid you'd ask it of me and put me on the spot before I could put you on the spot. Is there a Maya god or goddess of love?"

"Ix Chel, the rainbow deity," Luis said. "She's responsible for healing, childbirth, and benevolence in general. She was an oddity among our gods, who were generally severe."

"I saw a rainbow or two today. Speaking of vision, Luis, can I ask you, without your taking it as nagging, how's your eye?"

"Improving."

"You're cocking your head when we talk. You're on the other side of a room, I barely notice. We're nose to nose, like we've been, the angle increases. I took a photography class in college. It's called parallax. You're compensating. You're blind in that eye."

Luis clasped his fingers behind his head, on the pillow.

"You're not talking to me, Luis."

He smiled. "Since we're lovers, Denise, we therefore have to be completely honest with each other?"

Denise made a fist and tapped his nose with it. "You will if you know what's good for you."

"Today I thought I saw some light. A dull flash, a flicker. I'm making progress. I will recover, I will be okay, fine."

"A flicker of light is progress?"

"It is if it's your eye," Luis said. "I was happy."

Denise straddled him, groin to groin. It was not sexual. Sexuality at that moment was an impossibility. She massaged his chest, saying, "We'll get them, Luis, Gilbert and the goons, every one of the rotten bastards."

CHAPTER TWENTY-FOUR

igueroa, the curator, he's a prisoner," Denise said. "That's basically what he is."

"He is," Luis agreed.

They were having a late, leisurely breakfast in a café adjacent to Denise's hotel, trying to devise a method of spiriting the National Museum of Anthropology assistant curator out of the Club Estrada. Luis could not again approach Figueroa in the guise of a reporter. He could not step onto hotel property. Rojas's security personnel would be on the alert. Their best plan thus far required a joint naval and air assault.

"We have to lure him out," Denise said. "We can't drag him out kicking and screaming."

"We can't," Luis agreed. He had contemplated dragging Figueroa out kicking and screaming. It had been a momentary, whimsical thought. The distance from the pool bar to Kukulcán Boulevard was much shorter than from bar to beach and beyond, but the gauntlet of Rojas's storm troopers would be thicker.

"You said he was frightened."

"Extremely."

"Well, even if your captors are indulging you, picking up the tab while you eat and drink and sun yourself to death, you're still a prisoner. I imagine it's getting pretty tiresome."

Luis was catching her drift. "We don't abduct him. Like they say in gangster movies, we bust him out."

"Exactly. But does he want to escape? That's the tricky part."

Ravenously, they had consumed *huevos rancheros* and a second basket of freshly baked rolls. Luis drank his coffee and said, "We ask him."

"That's the trickiest tricky part. You can't go in there, Luis. You'll be shot on sight. I'm not a stranger to the bad guys or they wouldn't have searched my room, but I'm not as familiar to them as you. I could come and go in the hotel. Getting close to Figueroa is the key."

"He'll be at the pool bar drinking Coronas. That is a safe bet."

"Me as a waitress, that won't work?"

"No. The bar waiters are male. Since I posed as a waiter, employees will be under closer scrutiny. No employee who isn't an actual employee will be patrolling with an order pad and a tray. No Indian on the premises who isn't an employee will escape scrutiny. Rojas is slimy, but he's efficient."

"You won't reconsider involving Inspector Salgado?"

"No. If he orders Figueroa into the station, he'll receive a phone call from above. If he goes to the hotel and Figueroa resists, Estrada Estrada will accuse him of harassment to people of influence and Hector's career will be finished."

"So it's you and me. Okay, I'm game," Denise said, picking up the check. "How do I get next to Figueroa?"

Luis took the check from her and counted out pesos. "North American tourists wander freely."

"I'm not that cheap," she said, grabbing at the check he held out of reach, nudging his shin with a toe. "Okay, I'm a tourist. Hell, I *am* a tourist. Sort of. I just walk in and go up to him, just like that?"

"No," Luis said, appraising her. "You're not a—how should I phrase it?—sufficiently a tourist."

Denise looked down at herself. "I'm wearing tan slacks and a white blouse. I think I know what you're driving at. In Seattle I'm weekend summer casual, in Cancún I'm dressed in formal evening wear."

Luis smiled and nodded.

Denise stood up. "Well, I've never needed an excuse to go shopping. Onward!"

Denise negotiated the price of a one-piece bathing suit, a glossy garment of bold pinks, yellows, greens, and blacks that miraculously, in Luis's good eye, did not clash. He volunteered to bargain, but she said remember, negotiating insurance claims, bargaining, that's what I do for a living. Luis was impressed. He could not have reduced the final purchase price a thousand pesos.

She had looked at several bikinis. Luis had recommended against them. Denise asked him if he was being possessive. He lied—fifty percent of a lie—when he said no, you look too good, you'll attract excessive attention. They completed the ensemble with a waist-length terrycloth robe, a straw sun hat, huaraches, and sunglasses with lenses just large and opaque enough not to seem ridiculous or obviously an article of disguise.

Denise modeled the swimsuit in her room. A delay resulted. Eventually they showered, dressed, and Luis wrote a note in Spanish:

> Professor Figueroa:
> We have come to liberate you. Collect your family, bring money, plane tickets, but no bulk that would give you away. Thirty minutes. In front. Pretend you're going to lunch in the coffee shop. Run out the main lobby exit. We will be waiting.
> Your Friends

"Liberate" was Denise's idea. It had a Latin political ring to it, she claimed.

Luis said, "Walk into the water, sit next to him, ask him the time of day, hand him the note, walk out of the water, and out to the car. No risks, Denise. Take no chances."

"Yes sir. But what if he's a contented captive? What if he doesn't accept our liberation offer?"

"Then we devise a naval and air assault."

Luis dropped Denise off at the Club Estrada and parked in the passenger loading zone of the hotel next to it, the little Golf hidden in a forest of buses and courtesy vans. Denise rejoined him in ten minutes and said, "He was there, bellied up to the pool bar, apparently sober, but you could tell he was working on getting seriously hammered."

"Hammered?"

"Smashed, drunk, crocked. The water in the pool was fabulous. Warm. I didn't want to get out."

"How did it go?"

"I gave him the note. He read it, blinked at me with puppy dog eyes, and I left. He had a zombie kind of expression on his face. Señor Figueroa is not a happy camper."

"His family?"

Denise shook her head. "I didn't spot a chunky mama and two rug rats in the pool. How many minutes are left on the thirty?"

Luis glanced at his watch. "Eighteen."

"Time flies when you're having fun."

Luis drove onto Club Estrada's loading zone, a brick semicircle that ringed a fountain. Precisely thirty minutes and zero seconds had passed since Denise's delivery of the liberation note. A chain of Figueroas in shabby beachwear barged awkwardly out of the lobby, through the brass-and-glass revolving door, the professor clutching the hand of a flustered wife who was clomping along clumsily, struggling to keep up while clutching the hand of a sullen boy who was clutching the hand of a younger girl who, if jerked any harder by the boy, would explode into tears.

Luis was behind the wheel, engine running, right front and right rear doors wide open. Denise stood by the right front, waving wildly, yelling, "Come on, you can do it, come on, you can do it—!"

The Figueroas were twenty meters from them, escape

prospects looking good, when a man in a Hawaiian shirt burst through the main door.

"Oh hell," Denise said. "Luis, who's that?"

"Just hotel security. Nobody," Luis said, jumping out of the car.

He moved between the Figueroas and the security man, who was the height and girth of Estrada Estrada's Romero. The security man held a cordless phone to his ear and began to speak. Moving forward without a hitch in stride, he doubled a fist and swung at Luis, one arm plenty to deal with a sawed-off Indian, to swat the nuisance out of his path.

This fellow was narrower in the shoulders than Romero and much, much slower, and his flesh quivered when he delivered the punch. A fat, ugly mammoth retained for show, Luis thought. A Godzilla-like placebo for tourists who feared thieves, confidence artists, and international terrorists.

Luis ducked the blow and drove the heel of his hand into the telephone. He heard a satisfying crunch of breaking plastic. The security man screamed, fell to one knee, and cupped his bleeding ear.

Luis flung the telephone into the fountain. A second security type charged toward him. He was of average size, desk clerk size. He saw his colleague on the brickwork, writhing into a fetal position, whimpering and bloody. His masculinity would not tolerate cowardice, a halt or retreat, so he reduced his advance to cinematic slow motion. He was still coming, but Luis could have had lunch before they collided.

Luis backpedaled to the car. Denise was up front, a pile of Figueroas in the rear. Luis gunned the engine, gnashed the gearshift into first, and lurched into boulevard traffic. He avoided all vehicles, although a car rear-ended a car that had slammed on its brakes to avoid Luis.

"Jesus," Denise said, cringing. "Is there a Maya God of Demolition Derbys?"

The air was charged with a cacophony of skidding tires, horns, and obscenities. Enrique (Bud) Rojas was on one knee beside his fallen security trooper, resplendent in paisley necktie and maroon shirt. He was shaking a fist at Luis, who returned the salute—a universal middle digit—and said in English, repeating in Spanish, "Ten kilometers to the airport. Seven minutes."

"Hi, amigos," Denise said, turning around. "Trust him when he says seven minutes."

Luis saw through the mirror that Figueroa's mouth was agape. Luis said in Spanish, "Denise resembles the dead girl because she is the dead girl's sister, Professor. Compose yourself and do not make mention. She has enough reminders."

"What did you say?" Denise asked Luis.

"That your Spanish is excellent, although limited."

"Liar. Luis, can you slow down a little, please, okay? And can we stick to our own lane? This isn't England."

Luis smiled and said, "Professor, do you have tickets and money to get you home to Mexico City?"

"We stuffed our money inside our shorts and we can exchange our tour tickets, yes. You are that reporter. I cannot speak to you further."

"I am no reporter," Luis said. "I am an independent detective. Miss Lowell is my client. Neither of us is convinced that the evangelical missionary is Gilbert. If he is not, Miss Lowell desires to know who Gilbert is. Miss Lowell demands justice. She is paying me to learn the truth. Professor, you can and will speak to us."

"No!"

Luis pumped the brake pedal. The Golf slowed to within twenty kilometers per hour of the speed limit. "You win. I give up. I will let you out here."

"No, no!" Figueroa cried. "Step on the gas!"

"You were prisoners at Club Estrada?"

Figueroa evaded Luis's question with a question. "What is wrong with your face, your eye?"

"I tripped and fell down. There is an epidemic of tripping and falling in Yucatán. A young North American friend of mine tripped and fell to death in his sleeping bag on the Xcacel beach. It must have been one of those dreams where you fall through the air from great heights. Who was holding you prisoner and why?"

"So it is true. The gringo boy murdered at Xcacel was the subject of constant bar gossip. The rumor is that he came to Tulum to meet a flying saucer. Some gullible, lesser-educated hotel employees insist that he was incinerated by a space alien death ray. Naturally, the story of the murder was not in your newspaper."

"Not my newspaper. I am honestly not a reporter, I am a private detective on a case. Who was holding you prisoner and why?"

"Not in the company of my family," Figueroa said angrily. "When we are ticketed and lined up to board for Mexico City, I will speak to you."

Luis saw through the mirror the round, passive face of Señora Figueroa, the face of a submissive Mexican wife. Her eyes refracted to Luis's working eye. He read in them a peculiar serenity. She was younger than the professor, in her early thirties. The age lines on her cheeks and radiating from her eyes were freshly drawn. The professor had blunted the ordeal of his captivity with continual Coronas. She had not. She had endured her anxieties with clarity. As the strength of the Mexican family, the wife and mother, while her husband smashed and hammered his brain and liver at the pool bar, she had been the caretaker of her children and herself, their welfare and their sanity. He saw also in her serenity a latent defiance. Once they were free, there would be changes. The professor, the husband and father who had jeopardized them, would change his attitude or he would change his address.

The daughter was seven or eight years old, and terrified. She was on her mother's lap, head buried between pendulous breasts, mother stroking her long hair, kissing her forehead. The boy, two to three years older, stradled his father's leg while clinging to Luis's headrest. He was grinning and his eyes were wide.

"What strikes you so funny?" Luis asked, looping an arm behind him, tugging the boy's ear.

"Your driving, sir. Are we to be in a car chase movie?"

At least I can please one member of this family, Luis thought. He downshifted, floored the gas pedal, pressed the horn, and passed between two cars, missing them by inches, creating three lanes out of two.

The Figueroa boy squealed in delight.

Denise flinched and said, "Luis, even Unity Property and Casualty would cancel you."

In excess of one million people per year fly in and out of Cancún International Airport. They tend to congregate in clumps, herded by flight schedules, travel agents, and the demands of Immigration and Customs bureaucracies. On this occasion, the government officials looked bored and lethargic, but they were uniformed and in quantity, a deterrent if Rojas pursued. The Figueroas were able to swap their return tickets for a flight departing in thirty minutes. Denise stayed with Mrs. Figueroa and the children while Luis took the assistant curator aside.

"I apologize for speaking sharply to you in the car," Figueroa said. "You risked your life to release us from that wonderful jail. We were supposed to go home later in the week. I do not know if we could have. Thanks to you, we should be safe. I have friends in Mexico City. I do not think they can touch me there, especially if my lips are sealed. And they will be after I tell you what I can tell you."

"Were you threatened?"

"Not technically. When we were invited to transfer from our cheap hotel to the Club Estrada, two Cro-Magnons in the employ of Mr. Estrada assisted us in packing *before* I assented to move."

"Did you have contact with Mr. Estrada?"

"Yes, once. He and Mr. Rojas greeted us as we were becoming settled in our suite. He was gracious. He said he was also public-spirited and a friend of law and order. He was rewarding us for our role in the apprehension and conviction of Gilbert."

"Why were you at the Club Estrada that night?"

"My wife and I were splurging on dinner at the restaurant and dancing at the disco. One night of pampering ourselves was all we could afford. The Hotel Zone is incredibly expensive."

"How did you happen to identify the knife?"

"I was coming out of the lobby rest room. There was a disturbance upstairs, much yelling and screaming. I ran up the staircase to investigate. Everything that transpired thereafter is true."

"They frightened you without threatening you. What do you guess they planned to do with you?"

"They seemed to have an undetermined deadline. That was my feeling. Something was to occur at a subsequent date. Then we could go home. Or perhaps we would not, I feared. It depended on a factor that was not divulged to me. The full facilities of the hotel were available to us gratis, but security men always hovered nearby. Your plan for us to bolt out to your car surprised them, but only by seconds, as you are well aware."

"Did you feel the undetermined date would arrive soon?"

"I did, but how soon I cannot say. Mr. Estrada, in his greeting, told us that if we desired to stay beyond the end of my vacation, he could transact an extension."

"Is there any question in your mind that your imprisonment concerned the knife and the murder?" Luis asked.

Figueroa sighed. "None whatsoever. I had the unspoken assurance that their hospitality was mandatory. I am not normally a heavy drinker. The beer fortified my courage and my ability to provide a brave, unworried facade for my family."

"You certified that it was a genuine Maya sacrificial knife. That is significant for an unknown reason. What puzzles me is that you certified it at the murder scene. Do you swear that you had no prior contact with Estrada and Rojas?"

"That is the truth, yes."

"How could they have intimidated you into lying then, immediately, instantly, at the scene of the murder?"

Figueroa looked at Luis, blinking. "I did not lie. The knife is bona fide. It is not a counterfeit."

Luis could not summon a reply.

"I do not understand either," Figueroa continued. "They bribe me and hold us hostage because I gave a correct determination."

"You yourself said you were no Mayanist," Luis finally said.

"No, I am not a Mayanist. I have examined numerous Aztec sacrificial knives, real artifacts and fakes. Lowland Maya used flint. Maya in the southern highlands used obsidian. The Aztec used chalcedony. They each employed the materials that were available, but their designs were similar. The handles were ornamental—compositions of wood, leather, or decorative stones.

"The blades were chipped into shape, razor sharp, with stone tools that were of comparable hardness or harder. The blades, being of crystalline structure, would chip randomly. The works of the finest artisans were asymmetrical. They were beautiful. They had an abstract texture. The reproductions that are peddled to unsuspecting tourists are usually fashioned in a vise with tempered-steel chisels and an electric grinder. This method is substantially quicker than the techniques at the disposal of ancient Indians. The blades are more uniform and have a smoother surface. The copies are often extraordinarily good. They duplicate and weather the hilts well too. The blades give them away. A trained scientist can discern them as bogus in a—" Figueroa snapped his fingers.

Luis thought of Hugo, of his antiquity factory, of his labor-intensified knives and tempered-steel chisels, of his practical approach toward cheating those who sought to steal national treasures. He thought he might become sick to his stomach.

He grasped Figueroa by the biceps. "Is this the truth? If I cannot believe you, this I swear, I will drive you to Club Estrada and toss you in the fountain."

Figueroa's blinking accelerated. He said, stammering, "I swear to God, I swear to the Blessed Virgin, it is the truth. I had no incentive to lie in that horrible, bloody hotel room, and I am a professional. I would stake my life on my opinion."

Figueroa's flight was announced on a loudspeaker. Denise waved at Luis. He released Figueroa's arms and said, numbly, "Where would this authentic knife come from? Are they not scarce?"

"They are scarce, but not as rare as you would imagine.

Museums are robbed and the criminals are not caught and the items are never recovered. They are sold to private collectors in Mexico or to visitors who smuggle them out. Who can say? Do you recall the burglary at the National Museum of Anthropology on Christmas, 1985?"

"Yes," Luis said. "It was a famous crime."

"Infamous," Figueroa corrected. "A shameful incident that we on the museum staff will not live down in our lifetimes, whether we, individually, were negligent or not. I, personally, was not culpable, but I am periodically reminded, in the spirit of ridicule, how priceless artifacts were stolen under our noses.

"Two novice criminals entered and stole historical treasures. The guards were sleeping off a Christmas Eve drunk. Fortunately, most of the items were recovered four years later. The burglars had traded a few minor pieces for cocaine. I am illustrating how simple, comparatively simple, acquisition of a historical item can be."

"I am confused," Luis said. "The knife is genuine. You state that it is genuine. So they kidnap you to coerce you into standing by your evaluation."

"Let me present a theory. They—Mr. Estrada and Mr. Rojas in behalf of Mr. Estrada—believe my evaluation was incorrect. I saw the knife briefly, in a darkened room, blood-smeared, freshly removed from the chest of that poor girl, in a frenzied environment. They believe the knife is a fake and that I will reexamine it and recant when under legal oath. This is not true. The knife is bona fide and I will swear that it is. What motivates them to suborn justice, which is in fact being done, is a riddle I cannot solve."

"You authenticated the knife. Other experts can too," Luis said.

"But will they? Why bother? What bearing has it on the case? Has the prosecution or defense any reason to reauthenticate?"

Luis shrugged.

"Or, if a second opinion is requested and it differs from mine, it is not inconceivable that it would be discarded. My signed statement or verbal testimony will automatically be accepted. And, common sense leads me to question why it would not. The missionary killed the girl. Please, may we go?"

Luis thrust an arm toward Denise and the other Figueroas.

"Have you any other questions, detective?"

"Thousands," Luis said. "Thousands."

CHAPTER TWENTY-FIVE

At Denise's suggestion, they swapped the too-familiar Golf for a Beetle. As a secondary practicality, she said, you, Luis, have more experience in a Beetle than a Golf; you are attuned to its handling and less likely to kill us.

Luis's rental-agent friend wasn't there. His counterpart, a grim young man, circled the Golf, twitching his nostrils and glaring at Denise, saying to Luis in Spanish that he smelled carmelized fluids and metal-on-metal, and what the fuck did the gringo lady do to my car? Luis informed him that it was not *his* car, that his overly sensitive nasal passages were smelling imaginary mechanical problems, and that the next renter might destroy it anyhow. His logic and a ten-thousand-peso consideration expedited the Golf check-in and Beetle check-out.

Denise asked if they could drop by Inspector Salgado's. In a cracking voice she said she wanted a progress report on the release of Mary Ann's remains. Luis had been crestfallen by Figueroa's revelation. His approach to the investigation had been centered on a bogus murder weapon leading him to Gilbert, whether he be Proctor Smith or Raúl Estrada Estrada or whoever. Denise's renewed grief set his glum mood in perspective; being a bumbling detective was far preferable to being the custodian of your sibling's corpse.

Hector wasn't in. Luis refused to entrust Denise's request to a subordinate. They would revisit later on. He would also, if permitted, visit Proctor Smith. They could pass the time conversing about Bibles, prostitution, and locksmithing.

They went to the law office of Ricardo Martínez Rodríguez. Ricky was in. They entered as a client was leaving. Luis presumed he was a client. The man, middle-aged, with skin of leathery mahogany from a life beneath the sun, limped past them. One foot was heavily bandaged. Sombreros were stacked high on his head and silver bracelets covered the lower half of each forearm, clumping at the wrists. A beach peddler and his inventory, Luis knew. A walking souvenir shop.

"Come in, come in," Ricky said, looking at Luis alone, gesturing to folding chairs. "That poor wretch. A sad, sad situation."

Luis and Denise sat. Luis looked at President Cárdenas on the wall, wondering what the great man would think of Ricky's ethics, and said, "What happened to him?"

"A Jet Ski ran over his foot. Those tourist fools at the hotels rent them. They have no skills or experience to operate the machines safely, yet they race on the water in reckless abandon and skim onto the beach at breakneck speed when they are through."

242

"Is his foot broken?"

"No. By the grace of God, my client reacted an instant before impact and spared himself further injury. Essentially, his feet were grazed, but he is in excruciating pain and the skin of his toes is hideously scraped."

Denise sighed. Luis dared not look at her. "Whom do you intend to sue?"

"An addition to already clogged court dockets would be counterproductive and irresponsible. I have an appointment tomorrow with the jet skier. I will point out the perils that might befall a foreign national who negligently injures a Mexican citizen. I am confident that we will arrive at a mutually amenable settlement."

Ricky switched to Spanish. "Luis, could I proffer a piece of advice without offending you?"

"It depends."

"You and this lady are inseparable, yes?"

"She has a personal interest in the case," Luis said blandly.

"Yes, I found out her identity. She has my deepest condolences. But, Luis, you could have informed me at the Crazy Cow that she was the sister of Gilbert's fourth victim."

"I could have," Luis conceded.

"I sense that you are developing an affection for her. Luis, you are my friend and I do not wish to see you hurt."

"Thank you, Ricky."

"She is pretty and you are a normal man who is not as socially gregarious as I, your friend, would like you to be. You have a sexual longing for her, I presume. To spare yourself future frustrations, my advice is that you terminate any thoughts of romance."

"Why?"

"You were there, Luis. At the restaurant. I made a friendly, suave overture. She was a block of ice and she spoke like a brutish laborer to Attorney Ringner. You know what she is, do you not? Duress brought out her true colors."

Attorney Ringner? Luis wondered. Not Lard, his pal and colleague and nightclubbing cohort. "No. What is she?"

"A lesbian. All the signs were manifested."

"She is?" Luis said, his jaw falling.

"I am afraid so. If I possess a singular talent and insight, it falls in the realm of the fairer sex. Take my word for it. Touch her body and she will shrivel up like a prune."

"Your warning comes as a devastating blow, Ricky. I am very grateful. Forgive her her weakness, will you? She needs a lawyer to dispose of her sister's condominium and I recommended you."

Ricky smiled at Denise, startling her. Luis shifted to English and to business, describing their adventure with the Figueroas.

Ricky shook his head languidly and said, "You and your sacrificial knife fixation, Luis. The kidnapping connection is intriguing, but insubstantial. Mr. Estrada demonstrated intent to deceive in a situation that required no deceit. Physical evidence is absent."

"I know," Luis said. "Tracking a fake isn't easy, but it's possible. A stolen antiquity that has changed hands ten times, impossible. A bogus knife was sold to Romero, Estrada's goon who paid a call on you complaining about me."

Ricky spread his arms. "Luis, that monster probably uses it as a toothpick. You hoped it was the murder weapon and could be traced directly to Estrada? I empathize, but that is not the real world. A happy ending is unrealistic."

Luis nodded agreement, then said, "What's new with you and Ringner? What are you doing in behalf of Proctor Smith?"

"Attorney Ringner is a degenerate," Ricky said tersely. "Our infrequent communication is correct and business-like."

"Ricky, what happened?"

"The evening of his bullfighting injury, which I related to you at that grisly scene on the beach?"

"Ringner gored by a calf," Luis recalled, smiling at the mental picture.

"Yes. Well, I did not reveal the ending of the story. It was too mortifying, too disgusting. Hortensia and Carla and I assisted Attorney Ringner to his hotel room. I did not stay."

"I remember."

"The ending of the story is a later stop I made at his room to see how he was doing. Quite well, as it turned out. There is a French phrase for what I witnessed." Ricky snapped his fingers. "It is on the tip of my tongue."

"*Ménage à trois,*" Denise said.

"Yes." Ricky acknowledged her with a polite nod. "Thank you. I refuse to describe the lurid details. The consolation is that my eyes are finally open wide regarding Hortensia. The lady is depraved."

"I'm sorry you and Ringner aren't getting along," Luis said. "Have you and he anything new on the case?"

"You would have to ask him, Luis," Ricky replied icily. "He has been cutting me out of participation. This was going on prior to the pornographic event, incidentally."

"Have you been paid?"

"Hah! I realize now that payment is a dream. Ringner will regret his treatment of Ricardo Martínez Rodríguez, Luis. He will. To provide the minimum legal assistance, to throw his client to the dogs, still requires Mexican legal expertise. He can come to me on his hands and knees and he will not receive it."

"Is that what 'damage control' has come to?" Luis asked. "Is that what Ringner and Tropical Language Scholars intend to do?"

"Basically. He may have some tricks up his sleeve. He may not. You can ask him, Luis. He is anxious to see you. He came here this morning asking where you could be located."

"Why?"

"He would not confide in me. He was evasive."

"Did you tell him where to find me?"

"I did. I hope that was all right. I gave him directions to Ho-Keh. He made a crass comment concerning jungles, headhunters, and cannibals. He asked where else he might look. He was attempting nonchalance, but I sensed an urgency. I suggested the Tulum ruins. Since the fire, well . . ."

"My income is reduced to tour guiding," Luis continued after Ricky's hesitation. "If I am lucky."

"I am sorry, Luis. That was tasteless of me."

"Don't apologize. I'd like to see Attorney Ringner."

"Luis, let me proffer an additional piece of advice. They pound your face, they burn your shop. Ringner will never pay you. Proctor Smith will be convicted of the Gilbert murders. It is as if the forces of the universe are rolling over you like a celestial bulldozer. Raúl Estrada Estrada will produce on demand a thousand alibis for the Gilbert murders. Circumstantial evidence is irrelevant. Subsequent crimes against you and the ultimate crime against the flying saucer Anglo are irrelevant. This is Mexico, this is not the land of Perry Mason. Quit the case. Quit it while you can and proceed with your life while you are still among the living. I am taking my own advice. I am finished with Gilbert et al. Luis, I beg you, follow my example."

Luis looked at Denise. "You haven't seen the ruins in good light yet."

"I'd be delighted," she said.

Ricky crossed himself and moaned.

Conversation between Cancún City and Tulum was confined to Denise's asking what's with Ricky—he loves me, he hates me, he loves me, he hates me.

Lust, Luis said. Ricky is aroused by money. He cannot have your body, he will settle for a condominium-selling commission. They laughed and, for the remainder of the trip, enjoyed the relative quietude of their slipstream, which at one point throbbed through opened windows at one hundred twenty kilometers per hour. Like a finely tuned hurricane, Luis thought. Like a kamikaze plane that had lost its canopy, said Denise.

At the entrance to the ruins, Luis asked a friend and fellow guide how it was going.

"Slow," the man said. "Terribly slow, and, hey, two hours ago this weird guy was asking for you."

"That was what I was going to ask you," Luis said. "What did he look like?"

The guide friend slapped his hips and pointed his fingers at Luis, a fast-draw pantomime. "A gringo cowboy. I told him I didn't know where to find you. He gave me and three other guys standing around some pesos to send you to him if you showed. He said he'd be someplace close where he could wet his whistle. You can maybe catch him. Luis, you talk good gringo. What does 'wet your whistle' mean?"

"To have a drink."

"We thought so. He looked like the type. We sent him up to the corner."

The corner was a combination café and hotel at the highway intersection. The café had a thatch roof and specialized in pizza. Luis spotted Ringner at a table drinking beer, smoking long black cigarettes, and watching "Bewitched" on a wall-mounted color TV. Elizabeth Montgomery was performing her magic in dubbed Spanish. One other table was occupied, by three traffic police officers. Luis knew the policemen and they exchanged waves.

He pulled out a chair at Ringner's table for Denise. Ringner looked at her as she sat, saying, "Oh oh."

"Not to worry," she said, giving the peace sign.

Luis sat down. "You've been hunting for me, I understand."

"Boy, sure have, Tonto. You popping in like this, you're a sight for sore eyes. And, hey, what's the skinny on your left one? No offense, but you look like you've been in a turkeyshit shovel fight without a turkeyshit shovel."

"A sight for red eyes," Luis said. "That was your last 'Tonto.' "

Ringner tipped his ten-gallon hat at Denise. "Sorry about the loss of your sister, hon. I should've known a classy little gal like you wouldn't't've caused an uproar unless you were stressed out. Anything I can do?"

Denise shook her head.

Luis's attention drifted to the red-checked tablecloth. On it were bottles of Worcestershire sauce and green chili sauce. Incongruities, Luis thought. Bizarreness. Strange pizza condiments. Samantha on the television, tittering in Spanish, twitching her nose like the rental-car agent, making things disappear and reappear. W. W. (Lard) Ringner, cowboy and Texan and lawyer. He and a North American woman he had known for less than a week in love and lust or something in between. Perhaps this was the object of Dave Shingles's quest: zestful weirdness. Perhaps I have been beamed aboard a spaceship without realizing it, he mused, teleported to an alternate universe.

Luis snapped out of his fog and said, "What's on your mind, Ringner?"

Ringner swigged his bottle of Dos Equis, winked at Denise, and said to Luis, "Whoa. Take it easy. I thought it was *her* going through Midol withdrawal. Okay, here's the situation, the bottom line. We're fast-shuffling Proctor Smith off to Guadalajara for trial. Guadalajara's a big town. It's Mexico's second city and it's thirteen hundred miles from Cancún. You can get lost up there in the hills.

"Smith's going to cop on assaulting the arresting policemen in the hotel hallway. He'll plead not guilty to the fourth murder and it's up in the air whether they'll be able to bring charges on the first three, although I think they'll find a way. The trial will get mucho ink in Guadalajara, but it won't be the big splash it'd be here. It won't poison the Cancún tourism well to any greater degree than it already has, and that's foremost on everybody's mind."

"Cutting your losses," Luis said. "Damage control."

"Right. Proctor Smith, providing he cooperates with everybody, he's got a damn fine chance of skating through this thing with his hide intact. Of course, I'm expressing these developments in American legal terms. Criminal justice is a whole different ball game south of the border. TLS has okayed me to fly up to Guadalajara, establish a base of operations, hire us a crackerjack Mexican attorney, then scoot on home, mission accomplished."

"You already have a Mexican attorney on retainer to Tropical Language Scholars," Luis reminded him. "Attorney Martínez."

"Ricky. Yeah, but Cancún and Guadalajara, that's apples and oranges, you know. Like Dallas and Boston. Or L.A. and Dubuque. An out-of-towner'd be crucified in that situation. He'd look funny and talk funny. The jury'd crap in his hat. Besides, Ricky's nose is out of joint and I'll be damned if I can figure out how come. Ricardo's a good ol' skirt-chasing party animal, but he's kind of moody."

"How are your parasailing and bullfighting injuries?" Luis said.

"Hey, thanks for asking," Ringner said, lifting his beer. "I'm fit as a fiddle. Fun, sun, and semi-clean living. The secrets of health and happiness. Can I buy you kids a cold brew? They don't stock a decent brand of bourbon in this dive."

The kids said yes, he could. Cold bottles of León were brought. Luis said to Ringner, *"Providing* Proctor Smith cooperates with everybody? You have doubts?"

"Good ear. Smith's balking. Give me two more clients like him and I'd tear my hair out. I'd be a dead ringer for a handsome and charming Kojak. Smith can't make a decision. He does make one and he changes his mind. It's like he has to consult God on every damned thing and the line's busy. Hey, I don't blame the Big Guy. I was Him and I knew Proctor Smith was phoning, I'd leave the receiver off the hook too. It was the missus who finally booted him off the dime. I was concentrating on the embezzlement thing that had him tugged by the short hairs, but, hell, all that accomplished was to hold his attention. I start talking substantive defense strategy and we run smack into a wall."

"Ellen Smith?" Luis asked, measuring his respiration, concealing his surprise.

"Yeah. Shocked the hell out of me. That gal's got a head on her shoulders, you know."

"She was opposed to a venue change and concessions by her husband," Luis said. "She believed he was innocent."

"Still does," Ringner said. "But she's suddenly worked herself into a tizzy. Decided her Proctor can't get a fair trial in Cancún City. That's what I've been asserting from the git-go. Ellen lit a fire under Proctor. Boosters are firing and we're ready to lift off. There's just this one minor loose-end situation to resolve. That's where you come in, my friend."

"Me?" Luis said.

"Would you buy a used car from this man?" Denise said.

Ringner drained his beer and rotated it above his head like lariat, signaling for another. "Sticks and stones, hon. Here's the problem. Smith thinks mucho mucho of you. You're his Brother Balam Jaguar. The 'brother' tag is no mystery. These fundamentalist Jesus drummers, a stray dog on the street is their brother. Jaguar? Is that a nickname like Lard is a nickname?"

"No," Luis said.

"No? No? Balam has to translate into Mayanese as 'Man of Few Words,' that's how hard it is to have a conversation with you. Whatever you are to Smith, he won't sign on with the program till he has the green light from you."

"I should visit him?"

"Please. Yes indeed."

Luis extended an outstretched palm. "Pay me what you owe me."

"Whoa," Ringner said. "*I* don't owe you a nickel. TLS owes."

"You are their representative. Pay me."

"TLS owes Martínez. You're subcontracting for him. Wish I was authorized to help you, but I can't."

"Luis, are you selling out to this clown?" Denise said, touching his arm.

"No, at least not until he pays me."

"Sorry, Charlie."

"Did Tropical Language Scholars advance you some money?" Luis asked.

"If it's any of your business, a couple of bucks for expenses."

Luis rubbed thumb and fingertips together. "Then give me what remains outside of your basic living needs. You are doing nothing for your client and I want my money before the rest goes to whores and bartenders. I want Ricky's share too. We worked hard for you and we want to be paid. I have a family to support and Ricky yearns for an anti–'La Bamba' carpet."

"You're talking crazy, Tonto, and get that paw out from under my nose or you're gonna lose it."

Luis sprang out of his chair and slapped Ringner's face. His head snapped back and his cowboy hat flew off, rolling on the floor on its edge, like a coin. "I said no more 'Tonto,' Mr. Ringner."

"God, Luis," Denise said.

Ringner held his cheek. "I'm not retaliating on your home turf if that's what you're hoping for. I'd give my eye teeth to be in Dallas now, instead of this sorry excuse for a banana republic."

"Money," Luis persisted, not entirely seated, arm still extended.

Ringner removed five twenty-dollar bills from his wallet and handed them to Luis. "That's what I can spare. You bill TLS for what you think you're owed. Or you can take a flying fuck at a rolling doughnut. I'm expecting you'll see Smith and fulfill your obligation. After that you're fired, you and your buddy."

"I will see Smith, I promise," Luis said, taking the money.

Ringner turned and looked at the policemen, who were drinking soda pop. "I have half a mind to file a complaint against you with them for assault, extortion, and grand theft."

Luis waved and smiled at the officers. They waved and smiled at Luis. "Go ahead. They are traffic officers. Our dispute is a civil matter."

Ringner forced a smirk. "So the only way they'd throw you in the pokey is if you hit me with your car?"

"Don't press your luck," Denise said. "You haven't seen him drive."

CHAPTER TWENTY-SIX

*L*uis, was it necessary to slap Ringner?"

"Yes," he said.

"That's questionable as hell. Your traffic police buddies would have helped you make him pay what you're owed, wouldn't they?"

"Helped me how? I barely know them. They're young guys. I'd already been kicked off the force before they began."

Denise was driving. She had asked to drive. Now Luis knew why. She had intended to lecture him when she made the request. By driving, she could manipulate the conversation. If he were at the wheel and he cared to change the subject, he could merely perform a maneuver she perceived as dangerous, however erroneously. Terror would interrupt her monologue and her concentration. She was anticipating him and he was analyzing her anticipating him. Soon they would be reading each other's thoughts, fumbling inside each other's heads like pickpockets. A clever stunt for two people who thought in different languages.

"Luis, you could've had them come to the table and bluff Ringner. You know, three Mexican cops just being there, staring at him. He would have come through with the money."

"Excellent idea, Denise. I should have thought of that myself. He would have paid more than one hundred dollars. But he said 'Tonto' after I asked him not to."

"And you lost your temper. Ringner is a drunken sexist bigot. I don't blame you for being ticked off at a racial slur, but I think you were itching for an excuse to nail him."

"I lost my temper."

They passed the Pemex station and his car. The Volkswagen appeared untouched, thickly coated with dust, as if it had been there for ages, just waiting to become an archaeological find.

"Are you a violent person? And please don't feed me the stock Mexican machismo bullshit," Denise said. "I don't believe you're a violent person, but who knows anybody these days. I sure as hell didn't know my own sister. Do you have a mean streak? Am I some airhead who hopped into bed with a guy who has a mean streak? Am I setting myself up for a nasty surprise? I've got to tell you, I'm one of those old-fashioned girls who doesn't happen to believe that sex and violence mix. Luis, you bounced out of your chair before I could blink my eyes, and with your open hand you hit him so hard you gave him whiplash. You don't know your own strength. That's scary."

Luis had no defense, so he counterattacked. "Didn't Ringner anger you? Didn't you want to hit him? You're lying if you say you didn't."

"Of course I wanted to hit him. I wanted to set his clothes on fire. But I didn't."

"I wouldn't hurt you," he said, looking at her. "I never hurt either of my wives. I never hurt my babies."

She took the hand he offered. "I guess I know you wouldn't. I guess I'm more worried about you than anything else. You take a poke at somebody, it's a good way to get knifed or shot. That's a fairly common scenario in the States, you know."

"Knives," Luis said. "Don't remind me of knives. A great theory up in smoke."

"Figueroa gummed up the works big-time," Denise said. "May I suggest another line of thought?"

"Please."

"Opportunity."

"Explain."

"Okay, first of all, let's reject the origin of the knife as relevant. Whether the same knife was used for all four murders and whether it was or wasn't a real antique, who cares? Gilbert could have bought it on sale at Kmart for all we know.

"Mary Ann and the three other women were killed at roughly one-month intervals. That's the nearest to a pattern in the murders and it doesn't pass for an MO, not as far as I'm concerned. The killings took place on different days of the week, at different hotels, at different times. The women had entirely different backgrounds."

"They were slim, dark, and attractive," Luis said.

"Slim, dark, and attractive I don't feel is a pattern. There are a zillion slim, dark, attractive women in the world and we can't all remind this scumbag of his mother or of a girlfriend who dumped him in the ninth grade. Opportunity."

"Opportunity?"

"He killed when and where he killed because he could. He had access and escape. Assuming Proctor Smith isn't Gilbert, he blended in like wallpaper. He got in and out and nobody noticed."

"Hector told me in confidence that only the first victim was raped," Luis said.

"No evidence of sex?" Denise asked, surprised.

"No."

"Another nonpattern."

"I like your opportunity theory," Luis said. "Trouble is, that makes everybody a suspect. Hotel employees, deliverymen, guests. Mexico is a free country. People inhabit hotels day and night, mingling, working, whatever."

Denise sighed. "I know. Wait, maybe a tourist. The murders were in March, April, May, and June. Isn't it unusual to vacation in Cancún four months in a row? I realize Miami is an hour by air and New York is—what?—three hours."

"Unusual," Luis admitted.

"Could we run it by Inspector Salgado? Ask him to audit airline manifests and flag every person who traveled to Cancún during all four murder time frames?"

"We could ask. But a million people a year come to Cancún. I don't know anything about airline recordkeeping. They would maybe supply passenger manifests if we're lucky and ask nicely. Then what? Who's going to pay for the computer to process the names? Names that could also be aliases."

"Yeah, okay, okay," Denise conceded. "I get the message. Are we headed to the jail and Proctor Smith?"

"Yes. I promised Attorney Ringner. I didn't promise results. I'd like to see Ellen Smith before seeing Proctor."

"To learn why she flip-flopped and is pushing her hubby into doing something dumb?"

"Yes, and to see how well she's surviving."

Denise shuddered and said, "Proctor Smith doesn't have to be Gilbert and I don't have to meet him in person to get the heebie-jeebies."

"The what?"

"I wouldn't accept a date to the prom with him."

"Prom?"

"Fiesta."

"Finally understood," Luis said. "Why does he repel you?"

"The Bible he gave to my sister. He autographed it. You generally autograph a book when you write it. Who the hell does he think he is?"

If Ellen Smith's apartment house appeared substandard at night, in the daylight it was depressing. Any earthquake strong enough to quiver a seismograph needle on the opposite side of the world would crumble this building, Luis thought.

Ellen Smith looked haggard, as bleak as her home. Luis introduced Denise. Ellen told Denise how sorry she was about her sister, hugged her, and made tea.

"I was worried about you, Mr. Balam," she said, bringing a tray of steaming cups into the living room.

"You shouldn't have worried."

"By the looks of that shiner, I had cause to worry."

"I tripped and fell. I'm fine."

"Hah!" Denise said. "He's blind as a bat in that eye and he refuses medical attention."

Luis felt his cheeks and ears warm. "How is Mr. Smith?"

"He's the same in the regard that he's making the best of things. I gave Proctor your advice to keep his yap shut on the subject of locksmithing and he has, so he hasn't shot himself in the foot again. That's something, I suppose. Luis, is your investigation bearing fruit?"

"We haven't the evidence to free your husband, but I don't think he's Gilbert."

Ellen Smith looked at Denise. She nodded. "Me too."

"Well, I suppose I should be happy with that vote of confidence. A key turning in his jail cell door, that would make me happier."

"Ellen," Luis said, "I asked you last time if Proctor lied to you. I also asked if you had any information that would be useful to me."

"You're asking me again?" Ellen said with a small smile.

"Yes."

Ellen inhaled deeply, the kind of deep breath taken, usually unsuccessfully, to hold back nausea or tears.

She sniffled and said, "The Lord, He gave my Proctor too much manhood. It wasn't the first instance Proctor strayed. I was an ostrich. I suspected him all these years, but I never caught him in the act. How could I with my head buried in the sand? I know exactly what Proctor was doing in your sister's room, Miss Lowell.

"In the unlikely event you haven't been told, Proctor and I have been in a little hot water with Tropical Language Scholars concerning money. It's turned up missing or spent on things we didn't buy. In lean circumstances, you have to cut corners to accomplish the Lord's work. You dig into the cookie jar to buy gasoline for your car to go into the villages and translate the Word of God. You bribe a hotel manager to place Bibles in his rooms. Well, if you construe such things as misappropriation of funds, you can go right on ahead.

"Proctor, obviously, was not doing under-the-table Lord's work with the pilfered money. Luis, I said to you the other night, my man is human, he has feet of clay; but somehow, as I'm saying it now, it sounds ludicrous and stupid."

"Not ludicrous, not stupid," Luis said. "Did he confess to you?"

"That he was unfaithful? Did he ever! I confronted him with my suspicions. Luis, you pressing me on Proctor's honesty, you can take credit for nudging my head out of that sand and making me ask Proctor point-blank. He fell on his hands and knees and begged my forgiveness and the Lord's. I'm praying for Proctor, and Proctor is praying for Proctor. If he comes out of this mess alive, I'm content that I'll have a new, improved Proctor Smith to spend the rest of my days with."

"Did he confess to seeing women besides Denise's sister?"

"No, not in Yucatán. In Oklahoma he evidently was a Don Juan and I was the only person in the county who didn't know. He had an obsession for your sister, Miss Lowell. He says it wasn't love. He says he couldn't budge Satan's grip."

She paused and looked at Denise. "Oh, that *was* ridiculous and stupid, a lousy insensitive comment to make, implying that your sister was an instrument of Satan."

Denise said, "No problem. I'm agnostic. I don't lose sleep over Satan."

"No other women in Yucatán?" Luis asked. "Not Janie Foster. Not Judy Jacobson? Not Alison Hall?"

"No, absolutely, positively not. I asked—no—I interrogated Proctor about them. I had to be convinced one hundred percent of his innocence. His affairs shook my faith in him."

"And your faith is restored?" Denise asked.

"One hundred *and ten* percent. Proctor is a big, strong man physically, but in his heart he's weak. He's a little boy, but he's no murderer. I'd stake my life that he isn't."

"Lard Ringner, the Tropical Language Scholars lawyer," Luis said. "What is your opinion of him?"

"A lost, tortured soul," Ellen said, stirring sugar into her tea. "He has no allegiances, even to himself. He's a barren shell. He believes in nothing."

"Our friend Lard, isn't he an odd choice of legal counsel for a missionary organization?" Denise asked.

"He spoke an offensive expression. Damage control," Ellen answered. "I imagine Mr. Ringner excels at damage control."

"Ringner dropped a shocking news bulletin on us a while ago," Denise said.

"Give me three guesses," Ellen Smith said. "Pleading guilty to assault and moving the trial to Guadalajara."

"According to Ringner, you had decided that your husband couldn't get a fair trial in Cancún City," Luis said.

"I'm convinced he can't. I'm also convinced that Cancún City isn't safe for him or for me. Are you going to the jail, Luis?"

"Yes."

"Oh good. Please go as soon as possible. Proctor thinks the world of you. He has to hear what's best for him from your lips before he makes it official."

"What's frightening you, Ellen?" Denise asked.

"What should be frightening Luis. And you too, as long as you're with Luis and involved in the murders."

"What?"

"The fate that befell your assistant detective," Ellen told Luis. Her face was the color and texture of wax. Her eyes were recollecting demons.

"Dave Shingles?" Luis asked.

"Yes, that young American gentleman with the thick glasses. Mr. Shingles said he was working for you on the case. He interviewed me. He wouldn't identify his prime suspect, but he said he was close to solving the case. I learned yesterday that he was murdered in his sleep that night.

"Can you receive a fair trial in an environment where you can be killed for searching for the truth? Can you count on remaining alive throughout the trial? Can you?

"Can we have a happy ending like in detective novels? Can we, Luis? Can we?"

ector hadn't a clue how far the paperwork on the release of Denise's sister's body had traveled. He volunteered to walk her through the process. He refused to trust memoranda or telephone assurances. The status of a document in a Mexican bureaucracy, he said, was mysterious and unpredictable. Tracing one could be compared to chasing a mirage with a net.

Armed with Hector's permission slip, Luis called on Proctor Smith. The evangelical was sitting on his bunk, inert. The man had a remarkable tolerance for tedium, Luis thought.

"Brother Balam Jaguar."

"I just came from your apartment. I talked to your wife."

"Ellen's feet are itchy," Smith said. "She thinks we ought to skedaddle on up to Guadalajara and take what they're gonna dish out. She don't think we're safe in Cancún, neither me or her.

"I said, whoa, let's get us an outside opinion. They're gonna hang me out to dry irregardless of where I go on trial.

I can't be having Ellen endangered, so I'll abide by her desires just as soon as you tell me my defense is hopeless. You're the only person who's working on my behalf, far as I can see. That lawyer they sent down for me from Dallas is rinkydink and besotted. He's dancing to someone else's tune. The Mexicans, they got their Gilbert and that's all she wrote."

"I can't answer you until you answer me. Truthfully."

Smith looked away from Luis. "Ellen told you about María?"

"Yes. How often did you buy her?"

"Twice a month was all I could afford."

"On embezzled funds?"

"Admitting you're a nickel-and-dime sneak thief and an adulterer, Brother Balam, that's tough. Weaknesses diminish the man. You are reminded in no uncertain terms how far short you fall of the glory of God."

"Tougher than admitting you are a serial killer?"

"I can't answer that one, podner, because I'm not. I steal dollars to satisfy my craven flesh. I said to you last week, I don't take human lives."

"Did you always rendezvous with María López in a Club Estrada hotel room?"

"Not always. That condo of hers down the coast, you know about the place?"

"At Akumal? Yes."

"Yeah, I reckoned you would. Ellen told me María wasn't María, she was Mary Ann, and that this detective who worked for you who got killed too said you and María's sister was investigating the killings. Well, me and María met at her condo sometimes. I was the only customer she allowed to call on her there. I was the only customer she let into her life."

"Why were you so privileged?"

"Because I treated her as a person instead of an object, a living creature with value. I was worried for her immortal soul."

"You were attempting to sell her your religion?"

"I was bringing her the Good News of the Lord Jesus Christ. Satan had invaded her like a cancer. If I could boot the Stinko Prince in the rear, put him on the run, I'd be saving this lovely girl from eternal damnation and my ownself too. Sad to say, it was a losing battle from day one. Satan, I'd lay with Maria and his evil would transfer from her to me. I could feel him seeping into my pores. His powers are awesome to behold."

Satan, Luis thought. These evangelicals and their mythological demons. They belittle the Maya pantheon, yet they fabricate an animal-like creature with horns and a tail, a mutation of nature, and blame the figment for their own sleazy behavior. "Am I to understand that Satan had occupied Mary Ann's body and that you were occupied next? Like a flu virus?"

"Brother Balam, you're an atheist. I don't expect you to comprehend, but that's exactly how Satan goes and worms into unsuspecting lives.

"Why, María concealed from me her true identity and nationality. How do you figure she could do that to somebody who knew her as good as I knew her without intervention from the Prince of Darkness? Impossible."

"She was an actress," Luis said. "She wasn't Hollywood quality, but she was good enough for the Cancún Hotel Zone."

"She was a Jezebel, Lord rest her tormented soul," Proctor Smith affirmed.

"A what?"

" 'She painted her face, and tired her head, and looked out at a window.' Second Kings, Chapter Nine, Verse Thirty. 'Notwithstanding I have a few things against thee, because thou sufferest that woman Jezebel, which calleth herself a prophetess, to teach and to seduce my servants to commit fornication, and to eat things sacrificed unto idols.' Revelation, Two, Twenty."

"What?"

"A Jezebel is a wicked woman who corrupts. I'm not faulting María on account of how she turned out, Brother Balam. Satan overwhelmed her. Jezebels, they got a domination over men we can't altogether fathom."

Denise should be listening to this, thought Luis, listening to Proctor Smith characterize her dead sister as some legendary monster, destroying decent Christian men with the black magic between her legs. Satan's grip? Smith was portraying himself and Mary Ann as partners, them and the Jezebel third party.

If Denise had a sharp knife, he mused, she might be happy to do the evangelical a service, to geld him. Smith's Satans and Jezebels could depart with the offending organs.

"Mary Ann reminded you of the Jezebel lady," Luis said. "Not Lupe Velez?"

"Who?"

"Truthfully, then, that night, María López's door was not ajar."

"Ellen spilled the beans on my locksmithing training too, huh?"

"Yes. Your wife told me all the Proctor Smith secrets she knows. Tell me some Proctor Smith secrets she doesn't know."

"I unburdened my pustulating soul to her, brother. That was the extent."

"You snicked the lock and let yourself in?"

"Mickey Mouse excuses for dead bolts they installed in that hotel," Smith said, shaking his head.

"Go on."

"It's like I been saying to everyone. Strike out the lie about entering a door that wasn't shut tight and my story is God's truth."

"She was already dead," Luis said. "You took her pulse and there was none. The lights came on. You panicked and ran."

"Yep. That's how it was. They jumped me out in the hallway. And here I am."

"Review everything in your mind. Did you leave anything out?"

"Nope. The mob liked to of killed me in the hall. Lucky for me the manager was in the vicinity. He quieted them down till the police arrived. They would of tore me limb from limb."

"The manager?"

"Night manager, overall manager, I don't know. He knew good English and yelled at them that the cops was coming and I was entitled to a fair trial. The man saved my life and I never saw him again. Before they haul me up to Guadalajara and do what they're gonna do, I'd like to shake his hand and say thank you."

"What did this life-saving manager look like?"

"Homely little guy, homely as a mud fence. Maybe he had smallpox when he was a kid. Sharp dresser, though."

Luis did not reply.

"You gonna hold me in suspense, Brother Balam Jaguar? You ain't gonna say one way or the other, I got to ask you anyhow, how come you're sticking your neck out for me?"

"I dislike you less than Gilbert," Luis said.

"That's a booming vote of confidence. Should I fight extradition or should I throw in the towel?"

"Hang on," Luis said. "Hang on for every second you can."

CHAPTER TWENTY-EIGHT

Inspector Hector Salgado Reyes of the Quintana Roo State Judicial Police, seated at his desk, official of demeanor, slid the center drawer to his hemispherical midsection and flicked it shut.

"The knife is gone, Luis, property of the court, via Mexico City."

Hector paused and looked at Denise. "Forensic experts certified it as a Maya artifact dating from the eighth or ninth century. That was the tail end of the Classic Period, if memory of my schoolday history classes serves me accurately."

Luis had just signed out of the jail and joined them. He said, "I knew that. I knew the knife was real."

"Belatedly, you knew it was real, Luis," Hector retorted. "Belatedly. Furthermore and correspondingly, the tip removed from the late Miss Alison Hall makes a perfect jigsaw puzzle fit."

"I knew that too. Why are we on a subject you prefer to avoid?"

"Because you are at this minute wide-eyed and antsy.

You have come from Proctor Smith's cell and you are in possession of a revelation."

"In possession of a mystery clue," Luis corrected.

Hector laughed. "Smith will say anything. Did he convert you to Jesus?"

"Not yet. He converted me to belief in his innocence."

Hector whistled softly, shaking his head slowly, like a metronome. "Luis, Luis, Luis. You have always believed in the wretched Bible thumper's innocence. I must conclude that you married that position to be contrary, not to mention the billable hours the lawyers are generating."

"*Were* generating."

"Yes, my mistake. They have abandoned him. Pitiful, pitiful."

"I was skeptical that he was Gilbert. I didn't necessarily believe he was innocent, even after Estrada's goons attacked me and killed Dave Shingles and tore pages from his notebook and searched Denise's room and, meanwhile, kidnapped Figueroa."

"Kidnapped Figueroa? Detained, perhaps. Persuaded with luxury. The Corona brewery had to put on a swing shift to handle the increased sales."

"Funny, Hector," said an unsmiling Luis.

"Since we are on the topic of drunken, luxuriously detained museum curators, Luis, I received a report of your scuffle outside Club Estrada."

"Were criminal charges filed against us?"

"No."

"Hector, wouldn't Estrada and Rojas file charges? Wouldn't they, unless they had something to hide?"

"Not a valid argument. They are an exceptional pair, a rich man and his lackey who settle things however they so choose. Accordingly, their behavior is too unpredictable to categorize."

"You seem to be defending them," Luis said. "I confess to causing the disturbance. I confess to kidnapping Figueroa, who was being detained. Perhaps. I confess to assaulting a hotel employee with his portable telephone. I confess to vandalizing his telephone with the side of his face. I confess to giving Bud Rojas the finger."

"Don't forget reckless driving," Denise added.

Hector shook his head. "Luis, you are acting excessively immaturely."

"I wasn't acting immaturely at Xcacel when I identified Shingles. You weren't acting immaturely when you said Proctor Smith could not possibly be innocent, but maybe was. You weren't acting immaturely when you said the illogic was maddening."

"We are beyond logic and illogic. Luis, we can no more stop events now than we can reach out and stop a speeding train. Proctor Smith is going to Guadalajara for trial. That is his best hope for acquittal. Should he be not guilty, his case will not be prejudiced by Yucatán's hatred of Gilbert."

"Should he be not guilty, Hector, he will be hundreds of kilometers from evidence and testimony that could benefit him."

"What evidence and testimony?"

"Me."

"And me," Denise said. "Should he be wrongly convicted, the killer of my sister gets a free pass. I'll scream my head off to somebody. You're an expert on law and the Constitution, Inspector. Point me at the right somebody to scream my head off at."

"Children, children," Hector chided patiently. "This is Mexico. No article in the Constitution of the United Mexican States articulates the reality of political momentum.

"Momentum and inertia are the social, political, and economic engines of Mexico. One rolls over your face and flattens you like a tortilla. The other could not be budged with a nuclear device. This is not contradictory. They blitzkrieg you or they ignore you. They are exercising their will to your detriment. They are greedy or they are lazy. As far as you are concerned, it is the same.

"Proctor Smith is my alluded-to speeding train. The disposition of Miss Lowell's sister's body is, alas, inertial and nebulous."

"The paperwork has been lost?" Luis asked, looking at Denise.

"No, Luis," Hector answered. "The paperwork is not lost. You, like myself, are an alienated Indian, but we are nonetheless Mexican. We are enormously aware that paperwork is *never* lost. It is *never* misplaced. We were informed that the documents are not processed yet, but will be momentarily, though no processor of the documents, past, present, or future, can produce them on demand."

"No problem," Denise said. "Mary and I are here for the duration anyway. We're hanging around until we're reasonably satisfied who Gilbert is."

"Hector," Luis said, "we have to interview Estrada, his goons, and Rojas."

Hector laughed. "Your mystery clue? The junior and his manager will doubtlessly be delighted to cooperate."

Luis ignored the sarcasm. "Estrada first, then the goons, then Rojas. Estrada should be easy to locate. He hangs out at his Puerto Estrada resort project a lot, lazing in the sun, playing the boss, giving orders. He has a few minutes to spare for us."

"Luis—"

"Rojas was *there*," Luis interrupted. "He was at the Club Estrada when Mary Ann was killed. He told me he wasn't. Proctor Smith told me he was. Rojas lied to me."

"Luis, Proctor Smith is an abnormal and muddled individual. He is a crazy man."

"I think he is insane too. He was raving about Satan and Jezebel, but his mind functions when we discuss the case."

"So what if he is accurate? Rojas is the hotel manager. You expect him to be at the hotel. Perhaps you misunderstood the Polyester Asshole when he said he wasn't there."

"No. No misunderstanding."

"Luis, don't harbor any ambitious detective ideas regarding Rojas as Gilbert. The other murders occurred at other hotels. There is no evidence that Rojas was at those scenes."

"I'm not accusing Rojas of being Gilbert," Luis said. "I'm accusing him of covering up for Estrada."

"I should ask Estrada if this is true?"

"We should ask him what he was doing the night of Mary Ann's killing. We should ask him what Rojas was doing. We should ask him what his attack dogs, Romero and Hernández, were doing. Then we should ask Romero and Hernández what they were doing and what Rojas and Estrada were doing."

"Then?"

"Then we should ask Rojas those same questions."

"Then?"

"Then we compare answers. Somebody will slip up. There are too many lies, too many crimes. Somebody will be inconsistent. Then we pressure that somebody to cooperate and save himself."

Hector said, "Luis, you are living a fantasy."

"Maybe, Hector, but we have to try. After Smith is gone, it will be too late."

"It is already too late, Luis. Please rejoin the real world. Smith is already as good as gone."

"Wrong," Luis said. "Smith is going to resist. He isn't going to cooperate with anybody."

Hector yawned and rubbed his eyes. "Luis, it has been an extremely long day. It has been a bad day. You are not going to downgrade bad to abysmal, are you? You are not confessing to be—please say you are not—the instigator of a resurgent stubbornness on the part of Proctor Smith? He and his wife had a deal with the public prosecutor. Airplane reservations were made."

"It was a bad deal, Hector. Smith is afraid for his Ellen. Given the consensus in Cancún that he is Gilbert and the rampaging of Estrada's goons, who can blame the Smiths for gambling on a Guadalajara trial."

"Oh," Hector said, snapping his fingers. "I have a brilliant idea. I speak to Estrada, Romero, Hernández, and Rojas—in that order, Luis?"

"Please."

"Why did I not think of this clever plan before? I interview them, yes, and the interviews reveal nothing. Then you, Luis, advise Smith to accept the Guadalajara arrangement."

"A brilliant idea, Hector."

Hector, a blotchy crimson, hovering between amusement and anger, looked at Denise. "Pardon my English, miss, but even in the company of a lady I cannot indefinitely restrain my natural speech patterns. Luis is fucking me royally, isn't he? Slipping it to me. Blackmailing me."

Denise bit her lip and did not smile.

Hector shook a finger at Luis. "You listen to me. I shall do this thing for you, but I go alone. You are not to participate. I absolutely forbid it. Am I making myself clear?"

"Perfectly," Luis said. "Perfectly clear."

CHAPTER TWENTY-NINE

xhaust fumes wafted through rust-porous floor-
boards. Hector's Dodge Dart smelled like smog and perspiration. The backseat's resiliency was ancient history. Sag-
ging in the middle on flattened springs, Denise and Luis
were irresistibly joined at the hip.

Late in the day, they were headed south on the highway,
bound for Puerto Estrada. Hector's blackened windows were
the basis of a compromise. Denise and Luis would remain in
the car while Hector accomplished the interviews alone.
They would not wander, they would remain silent. They
could not be seen from the outside. Therefore they were not
present. They were not participants.

Twenty kilometers from Cancún City, Hector turned onto
the resort property, driving under a brick arch, along the
perimeter of a golf course, nine holes in service and clut-
tered with polychrome pastel foursomes, the back nine under construction; past asymmetrical brick-and-concrete
pyramids of condos and rental units, some done and occupied, others still skeletal; by cafés that sold enchiladas,

T-shirts, tequila slammers, and fun; and a strip mall of boutiques.

Ahead lay an artificial lagoon and beyond it the Caribbean. Charter fishing boats were tied up at a marina, as was
a cruise ship. Passengers were filing off a gangplank, an
endless single-file mob in quest of dinner, gaiety, and the
atmosphere of old Mexico. Tonight, proclaimed a banner,
was fiesta night.

"Fiesta," Hector said, pointing. "Traditional singing and
dancing. Mexican hat dances. Piñatas."

" 'La Bamba,' " Luis said, thinking that he hadn't seen a
cruise ship in a long time, that Gilbert had rendered it an
endangered coastal species, like sea turtles.

" 'La Bamba.' Unquestionably," Hector agreed.

"Wow," Denise said. "How do you say Disneyland in
Spanish?"

"Disneyland," Luis said.

"The junior's father, who is overlord of the family holdings, is a smart and industrious man. He foresaw the Cancún
Hotel Zone tourism boom spilling out of its confines. He
foresaw resort development along the coast. He foresaw his
Hotel Zone establishments under financial siege by destination resorts, by these sorts of enclaves. He decided that it
was advantageous for the competition to be himself. Fifty
billion pesos' worth of self-competition. A staggering investment by anybody's standards."

"A very smart and industrious guy," Denise said. "Did
any of it rub off on his baby boy?"

"Not noticeably," Hector said. "Ah, he is not difficult to
find."

Hector was referring to the gold Mercedes-Benz 500SL. It was parked in front of a three-story stucco building, a vertical hacienda that housed Puerto Estrada's general head-quarters, a ritzy souvenir shop, and the realty sales office. The road on which the Mercedes rested was cobblestoned. It curved gently toward the marina, where boats took clients out for battles with marlins and sailfish.

"Too rich for my car's blood," Hector said, backing into a vacant lot diagonally across from the headquarters build-ing, next to an idle cement mixer. "Besides, my hubcaps would shake off on those damnable round rocks. Wait for me, children, and be quiet. Don't even breathe hard."

"What did he mean by not breathing hard?" Denise asked when Hector was gone.

"Not what you imply. I don't brag."

"You'd better not. Those people out there, they can't see us. I feel like a voyeur."

Cruise boat passengers were wandering about in groups, cameras at the ready. Ten minutes passed, then fifteen, then twenty, then forty-five. Denise said, "When is the inspector coming back?"

"I don't know."

"It's gotten dark."

"I know," Luis said, not adding that he disliked the idea of his friend being in that snake pit after nightfall. He was a competent police inspector, yes, but Hector was also un-armed and in the den of a rich man who wrote his own laws.

"Oh my God," Denise said, pointing at the building. "Here he comes. With Heckle and Jeckle."

Hector had exited the building through an unseen door. He was accompanied by Romero and Hernández, the shorter goon beside him and big Romero one step directly behind. Hernández's mouth, recipient of Luis's elbow during the brawl at Black Coral, was puffy like that of an exotic fish. Hernández listed slightly as he walked and his face was bumpy, as if he had been stung by a swarm of bees.

"Is he signaling us?" Denise asked. "His thumbs in his belt loops like that, fingers kind of flexing. I don't remember him walking like that."

"Me neither. He's signaling me. Hector has an arsenal in the trunk, every gun he's ever confiscated. He rigged a remote release under the driver's seat. I've got to do it before they're too close, carefully, so I don't rock the car."

Luis, in slow motion, jackknifed over the driver's seat and pulled the lever. Denise, looking out the back window, said, "It only popped up half an inch or so."

"Hector put weights in the trunk lid for that reason."

"They'll be here in seconds. Frankenstein's holding his hand sort of stiffly at his side. Small gun? I can't make out what's underneath his paw."

"Hector wouldn't submit this passively unless they had guns."

"God, how can they think they'd get away with kidnapping, a police officer no less, with hundreds of people around, hundreds of witnesses. It's pretty obvious they're taking him for a ride, as they say in gangster movies."

"Those aren't witnesses," Luis said. "They're North American tourists, who might maybe see three Mexicans walking to a car. The image will vaporize. Estrada and his staff have seen nothing, have heard nothing, will speak nothing."

Luis lay on the backseat and braced his feet against the door. "Shift to your door, Denise, and hold my shoulders with your entire strength."

She slid to the door, twisted, and clutched him until her hands ached. "You're chancing that they'll make the inspector drive and get in the back?"

"They always do in the gangster movies."

Hernández opened the driver's door and shoved Hector roughly inside. He opened the left rear door. Survival was sufficient incentive to drive the door into him, but Luis summoned the memory of the goons at Black Coral and their sexual ambitions for his babies. *Indian girls excite me. They can do wonderful things to you in the dark.* Luis's bloodstream was fifty percent adrenaline.

He thrust his legs to full extension. The door slammed into Hernández, blunt-edged steel dead center to the groin and stomach. He gasped through his damaged mouth and caromed backward into Romero.

A shot rang out. A small automatic pistol clanked onto the ground. Romero fell on his ass, howling, clutching a bloody foot, cursing Hernández. He saw Luis coming and grabbed for his weapon.

Luis landed on Romero's wrist with one foot and kicked the pistol with the other. It clattered off into the cobblestoned darkness. Having exited the front seat and browsed his trunk, Hector was back, shotgun in hand, double barrel touching none too gently the bridge of Romero's nose.

"Police! You are under arrest."

Hector repeated his command in English, even louder. Romero, not unintelligent, went limp. But why in English too? Luis puzzled. The barrel of a twelve-gauge shotgun a centimeter from each eye socket and you would be inclined to consider yourself under arrest. Bilingual commands seemed redundant.

Flashing cameras, blinking hot white, solved the puzzle. Motors whirred like locusts, advancing thirty-five-millimeter Fuji and Kodacolor film. Tourists were shutterbugging from prudent distances, lenses stretched to maximum zoom. Hector was playing to them, warning them off, and they were photographing a priceless and unique vacation experience, superior to the tallest Maya temple, the whitest Caribbean beach, the happiest fiesta. They were recording on film a Mexican drug bust in progress.

Hernández was curled into a lumpy ball, keening, hands protecting damaged organs. No further problem with him either. Denise was out of the car, cupping an ear.

"Don't you hear it? Running feet."

"What?" Luis asked. "You and Rosa and your sonar ears."

"Shush. There!"

Raúl Estrada Estrada sprinted from his headquarters building into a partially completed dive shop, knees pumping high. Even in darkness, he was recognizable in tangerine-and-beige golfing regalia.

Luis pursued. He stopped at the headquarters building and peered inside the dive shop, a wooden skeleton. No Estrada. Luis got into the Mercedes. It smelled of leather and cologne. It started and idled so quietly that he had to race it to hear it running.

Denise got in with him. "Hector has the situation under control and somebody's calling for reinforcements. I'll help you search for Estrada."

Luis fumbled with his left foot for a clutch. Denise moved the shift lever and said, "An automatic."

Luis jerked, squealing rubber, startled by the pickup of the eight powerful cylinders. Tourists leaped out of the car's path, one hand extended to break a fall, the other protecting their cameras. Luis drove around the lagoon and back-tracked along a parallel street, past townhouses and a circular building with a thatch roof designated as the Estrada Nautical Museum. Denise saw the junior on the other side of the entry road, trudging now instead of sprinting. He was headed for the golf course.

Luis visualized the Maya family that black night, balanced on their bicycle like a circus act, the junior in this Mercedes's predecessor, drunk and speeding and oblivious. . . .

He floored the gas pedal. The car fishtailed, corrected, and Luis took a shortcut through the vacant tennis courts. The clay had been laid, but nets were not up and the area was not yet fenced. The tires spun, gouging ruts in the slick, soft playing surface.

They raced across the road toward the golf course and struck curbing higher than it looked. Something exploded.

Luis was hit in the chest and the face by what felt like a pillow shot out of a cannon.

"Jesus Christ, Luis, will you please slow down!" Denise yelled. "You triggered the air bags."

Luis saw the cloth balloon that had burst from the steering wheel. It was deflating, as was the one attached to the dashboard on Denise's side.

"Sorry."

"Sure you are. He saw us. He's going for the bushes and trees on the other side of this fairway. If he makes it, he has cover until he reaches the highway. What's wrong with the car?"

Denise's voice was vibrating. Despite the softness of the fairway grass beneath, their ride was jarring. Luis said, "Flat front tires. The wheel may have sheared off on my side too. But we're still moving. Mercedes-Benz builds a good car."

"Luis, veer right and speed up, or he's gonna make it."

"You ask me to speed up?" Luis wondered out loud. He obeyed, cresting a raised green, flattening a marker pole impaled in the cup and scattering a foursome. How and *why* did they play in the dark?

"Yes!" Denise yelled, shaking a fist. "We've headed him off at the pass."

The crippled 500SL reached the tree line in advance of its owner. Estrada reversed field, head twisted toward his pursuers. He didn't see the sand trap. His legs buckled and he fell in.

When he had recovered to his hands and knees, the prow of the Mercedes extended beyond the lip of the bunker, shredded tires planted at the edge, engine revving.

"Luis, honey, don't."

Luis's hand grasped the shift lever, which was set on PARK. Denise's fingernails dug into his forearm.

"I wouldn't," he said. "The junior and I have to talk."

CHAPTER THIRTY

ho am I?"

"I do not know."

Luis was squatting in front of Estrada, who remained on his hands and knees, eyes turned upward, mesmerized by the Mercedes, which was revving at fast idle. Luis grasped Estrada's chin and wrenched his face and his attention from this distraction. "Look at me. You know me. Who am I?"

"The Indian in the shyster lawyer's office, the evangelical's independent detective."

"Correct. Excellent. Who else am I?"

Estrada shook his head.

"Let me give you some mystery clues. Traffic police, bicycle, dead Maya family, massive bribes."

"I was vindicated. The law ruled me innocent. You are hurting my mouth. And what have you done to my automobile?"

"As you wish. Have it your way," Luis said, releasing him. "I will tell you who I am. I am the Indian who controls your two-ton Mercedes-Benz. Watch and listen."

Luis raised an arm and twirled his forefinger. At this signal, Denise raced the engine. Luis hoped the power plant would survive long enough to play the game to its conclusion; the needle on the oil pressure gauge had been flickering, symptom of a ruptured oil pan and a trickling loss of lubricant.

Estrada flinched. Luis said, "Talk to me or you will look worse than your Mercedes-Benz. Why did you and your goons panic? Why were you taking Inspector Salgado for a ride?"

Estrada's winning white smile came out of nowhere. "You listen to me. I promise to forget what you have done to me, what you have done to my new automobile. Do you have any conception what a 500SL costs? I forget everything, you let me go."

Luis stared at him.

"I can pay you. You need not work another day in your life."

"No sale, Estrada. Your money and your influence and the European nose you bought, they mean nothing. They mean less than nothing. The woman in your car, who will drop it on your head at my command, she is the sister of your fourth victim, Gilbert. I knock you groggy with a punch, lower my arm like the starting official at a car race, and jump aside. Splat! You cannot buy her. You cannot buy me. We hate you too much."

Estrada laughed bitterly. "Gilbert? Me? You pray every night for me to be Gilbert, Indian. You have prayed for my fall since you lost your police job. That was your fault. You should have minded your own business. You were a flunky traffic cop. I did not intend to hit those Indians, but it happened. You could not touch me. You should have known that you could not touch me."

Luis seized Estrada's throat. He summoned every ounce of restraint and somehow kept from tightening his grip until fingers met thumb. "I am touching you now, junior. Bribe me with information, not money. It is your word against an Indian's, you know. Speak freely. Who, if not you, is Gilbert?"

"Enrique Rojas," Estrada said, gagging.

Luis withdrew his hand. "Rojas killed four women, had Dave Shingles killed, and me beaten?"

"Yes and no," Estrada rasped, massaging his neck. "Rojas is Gilbert. I ordered Romero and Hernández to eliminate the flying saucer gringo and to discourage you."

"Why?"

"To protect Rojas."

"How did you know?"

"I knew he and Romero were partners in a counterfeit knife fraud. They bought fake knives from a guy in Tulum City and sold them for big profits to gringo suckers. Romero bought them from the craftsman. Rojas, through his contacts as one of my hotel managers, peddled them. I am generous to my key employees and I close my eyes to their shady business ventures so long as they do not embarrass me."

Luis remembered Shingles's last words to him: *Those hotel managers were bordering on hostile. Randomness.* The murdered Dave Shingles and the missing notebook pages; he may not have solved the equation, but the prospect had cost him his life.

Denise's opportunity theory. Rojas, present manager of

the Club Estrada, past manager of others in the Hotel Zone. *Opportunity.* Rojas could move freely, camouflaged by his profession. He could own a passkey for every hotel room on Cancún Island. Randomness is a pattern, Shingles had said. Rojas could have killed not by phases of the moon or the stars, but by sporadic urges he could not or would not suppress.

Luis felt stupid. What was the North American slang? Tunnel vision. That was the expression. His obsessive hatred of Raúl Estrada Estrada had infected him with a blinding dose of tunnel vision. He felt stupider than stupid. His bluff of Estrada in Ricky's office had probably impelled him, among other things, to have Dave Shingles killed.

"When did you come to the conclusion that Rojas was Gilbert?"

"Last month, when the third girl, the stewardess, was murdered in the Maya InterPresidential. That and the scene of the first killing, the InterPresidential, are our hotels. Gilbert was driving me to distraction. He was destroying our Cancún operations. Our Puerto Estrada investment was endangered. We borrowed heavily to finance it, using our Cancún and West Coast hotels as collateral.

"After they found the flint knife chip in the girl's chest, I became suspicious. I spoke to Rojas. He is a sour, ugly little fellow. He has no success with the ladies unless he buys their bodies.

"I questioned him with Romero. You have been exposed to Romero's techniques, although I would have loved to fire him afterward. Obviously, his job performance was poor. He and his partner look worse than you.

"Rojas denied everything, but he was sweating. He was lying. The bogus knife business was good to Romero and he had ambitions to expand their volume and make a lot of money. Gilbert and his Maya knife made the Maya knife business impossible. Romero lost his temper. I could not manage him. The man is a psychopathic giant and a master at torture. He came within a punch or two of killing Rojas, but he didn't leave a mark. Rojas confessed to being Gilbert.

"The first girl he killed, the secretary, she was a potential customer. She was going to buy a knife to surprise her father on his birthday. The price was too high, so the deal fell through. Rojas, if you study the victims' physical appearances, is quite strongly attracted to slight, dark ladies. Why, he did not explain to us. His mother was probably slight and dark. Is that not how a sex murderer's mind is supposed to work? He tried to seduce—what was her name?"

"You are lousy with names, Estrada, you and your selective memory. Janie Foster."

"Yes, Janie. Well, of course she was having none of him. She laughed and called him names and slapped him. He raped her and killed her with the knife. It was his handiest weapon. He killed her to remove her as a witness against him."

"The pathologists say that the second, third, and fourth women were not raped," Luis said.

Estrada paused. "I was aware that Rojas had problems. But to this extent . . . He discovered that he derived, uh, satisfaction from the killings. The orgasms were twice as intense as any he had ever experienced in normal sexual relations. The man is a monster."

"A monster confesses three murders to you and you do not give him to the police?"

"He assured us he would restrain his impulses. It was a business decision on my part. Should it be known that an Estrada manager was Gilbert, imagine the scandal. Would anyone ever stay at an Estrada hotel again?"

"Wonderful," Luis said. "And he kept his promise for a whole month."

"I made a mistake."

"My friend's sister was your mistake."

"She was a whore," Estrada said.

"You son of a bitch." Luis raised an arm and doubled a fist.

"I am sorry, I am sorry!"

"How did Proctor Smith become the fall guy."

"The evangelical walked in a moment after Rojas killed her. It was perfect. We had a dream Gilbert."

"You also had the assistant curator and his family. Figueroa was a pampered hostage. Why?"

"He was at the right place at the right time. The evangelical and the curator, they were—providential, gifts from God."

"Figueroa stated that the murder weapon was a genuine sacrificial knife."

"He did, yes. Rojas confessed to us about the whore. In his twisted reasoning, he thought he could continue without my condemnation if he did not risk implicating Romero with one of their counterfeit knives. He had purchased the knife from a grave robber seven or eight years ago and was holding on to it for appreciation, as a long-term investment."

"He could have killed with some other weapon," Luis said.

"He could have, but a Maya knife, when Rojas thought about it, was the perfect weapon. A Maya knife is found and a disgruntled Indian is assumed to be the killer. Until Proctor Smith, that was rapidly becoming the accepted scenario."

"He left it impaled in María López/Mary Ann Lowell on purpose?"

"No, not consciously. Do not ask me to analyze his subconscious. It is a putrid hell. He had just killed her when he heard the door lock clicking. He was rushed. He hid in the bathroom. Proctor Smith came in, bent over the girl, then ran out. Rojas followed. Smith was captured. Rojas assisted by maintaining order at the scene and slipped away just before the police arrived."

"You did not swallow Figueroa's assertion that the knife was genuine?"

"We thought Rojas had bought his expert testimony. I wanted Figueroa under my thumb until the authenticity of the knife was settled officially."

"Figueroa swears it is real and I believe him."

"It *is* real," Estrada said. "The expert examination confirmed that it is."

"Convenient," Luis said. "One less person to bribe."

"We were releasing Figueroa anyway. Your dramatic rescue was irrelevant."

"Would it have been irrelevant if the knife had proved to have been manufactured by Hugo of Tulum City? You could bribe the forensic expert, maybe. But Figueroa in Mexico City at the National Museum of Anthropology? Out of your reach? Would you have risked a twinge of his conscience? He reads the newspapers, he reads the consequences of his involvement. Tell me the truth, would you have turned him loose?"

Estrada did not answer.

"Proctor Smith is tried and convicted, Proctor Smith the ideal Gilbert. That is well and good for you, but what of Rojas? He broke his promise to you and killed a fourth woman. Estrada, you are a despicable human being, but you are not naive. Did he promise not to murder a fifth woman? Did you believe him?"

"He promised and I did not believe. My people are watching him night and day. When the Gilbert flap subsides, I will quietly promote and transfer Enrique. He is an outstanding employee."

"To where?"

"Ixtapa. The West Coast, the Mexican Riviera, is booming. We have two hotels at Ixtapa. He will be promoted to general manager of both."

"The change of scenery, naturally, will transform the maniac into a happy, benign *Homo sapiens.*"

"We will observe him."

"You will make him guest of honor at a fatal accident," Luis said. "Far, far away from Cancún, tragically, your loyal, hardworking executive steps into an elevator shaft or whatever. How is my guess? Is that an upcoming business decision on your part?"

Estrada did not answer.

"Returning to an earlier question, why did you and your goons panic?"

"Hernández, the idiot, he panicked. The cop asked blunt questions. He is a skilled interrogator. We may have stumbled on our tongues slightly. We did not incriminate ourselves substantially, but Hernández thought so. He pulled a gun on the cop. We were then beyond the point of no return. We could not let him go then, could we? Could we?"

Luis did not answer.

"What are you going to do with me?"

"We are going for a ride."

"Not in my car. What have you done to it? The wheels and tires are broken and it is sort of lying on its belly. It has been sounding truly awful. Do you realize there is a waiting list for new Mercedes-Benz SLs? I own the *only* 500SL in Yucatán."

The engine wheezed, chugged, imitated the noise of a wrench falling on a concrete floor, and seized.

"They do not build them like they used to," Luis said. "Now you can sign up on a waiting list for an engine."

CHAPTER THIRTY-ONE

This is indeed an honor," Hector said. "An upper-class gentleman in my humble police department vehicle. I do eternally and relentlessly appreciate your cooperation, Mr. Estrada."

Raúl Estrada Estrada shrugged indifferently and continued gazing out his window at the night. Luis thought Hector carried off the comment as sincere, although he knew he was being joyously facetious.

Denise, sitting alongside Hector, said, "Inspector, don't you have seat belts even for the front seats?"

"Next, miss, you would be expecting those steering-wheel-mounted air balloons that are the current North American automotive fad. I'd spend a fortune installing them and make the fatal error of lending my car to Luis, who would crash and inflate them for fun, to see if they worked.

"Which reminds me, Mr. Estrada, the air balloons on your Mercedes-Benz, can you reinsert them in their receptacles or are you required to pay millions of pesos—or, preferably, from the manufacturer's standpoint, thousands of hard-currency German marks—to purchase replacement units?"

Estrada sighed. "How should I know? Am I a mechanic?"

"Forgive my foolish gaffe," Hector said, slapping the sides of his head. "How on earth should I expect you to be concerned about automotive safety systems when your motor is cooked? I fear I shall always be the ill-educated part-Indian and midlevel police officer who will never transcend his station in life, this deficiency due to my inability to communicate effectively with my socioeconomic betters."

"Inspector, hands on the wheel, okay, please?" Denise said. "It's late in the fourth quarter on this case and it would be kind of tragic if we wrapped ourselves around a banana tree."

Hector laughed, saluted, and obeyed. They had departed Puerto Estrada to a throbbing light display of camera flashes and police car roof blinkers. Luis imagined an exploding galaxy. Some lucky merchants would be selling roll upon roll of film tomorrow.

And the police cars. In Mexico, either you cannot find a policeman or they materialize in quantity. Every cop Luis had ever seen along the coast and some he hadn't were at Puerto Estrada. Federal, state, traffic, private security. Hanging out, posing for photographs, belatedly participating in the arrest of two notorious hombres who had abducted an officer of the law and were also, per rumors, allegedly associated with the serial killer, Gilbert.

Hector had relinquished custody of Romero and Hernández to his own state judicial police officers. Their orders were to transport them to the Cancún City jail, while Hector personally took charge of an "extremely material witness and prime suspect," namely Raúl Estrada Estrada. It might be a long trip for the goons, thought Luis. Law enforcement egos were being energized by the excitement of the moment and the ramifications of a major arrest. Also, Luis recognized a couple of grim-faced *federales,* men who, according to other rumors, had axes to grind with their former peers.

Hector could and should have spared a carload of his state officers, Luis argued, as an escort for their upcoming confrontation with Enrique (Bud) Rojas. Hector conferred with Estrada and overruled Luis. He had made vague promises of leniency to the junior, conditional on cooperation. Coercion, retorted Estrada. "Coercion" had brought Hector to booming voice. Slice it any way you like, boy, he said. Just remember, you are in so much fucking trouble that a bribe as large as the Mexican foreign debt could not save your pedigreed ass.

Hector then assisted Estrada out of the sand bunker, escorted him to privacy at the edge of the fairway, and discussed tactics. Hector's strategy was this: Arrive quietly so as not to spook the suspect. Estrada to query employees and discern Rojas's location. Estrada to instruct employees to gently evacuate guests from the immediate vicinity of the confrontation. Hector, not yet entirely sold on Rojas as Gilbert, to interview Rojas, Estrada on standby to cajole his manager into submission in the event he barricades himself or flees.

For these favors, Hector assured Estrada that he would testify in his behalf. Hector was a man of his word, no matter how disgusting the recipient of the promise. Luis hoped he was making a moral exception—lying.

So there they were, crossing from the highway onto Cancún Island, and Luis still did not approve of Hector's bargain with Estrada. Should Rojas be Gilbert, multiple killer and madman, he would in all likelihood disrupt Hector's plan. Much too much depended on the junior.

They stopped on the brick semicircle and got out, Hector quick to emerge before his prisoner. The security man in the Hawaiian shirt came toward them from the revolving brass-and-glass door. He saw Estrada, stiffened, and increased his pace, quickstepping while trying to stand at attention. He saw Luis and shortened his stride. A patch of gauze was taped to his ear. "What is Jumbo's problem?" Hector asked Luis. "One look at you and he swallowed his cud."

"Aversion to telephones," Luis said.

Estrada motioned the security man with a head flick Luis hardly saw, the way juniors did it. He asked where Mr. Rojas was. In his office catching up on paperwork, sir, said the security man, whose eyes never moved from Luis.

Denise tapped Luis's arm and pointed to the sky. From the beach, a spotlight beam was glued to a parasailer. Hector browsed his trunk, removed a long-barreled handgun, wrapped it in a towel, and said to the security man, "What is this vulgar shirt you are wearing? Hawaii, for God's sake, it is tropical Mexico's biggest competition. Dress appropriately, *guayabera* shirt and sombrero. Learn a musical instrument and serenade your guests with 'La Bamba' when you have nothing else to do. Exercise some common sense and patriotism."

The wide-eyed security man looked at Estrada, who said, "Dynamite idea. If I see you again in a Hawaiian shirt, you are fired."

"Jesus Christ," Denise whispered to Luis.

"Hector is nervous. He's silly when he's nervous," Luis whispered back. "Don't worry. Hector is at his finest when he's nervous and silly."

Hector said to the security man, "What special activities are scheduled at the Club Estrada tonight?"

"Night parasailing. The hotel next to us on the north has bullfighting. The gringos shuttle back and forth."

"Baby bulls in a baby bullring," Hector said, sneering. "Is your disco open?"

"It does not open for another thirty minutes."

"Where is Rojas's office?"

"In the lobby, behind the front desk."

"Good," Hector told him. "Go inside and clear the lobby. I want it deserted. Padlock the disco for good measure."

"How, sir?"

"Conduct an incredibly happy hour. Tell everyone there will be free drinks on the beach. On the beach, I emphasize. Go! Five minutes."

The security man looked at Estrada, who said, "Go."

Hector stared at his watch, lipped three hundred ticks of the second hand, and led the group inside. The lobby was vacant. Hector nodded thank you to the security man and jerked his head, saying get lost. He dropped the towel concealing his handgun and cocked the hammer. Luis was not familiar with guns and could not identify this one, except that it was a revolver the size of those fired by movie cowboys and Dirty Harry.

Estrada said, "Wait, I will go in and talk to him."

"No. Too dangerous."

"It is less dangerous if I see him first," Estrada argued. "He worships me. I can talk sense into him. I am the one person who can persuade him to surrender. I alone can prevent a violent reaction."

"Why do you want to?" Hector asked suspiciously.

"My reason is selfish, Inspector. You should have no problem accepting that. If you have to kill Rojas, he may take the secret of Gilbert to the grave with him. You are not convinced I am telling you the truth about him. You said you would recommend leniency for me. The greater my contribution, the stronger your recommendation, yes?"

Hector said, "Covering your miserable ass is a motive I can understand, junior. Be careful. I'll give you five minutes."

Again, Hector counted ticks. At two hundred forty, he said, "Four minutes. Plenty long enough. I don't like this. I should be in there. Luis, does Rojas worship Estrada?"

"He licks his boots."

"And hates him deep down inside, I am willing to wager. Thank you for the optimistic words, Luis. If Rojas is a maniac and kills Estrada, I will be held personally responsible. I'll have to pack my bags, crawl up my own asshole, and disappear. Pardon my vile tongue once more, miss."

"Apologize to me again, Inspector, and I'll send those bags on ahead for you."

Hector rapped on Rojas's office door with his revolver barrel and yelled, "Police! Come out with your hands up!"

"We are!" Enrique Rojas yelled back.

They came out, but nobody's hands were up. Rojas and Estrada were lockstepping in close formation, Estrada as shield. Rojas was steering him by a clump of his thinning hair, the flat of a flint Maya sacrificial knife on his Adam's apple.

"Shoot me and you shoot him," Rojas said to Hector, who lowered his gun.

Luis said, "Gilbert?"

"What do you care, Indian?"

They were backpedaling toward the pool-bar exit, Estrada lurching mechanically, a robot, his gaze trancelike.

"Yes or no?"

"Luis," Hector said.

I'm distracting him, Luis could not explain. "Is that knife the real thing, Bud?"

"Hugo is an artist."

They were moving with Rojas and Estrada, steps from the pool-bar door, cautious not to gain on them. Luis said, "Answer me, Bud. Yes or no?"

Tears streamed, glistening in vertical streaks on Rojas's face. He kissed Estrada's cheek and said, "Good-bye, Judas."

Rojas pulled the knife across Estrada's jawline. The junior clutched his jaw and fell to his knees. Blood seeped between his fingers. He tried to speak, gurgling instead.

Rojas bolted outside. Denise went to Estrada's aid,

screaming for a doctor, nurse, anybody. Luis and Hector pursued. The pool bar was deserted. The beach had been narrowed by Gilbert, the hurricane, to a ribbon of white sand. Nature's confiscation of the sand, Luis thought; storm gods having their cynical fun. People packed the beach to water's edge. Harried bartenders and waiters scrambled to deliver the complimentary drinks, some muttering sullen commentary on management's largesse.

The parasailing spotlight was off. A customer was being briefed and strapped into the harness. Rojas had plowed through the mob in exceptional time and was now shouting orders to the customer and to the parasailing employees, winning his argument with hysteria and, especially, the knife blade.

Hector held the revolver to his leg, saying excuse me, pardon me, shoving through, loathe to create a commotion. People were enjoying the free booze and each other, gulping their drinks and reordering before the spell was broken. Nobody was paying attention to him or to Luis, who was following close on his heels. Nobody was paying attention to Rojas, who was already airborne.

Hector told the trembling parasailing employee to switch on the spotlight and follow the customer. They watched Rojas and his parachute rise. The line was taut and the motorboat was speeding due south.

"Cozumel Island," Hector said. "He's not circling. He's escaping to Cozumel."

The hammer of Hector's revolver clicked. Luis grabbed his wrist. "No. Don't. If he were escaping, he'd steal the boat. He wouldn't hang in the air like a shooting gallery target."

"Luis, the spotlight is losing him. He's sailing out of range. What are you telling me?"

Luis did not respond. He didn't have to. Enrique (Bud) Rojas released the harness and fell. His arms and legs pumped and flailed. The suicide's remorse, thought Luis. You flap your wings, but you cannot fly and it is too late to learn.

CHAPTER THIRTY-TWO

Softhearted schmuck that I am, I went to the hospital to check on Estrada," Denise said.

"When?" Luis asked.

"On my way here."

"Will he live?"

"Yes. I didn't go to visit him. I went out of morbid curiosity, to inquire on his condition. A nurse told me that he'll be okay. Rojas missed the carotid artery. They pumped a few pints of blood into him. He'll have a dandy of a scar, though. The nurse traced a finger from ear to ear. From the gleam in her eye, Estrada hasn't lost his sex appeal, though. Maybe the scar will give him character, make him look like a pirate or a soldier of fortune instead of an aging brat. All things considered, they'll be lining up, taking numbers to hop in the sack with him. How's he faring with the law?"

"Hector keeps his promises. His intervention, combined with the junior's money and influence—don't worry."

"I'm not worrying, Luis. Are you glad he isn't dead?"

Luis just smiled. He was too content to be provoked.

Rosa and Esther were on duty at the new Black Coral, inside the tent on which Luis had put a down payment. His Beetle was parked outside, resurrected, gas gauge needle on FULL.

Ricky had paid him a portion of the fee he'd received from Tropical Language Scholars. Faith in the Lord and the power of prayer had cleansed their good name and delivered Proctor Smith home to Dallas. Since they were thanking God instead of the mortals who'd risked their lives in Smith's behalf, Denise drafted a letter that Ricky faxed to TLS with a bill. The gist was this: Jesus might be responsible for the miracle of your missionary's exoneration, but if you want him out of Mexico in this century, if you want the paperwork greased, pay up.

It was an admirable bluff. Funds were telegrammed the same afternoon.

And on that very day Ricky also received a settlement on the Jet Ski case, from which he withheld a sizable percentage for legal expenses. Stunned by his sudden wealth, not to mention the assignment by Denise of Mary Ann's estate, Ricky proved unusually generous with Luis, who demanded his cut at once, before the balance evaporated in quest of cold drink, hot women, and thick carpeting.

Most happily, while his babies were tending to commerce, Luis and Denise were alternately at play and at rest in his hammock. Hammocks, she had said aptly, they make a sausage out of a couple, hot and piquant and compressed.

"Come on, are you glad he didn't bleed to death? I wouldn't hold it against you if you weren't."

"I don't know," he said.

"The straightest answer you could give, I guess. How's

your eye? I notice you haven't been turning your head like you were in the beginning."

"It's improving. I can see light and fuzzy shapes. It's like I'm looking through stained glass. Anything else?"

"Sorry to be a nag. Inspector Salgado rammed the paperwork through the system for me. Mary Ann and I are going home tomorrow."

They listened to each other's breathing for seconds or minutes or hours: neither could judge the length of the silence. Denise broke it with, "I have to go home, you know. I can't stay indefinitely. I've already run out of vacation days. I'm on unauthorized leave of absence and you have to resume your life.

"To paraphrase Kipling, north is north, south is south. God, did I actually say that?"

"Rudyard Kipling," Luis said. "British author, 1865–1936."

"The 1974 World Almanac?"

"Page 373."

"Do you want me to come back?"

"Yes."

"Not just for guard duty in case the God of Death swings by for a second crack at you?"

Luis grinned. "No."

"Then I will."

"I'll be here," Luis said, holding her. "I'll be waiting."